The Book That Must Not Be Named

By Pepper Phoenix

ISBN 978-0-9975616-4-7

Published by Piobar Publishing

Lenox, Ga.

Cover design by Mackenzie Pendragon

Contact information: pepperphoenix.13@gmail.com

In the year of 1675 the small village of Torsaker, Sweden became infamous.

Infamous for being the location of the largest single mass killing of accused witchery in history.

Beheaded, stripped, placed on stakes and burned; seventy-one innocent souls lost their lives to fear, bigotry, and hatred.

The village people, friends and family members of six men and sixty-five women, turned their backs and let evil, in the form of Priest Laurentius C.H., guide their actions.

One year later, Sweden authorities declared all witches to have been removed from Sweden and a secret society was born. In hopes to atone for their blind faith, indifference, and intolerance, it based itself on the very magic that ignorance attempted to stamp out.

The soul responsibility of these members was to ensure that history never repeated itself. That no man, woman, or child, innocent or guilty, would go unprotected or undefended from bigotry.

They would call themselves,

The Witches Guardian's Alliance.

CHAPTER 1

"We have a problem," Ivan said lighting his cigar. With the only light in the room being the banker's lamp on the desk, the glow from Ivan's match created an eerie shadow across the man's face highlighting his red hair, beard and moustache. Ivan Bronius looked as if his entire head was ablaze; which with his temper was not entirely inconceivable and Max's lips twitched involuntarily at the thought. Knowing his employer would not find it amusing, he gave the carpet his fullest attention as the large man got his cigar lit and continued. "A.R. Martin is making a series out of that damn witch book. With the first installment we were able to force the author to make a lot of revisions in order to protect our people. This time we may not be so lucky. Success, as you know, tends to make people more difficult to deal with." Immediately noticing Ivan's not so subtle dig, Max shrugged his shoulders. He knew he was considered by many as the best guardian in the alliance. Apparently he was also considered difficult to deal with. In no way insulted by the description, he matched his employers raised eyebrows as the big man continued, "I want A.R. Martin dealt with; permanently, quietly and quickly." Max took the file Ivan extended to him and proceeded toward the door. "Gunther," Ivan said, stopping him just as he'd stepped one foot across the threshold. "I expect my orders in that file followed to the letter." The two men watched each other a moment then Max bowed slightly, shut the door and proceeded down the dark hallway. The entire building was empty at half past the witching hour of midnight. As the elevator door closed taking him away from the twenty fifth floor of the publishing firm, Max couldn't help wonder why he always felt the need to go home and brew a strong cup of coffee after any meeting with Ivan the Terrible.

♣

Walking into the convention hall a few days later, Max wasn't exactly sure what to expect. He was supposed to be looking for an author, but he had no idea what the person looked like or even if the person was male or female. The book and file his employer had supplied him with merely said A.R. Martin. Thinking of the last time he was in a bookstore, it seemed odd that there wasn't a picture of the author on the book. It appeared everyone did that these days. For some reason this author had chosen not to. Looking at his watch, knowing these things never start on time, he walked past several tables set up for the authors to sit and sign autographs plugging their books. It was going to be a busy place in a few minutes and he was rather hoping to find his quarry before the mayhem of book signing and photographs started. He glanced at his watch again as he walked over and fixed himself a cup of complimentary coffee. It tasted like complimentary coffee; the kind they give away because no one really wants it they just want something to do with their hands. Another unsuspecting coffee drinker came up to the table and fixed herself a brew. Cream and two sugars, stir three times. *Why did the minute hand on his watch not seem to be moving?* He thought to himself, irritated at how slowly his morning was moving, or more precisely, wasn't moving. The woman next to him fixing her coffee was quite attractive. Her hair was black and shiny and cascaded over her shoulder with a saucy little upturned curl. When she glanced his direction he wasn't quite sure if her eyes were green or blue, but they had a charming slant to them and he couldn't help smiling at her. Giving him no more than a curious look, she turned her attention back to her coffee. He watched her take a sip and grimace at the terrible flavor.

"It's not really gourmet day at the coffee table," he quipped with a little grin.

She offered a small smile showing no teeth, but an exquisitely positioned dimple right at the corner of her mouth. "Obviously not," she said in a soft whisper that made the hair on the back of his neck tingle.

Her voice was as soft as the sweater she was wearing looked; *cashmere,* he guessed. She walked away and sat down behind one of the tables being set up. *An author,* he thought maybe. He wandered around a little while as the tables were laden down with copies of each author's books and banners with the author's name and book titles were hung. As her banner was hung, he couldn't believe his luck. *So that's what an A.R. Martin looks like,* he thought to himself not even attempting to hide his grin.

Astrid glanced at the handsome man standing by the pillar next to the door. It was obvious he was an executive of some kind; his clothes were expensive looking, he was accessorized tastefully, and he held himself with an air of importance. The baby blue silk shirt he wore perfectly matched the blue in his eyes. The hand holding the terrible tasting coffee was well manicured with a large gold ring on his right hand that his other fingers absentmindedly played with. The large watch on his left wrist had a deep blue face and as he glanced at it, he raised an eyebrow seemingly annoyed at his present situation…whatever that was. Considering him far too attractive, she fervently hoped he didn't come by her table. Just as she stole one last glance at him, he turned her direction and a slow grin spread across his face. Astrid quickly buried her nose in her book trying to seem as though she hadn't noticed him. She also tried not to notice the attractive red-head that sauntered up to him in a clingy black dress that perfectly accentuated her every curve. Taking his arm in a friendly yet provocative way, pressing her bosom against him, she smiled beautifully and Astrid thought her definitely his type; attractive face, perfect body, and high maintenance. Again, she tried to concentrate on her book.

"I'm working, Felicity," Max said scanning the room, but appreciating the well-practiced pout on the ruby red lips of the woman stroking his arm.

Her hand played with the buttons of his dress shirt as she practically purred, "You know you only danced with me once at the party last month."

Max cast his mind back to the party she referred to. He'd only attended because another agent was there and he'd needed to get information. Since she was wearing a red dress, as soon as the song came on about the woman in red, Felicity decided she should have her pick of any man in the room to dance with and she'd picked him. "I'm sorry if you somehow felt neglected," he said casually.

"Neglected? I was rejected. I saw you leave with Mandy Simons." Again the pout emerged.

"Felicity, I am trying to work."

She leaned against him to whisper in his ear, "I'm in room three hundred and four, come to me tonight and make it up to me."

Max gave no answer, but patted her hand before walking away. If things didn't go well with A.R. Martin at least he had a backup plan.

Before he had a chance to walk to the pretty author's table, the doors opened and at least a hundred people came rushing in to get in line at various tables. Hers was no exception as twenty or more men and women got in line to have her sign their book or have their picture taken with her. There was a lot of interest in her book, good for her, bad for his people. As he watched her, smiling and talking to her fans, the smile he'd had before faded from his face. Almost as if his employer was hovering over his shoulder, he remembered the file he'd been given with strict instructions to follow the directions to the letter. Of course, he rarely followed anything to the letter. He prided himself on using his own judgement especially on assignments when he was being asked to put a period to someone; he was not, after all Agent Heiss; the Latvian machine. Max stood back waiting for the crowd to die out, but it didn't. There was a steady stream for three long hours. It was nearing time for the signing time to be over and he watched as the last stragglers walked out of the convention hall. As other authors packed up their belongings, Cashmere just seemed to sit frozen in place. She looked a bit frazzled and shell shocked. It had been her first signing and she put her head in her hands taking deep breaths trying to finally relax a bit.

"Are you alright?"

Astrid looked up into the face of the blue eyed coffee guy and her heart jumped to her throat. They weren't baby blue eyes after all, they were more of a crystal blue; icy and sparkling and she imagined could be termed cold if he was angry. She was already exhausted and a bit quivery. Of all the people to come up to her right now why did it have to be him? "Yes…yes of course. Just a bit tired," she said in answer to his inquiry. "This was my first time and…" Her hands shook slightly as she picked up her pens and put them away. "I'm not really very good at social…anything."

"Is that why you write?" Max asked casually.

"Yes, sir," she said bowing her head slightly then suddenly frowning as she said, "Oh, I'm sorry, sir."

"For what?" Max asked irritated that she had gone from sweet to subservient in seconds.

She motioned toward the book in his hand. "Did you want that signed? I'm afraid I wasn't paying attention. I'm very sorry."

It took Max a moment to realize he was holding her book. Gruffly he said, "It's understandable. You're tired and the signing is over," he put the book behind his back. Remembering his mission, he found his smile again and said, "I was going to ask if I could take you somewhere for a cup of coffee."

"What…," she looked up at him. "Why?"

Never in Max's entire life when he'd asked a woman out had she asked him, *why*. He wasn't sure how best to answer the question. "Well…I uh…I just thought since you've been here for three hours drinking that stuff," he pointed at the complimentary coffee table, "you could use some coffee with actual coffee flavor and perhaps a bite to eat."

"Well, that's very kind of you, sir, but I'd like to go to my room and rest a bit." She stood with her bag on her shoulder and started for the doors.

9

"You're staying in this hotel?"

"Yes, sir." She fidgeted with her bag and brushed her hair away from her face. "My uh...my publisher said they always do it for their new authors and...I just thought..." Max bent down and retrieved the room key she'd dropped, "It just seemed like a nice gesture and since I knew I'd be tired...and all."

There could only be one reason Ivan Bronius would offer to pay for her hotel room and it wasn't to be nice. It was obvious he wanted her home empty to either find something he wanted or to set up surveillance. Why she seemed so nervous about accepting the free room was much more difficult to figure out. "Well, there is certainly nothing wrong with accepting a gift," he said smiling trying to put her at ease. "Could I possibly take you to dinner tonight, then?"

"I'm sorry. I don't know you and I really don't think..."

"Forgive me," he said with a slight bow, "I should have introduced myself." He escorted her out of the doors and to the elevator. Offering her a sheepish grin that usually had the effect of putting most women at ease. "I'm Maxim Gunther," he said cordially, "I work for your publisher Iron Press."

"Oh," she said stepping back away from the elevator doors. "Is this regarding work, Mr. Gunther?"

"Max, please," he said placing a hand on his chest. "No, this has nothing to do with work. I understand you're a bit tired. It's no surprise. For someone not used to it, all that smiling and making small talk gets exhausting."

"Yes it does," she said with a shy smile he found captivating.

"How about I meet you down here in the lobby about seven o'clock? We'll eat at the hotel's dining room. There will be plenty of people around in case you find my behavior...ungentlemanly," he said, oozing charm. The way her soft eyes twinkled he knew he was winning her over, "You have to eat anyway," he added.

For the first time, she directed a full smile his direction. "Alright, Mr. Gunther, I'll meet you in the lobby at seven o'clock." She turned and stepped into the elevator.

Max didn't move. The smile she'd sent him gave him an unnerving feeling. He frowned rubbing his chest absentmindedly staring at the closed elevator doors. *Those eyes,* he thought to himself, recalling the odd greenish-blue tint and the slight slant. *I know those eyes,* his frown deepened as his phone rang startling him back into the present. "Hello?" he said, "Yes, I found her…I haven't had a chance to discuss things with her yet." He walked away toward the restaurant to make sure they reserved a private table. "You mind telling me your purpose for having her place empty tonight?"

♣

"You have a very faint accent. Where are you from?"

For a moment Max simply stared at the little pixie seated across from him. She'd worn a lovely little powder pink confection made out of a fabric that was so light it seemed to float around her. Together with the light green jewels she'd paired with it, it reminded him of picture he'd seen of fairies in one of his little sister's story books. Now, this fairytale creature was picking up on something that no one had picked up on for at least ten years. Blinking a few times and attempting to hold back a look of confusion he said, "I was born in Sweden." His brow wrinkled as he added, "My accent is not something people generally detect."

"Oh, I'm sorry. I didn't mean to…I sometimes point out things I shouldn't. I didn't mean to offend you in any way, Mr. Gunther."

Her hand that had been relaxing on the table went to her lap and Max had a pretty good idea she was clasping her hands together to the point of turning her knuckles white. "It's, Max, remember? I didn't say you offended me. Far from it. I am very proud of my Swedish heritage. It just surprised me because it's so uncommon for someone to hear it." Shyly she looked up at him and returned his soft smile. "I've been in this country since I was eighteen," he said trying to put her at ease.

"Do you go back and visit often," she asked.

"No, just…once," he said looking down at the knife on the table cloth. He didn't elaborate and she looked at him as if she expected him to say more so he said, "Have you traveled much?"

"Me?" She giggled placing her hand in front of her mouth. The smile gave an even more mischievous slant to her eyes. *Ermina's eyes*. Finding himself caught up in the memories those eyes evoked, Max quickly recovered to hear her say, "I've never been outside of Minnesota." He gave her a little smile, but was too lost in his own thoughts to have an intelligent response.

The waitress came with their meals all the while smiling coquettishly at Max. With her long blonde hair, pretty blue eyes, and attractively portioned figure, she flirted with Max with the ease of someone quite used to having a man's attention. Astrid had noticed when they'd given their orders that the woman barely noticed her existence. Even now she held Max's plate aloft, right at the level of her bosom, as if holding it for ransom until he looked up at her. "Your dinner, sir," she said sweetly, but with a bite, as if tired of waiting for his attention.

"Thank you," he said briefly then turned his attention back to Astrid. "I hear your book has done so well you're thinking of doing a second, maybe even making it into a series."

Astrid smiled at both the waitress' put out expression and Max's look of genuine interest in her book. "Yes, I...think I may make it a series. A lot of my readers have mentioned it when they come by for autographs." The lovely blonde set the plate down rather noisily and walked away.

"It always strikes me as interesting where authors get the ideas for their stories." Looking away from his salmon, Max waited for some kind of response to his statement. Upon receiving none, he pushed on, "How did you come up with the concept of your witch book?"

"Fairytales, witches and folklore have been a part of our society for generations," she said, shrugging her shoulders and taking a bite of her pasta.

"Yes, but...,"

"That's a beautiful ring."

Max looked down a moment as if he wasn't aware what he was wearing. "Thank you," he said, "what specifically led you to do a story on witches?"

"What is it?" When he only frowned she used her fork to point, "Your ring. What is it?"

"Oh, uh…it's a lynx," he said disregarding it.

"Why do you wear a lynx? Does it have some family significance or something?"

"It's just a ring," he said dismissively wondering if she was avoiding his inquiries intentionally.

"Oh, I'm sorry. I didn't mean to be nosy or…or anything."

Realizing his brusque tone had made her uneasy, Max reminded himself of his goal and slipped a smile onto his face. "No, I'm sorry. This salmon is a bit over seasoned and coming from a country that knows how to cook fish, I guess I'm a bit intolerant of amateur's attempts." The white knuckled grip she'd had on her fork eased and a little smile played around her lips. "The ring has no family connection; only a Swedish one. Although the lynx is one of Sweden's largest predators, they're quite shy and elusive and I guess the paradox has always interested me. I don't honestly know why, but I've just been drawn to them since I was a little boy," he said quietly as he ran his left thumb over the gold ring on his right ring finger. The gold head was perfectly carved and inset with two onyx stones for eyes. The craftsmanship was impeccable and Max had paid an exorbitant price. "I read a book once about a lynx named Timorous." He smiled remembering the character. "He had this funny habit of…," he paused suddenly remembering more than he wanted to.

"Yes?"

"Nothing, it's just an old children's book," he said, clearing his throat.

"Do you still have it?"

"No," he said quietly, not really wanting to relive the memory of what happened to that and all his other books. Her gaze being altogether too inquisitive, he concentrated more fully on finishing his salmon.

"Once upon a time I'd thought about writing children's books," she said timidly.

"Really," he said looking up at her.

"Yes, I...I love the idea of my story being there for a child when they've had a bad day or just need a friend to take them to another place or time. Books can become like old friends to a child," she tucked her head down, embarrassed. "I guess that sounds silly to you."

"No, I...I know what you mean," he said thoughtfully. After a long pause he asked, "So why did you decide to go the adult fiction route?"

"I don't think I really did decide," she said with a hint of sadness to her tone that perplexed him.

"I don't understand."

She sat up a little straighter in her chair and said with a smile, "I'm sorry your salmon is a disappointment, but the shrimp scampi is quite nice."

Three hours later they were still sitting at the table drinking mocha cappuccinos in lieu of dessert. "I asked you out to get to know you better, but I feel like you've asked more questions than you've answered," Max said to the beautiful creature sitting across from him. They'd talked about his Swedish ancestry, his thought that coffee was man's greatest discovery, and even why he wore boots instead of loafers. What they hadn't discussed was nearly anything about her. If he didn't know better he would think she'd intentionally steered the conversation away from herself. The way the candles on the table created a soft glow around her heart shaped face and the little dimple that occasionally peeped out next to pretty pink lips, made time simply slip away. For someone who prided himself on being time conscious, it was a new experience for him.

Astrid smiled at him, but didn't offer any apology or explanation for the evening's conversation. It was interesting, she thought, that the jewelry she'd worn matched his shirt he'd changed into for dinner. As if they'd somehow connected on a deeper level. *Now you're being ridiculous, Astrid*, she quickly reminded herself, *but why do his eyes look so much bluer against the green?* Earlier his eyes had appeared almost crystal clear, but now the green shirt brought out more of the blue and it had the effect of warming them a bit.

Max looked down at her left hand slowly stirring her cappuccino and noticed she wasn't wearing a wedding ring nor did she have the tell-tale tan line exposing that one had been there at one time. Before thinking better of it, the question slipped out, "So why aren't you married?"

"I guess the easiest answer is that no one wanted me," she made her statement so matter-of-factly that it took Max by surprise. There was not the slightest hint of embarrassment or anxiety in her features by the self-imposed revelation. Max however wasn't buying it. There had to be more to it than that; the woman was beyond beautiful and he knew from reading her first book that she was intelligent. There was definitely more going on than met the eye.

"Why aren't you married?"

Max looked at her and a smile slowly spread across his face. He knew the game, 'be warned, you ask me and I'll ask you.' "Well, I guess the simplest answer is that I never met a woman that inspired me to promise faithfulness. Without it," he looked down at the tablecloth a moment and blinked his eyes rapidly, "without it, what is the point of marriage?"

Astrid smiled, but felt there was more to his answer than he was willing to say. There was a sadness about him that made her want to comfort him. Since prying into other's lives was not in her nature, she let it go. "I should be going, it's getting late." Max stood as she did, "Thank you for a lovely dinner."

"You're very welcome." The dinner was over and Max hadn't even come close to getting the answers he was supposed to be getting. As his mind began racing trying to think how he could see her again, he took her hand, but she quickly took it away. She frowned down at the floor and held her hand as if he'd injured it. "I'm sorry...I meant no offense." The idea of her being even the slightest bit afraid of him rankled a bit, but he tried not to let it show. Placing his hands safely in his pockets he said softly, "Good night, Astrid."

"Good night," she said without looking back up at him.

Max frowned and took out his phone as the elevator doors closed obscuring her from his view. He'd missed three calls from Ivan during dinner. He raised an eyebrow congratulating himself on having the foresight to turn the damn thing off. Standing in the lobby watching the numbers above the elevator doors lighting up, eleven...twelve...thirteen, pause…then descending back down, Max thought about whether or not to return Ivan's calls. He got onto the elevator and pressed the button for floor thirteen. He hadn't exactly followed the file to the letter, per Ivan's instructions so deciding he wasn't in the mood to explain himself, he put his phone back in his pocket and walked toward room thirteen seventeen. Pausing only long enough to put his hand on her door and give himself a moment to sense that everything was alright, Max wandered down to room three hundred and four where he knew a warm and willing body was waiting.

CHAPTER 2

The next morning Astrid stepped off the elevator to find Max waiting for her in the lobby. "I...wasn't expecting to see you here," she said with an air of curiosity.

"Well, I had some business in the area and remembered that I hadn't gotten your number last night."

"If you work for Iron Press wouldn't you have been able to get it from them...if you needed it?"

Max sent her his most charming grin, "I wanted to see you," he said.

"Why?"

He smiled, "You intrigue me."

"Me? You've got me confused with someone else. I don't intrigue anyone."

"You intrigue me...I'm someone."

She smiled shyly at his gallantry as he took her bag and carried it out for her. He offered her his other arm to walk her out, but she ignored it. "Valet or parking garage?"

"Garage," she looked down and said quietly, "I didn't want to have to tip the valet," chuckling she added, "That sounds horrible."

"No it doesn't," he said sincerely, "you know what's horrible?" He waited for her to look at him and timidly shake her head. "I don't park valet because I don't want someone else driving my car!" They boarded the elevator and she was careful to keep a few feet between them. The file he had on her was vague to say the least, but the bit about her being suspicious and withdrawn was accurate. The question was, why. "I get

17

the distinct impression that you don't trust my attention toward you. Or is it just me in general?"

"I'm sorry, Mr. Gunther," she said causing his smile to slip, "But it does seem a bit strange to me that someone like you would even notice someone like me was in the building."

The elevator stopped. "What do you mean someone like me and someone like you? We're both human aren't we?"

She stepped off the garage elevator only to stop short and exclaim, "Wow, that's pretty!"

"Thank you," Max said acknowledging that his new midnight blue Jaguar F-type SVR was indeed...pretty. "You like cars?" he asked surprised as she walked over to it and gently ran her hand over the hood.

Her head bent down shyly, "I have a weakness for hot foreign cars."

"So have I," he said with a chuckle.

"A machine like this isn't just a car; it's an experience. I can understand why you don't want others to drive it. If I was a valet I'd take it for a spin before I parked it." Seeming to realize suddenly what she'd said, she quickly added, "I'm...I'm only kidding. I wouldn't...I mean I'm sure they don't..."

Max laughed cutting off her nervous ramble, "I wouldn't blame them if they did!" Her smile surfaced again as she looked at the car and Max temporarily forgot what a timid creature he was with. "I have this overwhelming desire to kiss you right now," he said.

She jumped back like a frightened rabbit. "Don't! Please, just...you don't want to do that."

Max stepped back not wanting to make her feel threatened. Keeping his tone even he said, "Are we back to that someone like you and someone like me thing?"

"Some...something like that," she stammered then looked into his eyes to say, "People don't like my touch. It sometimes makes them feel funny." Although she shrugged her shoulders as if it didn't matter, there was a sadness to her tone, "It makes some men...angry." The curious expression from his crystal blue eyes encouraged her to elaborate further.

"I like you, Mr. Gunther. You seem very nice. I wouldn't want to ruin a new…whatever this is."

Max came toward her and watched as her eyes watched his lips. When her tongue came out and licked her own, he knew the idea of a kiss wasn't completely unwelcome. As soon as his hand caressed her cheek, he understood what she'd said; she was a witch, he could feel it. It explained why some men, the type with negative intentions, wouldn't like her touch. Naturally her magic would repel them, but it seemed odd that she was confused by it; as if she didn't understand how it worked.

The aftershave he wore had a warmth about it, just like the hand that held her face so gently. It felt like a safe cocoon and the very idea made her nervous. He was a stranger, a complete stranger. Max toyed with a tendril of hair next to her cheek causing a warm sensation throughout her body and she slowly closed her eyes at the pleasure of it. As he leaned in for a kiss, the moment was lost as he was forced to his knees by a kidney punch from someone behind him. Max gave Astrid a shove trying to get her out of the way of whatever was coming next. "Run," he shouted. His voice echoing throughout the nearly empty parking garage. "Run!" Recovering quickly he got up and spun around to face his attacker just as another man punched him in the face. Astrid backed up against the car trying to stay out of the way of the flying fists. She'd never seen a brawl in real life before and the sound of fists hitting faces gave her a sick feeling in her stomach. Fights on television looked and sounded very different from the real thing. Max's fist collided with the tallest man's nose and Astrid turned away at the spirt of blood as the man howled in pain.

When it looked as if Max might actually win the two against one battle, one of the men pulled out a gun. Astrid screamed, "He's got a gun!" Max kicked the gunman's hand sending the gun sliding across the ground. Punching the one with the broken nose in the stomach with a solid right and doubling him over, he took a nasty blow to his jaw making his head spin. The men continued to grapple each other until eventually the one who'd made Max's head spin, kicked him in the back of his knee sending him to the ground. They continued their assault kicking him repeatedly and he was unable to silence a groan when a shoe made contact with his rib cage. Max used one hand to protect his head and the other to grab one of the guy's legs sending him down to the concrete on his back. Using her foot to slide the gun toward her, Astrid bent down and picked up the weapon. "Alright, enough!" A shot fired into a nearby car's front tire got their attention and they stopped fighting to look at her. "This is not the first gun I've fired and you're not the first man I will have shot. Get away from him or I start firing; starting with your manhood and working my way up." A car suddenly appeared and the two men scrambled to get into it. As it sped off, she said to Max, "Give me your keys they may come back." He handed her his keys and she opened the passenger door. On one hand it was good he was built so well to survive the attack, on the other hand it made him extremely heavy. She pulled and he crawled and eventually he was in the seat. Jumping into the driver's seat and trying to catch her breath she said, "I have no idea where I'm going, any ideas?"

He was breathing heavily and holding onto his ribs. There was blood all over his face and hands and his slacks were torn in a few places. In a raspy voice he told Astrid, "Turn right up here." Resting his head back against the seat he took a deep breath and retrieved his cellphone from his front pocket. His ribs didn't appreciate it and he began coughing.

"Shallow breaths. I know you think you need a deep breath, but don't try it. Shallow breaths will be easier on you. You may have broken ribs."

"*Lagom,*" he said quietly and did as she suggested and relaxed a little. "Go four blocks and turn left," he said and then spoke into his phone, "Hey, we're headed to your place. I got jumped. ETA about two minutes," and hung up. With his breathing still labored and his words a bit slurred, he closed his eyes and told Astrid, "At Carson Avenue go…go five miles to a road called," he swallowed hard and she glanced at him again, "a road called Spruce and turn left."

Astrid tried desperately to concentrate on the busy city traffic, but she couldn't help glancing back at Max every few minutes. His head rolled carelessly against the headrest and with every turn she made he clutched at his ribs obviously in pain. "Don't go to sleep. Okay?" Stopping at a stop light, she gently placed a hand on his arm and pleaded, "Mr. Gunther, please, don't go to sleep!" She was a little out of breath and her hands were shaking as she turned back to grip the steering wheel.

"I won't go to sleep if you…if you stop calling me Mr.…Gunther," he said in too much pain to effectively keep the sound of irritation from his voice. Taking another shallow breath to calm himself he said, "Four miles down Spruce, sixth condominium on the left, pull in."

"Yes, sir," she said timidly and Max's scowl returned.

A few minutes later she pulled into the driveway of a redbrick condominium. A tall, dark haired man came rushing toward them and Astrid quickly locked their doors and held up the gun she'd gotten from the thugs.

The man stopped and looked from Astrid to Max, sitting in the passenger seat with his eyes closed. "Max!" he shouted, "Max!" He looked back to Astrid, "Please, let me help him."

Max opened his eyes and looked out of his window. "It's alright, Astrid. That's my little brother," he said softly closing his eyes again. If she hadn't been so terrified she'd have thought it funny that Max called this man several inches taller than himself his *little* brother. Younger, okay, but little? She put down the gun and unlocked the doors.

Jackson quickly went to Max saying, "I've called Tom, he's on his way."

"*Lagom,*" he said.

"He said that before, I…I don't know why," Astrid said softly.

Jackson smiled, but didn't offer an answer. He and Astrid dragged Max into the condo. "Boy, you really pissed off somebody!" His comment only earned him a grunt from his big brother.

Moments after getting him on the couch a man burst into the room followed by a small young woman with sandy blonde hair. She quickly knelt on the floor beside Max and took his hand gently into her own. "How badly is he hurt?"

"I don't know he hasn't said anything yet. They just got here," Jackson said and pointed to Astrid, "She brought him."

The man that had come in with the young woman turned to her. "Were you hurt as well?" he asked kindly. Three sets of eyes looked at Astrid. Shaking her head, no, she stepped back into the corner. Quietly and calmly the man said, "Sara, why don't you see if she needs anything while I take a look at Max?"

"Of course, Tom." Giving Max a final look she reluctantly laid his hand down by his side and came over to Astrid smiling warmly. "Are you a friend of Max's?"

Astrid wasn't sure how to respond. The way the young woman had gone to her knees at the sight of him, it was clear Max was something special to her. Shyly turning her head away, she watched as the men used a bath towel to wipe the blood from his face. There was bruising on his cheek, a sizeable cut along his jaw, and his bottom lip was bleeding. "I just met him yesterday," Astrid said looking at Max's badly beaten body. They'd managed to get his shirt off and along with the fresh bruising she noticed he had a scar on his left shoulder that was at least five inches long. The jagged edges of it made her wince thinking of how much pain he must have endured at the time of the injury. He also had what looked to be burn marks on his upper right arm.

"Bruised or broken?" Jackson asked as Tom felt Max's ribcage.

"Bruised, he got lucky. I'll get you wrapped up Max just hang in there." Max kept his eyes closed, but gave him a short nod of awareness. "Jackson, there is some pain medicine in my bag, he's going to need it."

Sara escorted Astrid to the breakfast nook. The small place had the look of a single man's condo. There was no decoration anywhere. Everything was clean and tidy, but with no hint to the personality of the human being that occupied the space. It was a bit cold and sterile looking to Astrid and she subconsciously wrapped her arms around herself as she sat down.

Sara watched her curiously. She claimed to have just met him, yet the way she watched Max, the look of concern that crossed over her face when he winced in pain, made Sara believe there was more to the story. "Did you say you were a friend of Max's?"

"Yes, well…kind of. Really, I just met Mr. Gunther yesterday."

"Thank you for helping him and bringing him here. What's your name?"

"Astrid…Astrid Martin." She rubbed her arms feeling chilled suddenly. So many new faces, so many questions.

"Oh, you're an author, aren't you? You write about magic and things?"

"Uh, yes," she said faintly, "yes."

"Would you like a cup of coffee or something?" Sara asked her as she began to shake slightly. "Are you cold, honey?"

Astrid heard her ask as if from a distance and shook her head slowly whispering, "I'm…fine."

"Tom!" Sara called suddenly. "Tom!"

Tom came rushing into the kitchen and immediately saw the object of Sara's distress. Astrid was shaking badly and her lips had turned purple. Kneeling down in front of her, he took her hands and never taking his eyes away from her, he asked Sara calmly, "What's her name?"

"Astrid."

"Astrid," he said quietly, "my name is Tom. Can you look at me?" She started to close her eyes as Jackson wrapped a blanket around her shoulders.

Hobbling into the room Max asked, "Tom, is she alright?"

Tom ignored him, "Astrid, you're in shock, but everything is alright now." Again her eyes began to close, but he called out to her. "Astrid, look at me. Look at me, honey." She did as he requested and he gave her a warm smile. "You got Max some help and everything is going to be fine." His voice was calm and quiet and as her shaking stopped her lips turned back to pink. "Nod if you can hear me." He rubbed her hands warming them and she slowly nodded giving the patient man in front of her a timid smile.

Max stood behind Tom holding his ribs with one hand and grabbed for the back of a chair with the other unable to stand up straight, "Tom? Is she alright?"

Tom glanced over his shoulder, but brought his eyes back to Astrid, "She'll be fine. It's just hitting her how scary everything was, but it's all over now," he said looking into her eyes to make sure she was still with him. He turned briefly to Max, "Go back and lay down or I'll put you down. You may be bigger, but right now I'm stronger."

Astrid slowly looked up at Max and he said, "Hey, hero," and smiled at her, "You with us?" He waited until she nodded and then afraid at any moment he may fall down making a fool of himself, he went back to the couch and let the others look after Astrid.

Over dinner Max told everyone about Astrid's heroic rescue of him. A blush or grin or shyly looking away as he told the story wouldn't have surprised him, but the curious expression on her face wasn't what he'd expected. She seemed to do quite a few things different from what he expected. He couldn't recall another woman in his life that so baffled him. "I hope my sister hasn't been warning you away from me," Max said giving his sister a playful nudge.

"Sister?" Astrid said.

Max grinned at the wide eyed, open mouthed expression on Astrid's face and turned to his sister with a mock frown, "You didn't tell her who you are?"

Sara looked genuinely muddled, "I guess I forgot. With brothers like you two, who could blame me for wanting to put it out of my mind?"

The affronted expression on Jackson's face caused laughter all around the table. "I'm not just a brother, I'm your twin!" he said with his hand on his chest as if she'd truly hurt him, but the twinkle in his deep blue eyes told a different story.

Max was looking only at Astrid. She hadn't blushed from the story of her bravery, but she was blushing now and he liked it. He could imagine who she thought Sara was. Smiling at her he said, "Yes, that five foot two inch monster is just my sister, not my girlfriend…or whatever you thought she was." Astrid couldn't help a shy grin, at being caught. "She and her twin are my younger siblings."

"Twins?" Astrid asked, clearly surprised. Although they both had the same deep blue eyes, that was where the similarity ended.

Max laughed at the expression on her face. "Yes, twins. I have a feeling that in the womb Jackson took all the food!" Astrid looked at the petite little Sara with sandy blonde hair and a bright, open smile, to the tall, broad-shouldered Jackson with deep set eyes, bushy black eyebrows and jet black hair and grinned as Max continued, "The doc over there is Tom, a family friend. Although, with how tightly he wrapped my ribs I wonder how much of a friend he really is. By the way, how did you know to tell me to take shallow breaths?"

Astrid's shy smile melted from her face. She looked down at the table and shrugged her shoulders, "I just...knew," she said softly, not elaborating.

Not getting much from her verbally, Max watched her body language. She wasn't laughing or bragging or making fun of things the way people usually did when they'd had some sort of accident. She was embarrassed, ashamed, and frightened. Someone had hurt her and if his instincts were right, as they usually were, they'd not just hurt her physically, but psychologically as well.

Feeling the need to break the sudden tension, Jackson asked, "Astrid, I have to know. Where did you learn to handle a gun like that?"

Astrid looked up at Jackson surprised, "What? Oh...well, that bit about me having fired a gun before and having shot someone...I made that up."

"What?" Max quickly set his coffee cup down before he spilled it.

"I had to think of something quickly," she said shrugging her shoulders and taking another bite of her pizza. "I am a writer...a storyteller."

The people at the table were quiet as they all digested what she'd said. Max watched her intently. She seemed so confident, so in control when he was under attack; then once things calmed down she was quivering in shock. He'd seen some pretty cool in the crunch heads before, but this little female took the prize. A grin spread across his face. He'd been ordered to get to know her better. Well, he'd been ordered to silence her, but that alone required getting to know her better. *Sometimes,* he thought, *you just had to love your job.*

25

CHAPTER 3

"So who do you think was behind the attack on you and your little friend yesterday?" The sun was shining brightly on Max's new Jaguar and Tom ran an appreciative eye down it. He glanced over at Sara's red Z28 and then at his own beat up, ten year old beige Jeep and frowned. Maybe he needed to clean up his image a bit. *A lady like her wouldn't want to go out in a...*

"I know exactly who it was," Max said bringing Tom out of his musings. "It was Ivan. I recognized his thugs as they were beating the...as I allowed them a few practice punches."

The humor was not lost on Tom and he gave an appreciative bow, "And the reason you didn't pull out that rather daunting Beretta of yours when they pulled out their weapon?"

Max grinned, "Even thugs can be useful. I may need their services one day! Besides I think they just meant to get me out of the way. Ivan wants Astrid terminated and I haven't done it yet so I think he's getting antsy."

Sara's quick intake of breath alerted them to her presence in the condo doorway. She quickly shut the door so that Astrid wouldn't hear their conversation and rushed down the steps to where the two men stood talking. "Why? Why would he want to kill her?"

"Sara, its business," Max answered her. He looked into her enormous, worried eyes and confused expression. "Don't worry, everything will be fine," he said giving her the placating smile she'd experienced all her life.

Quite used to her brother's charm, she ignored his smile. "I thought you and Ivan and the rest of them were sworn to protect people."

Tom flinched at the pain in her voice. It was a contentious subject between himself and Max that she know anything about her brother's work. Although they were both part of the alliance, Max's particular area tended to get ugly. In Tom's opinion it was no place for someone as tender hearted and compassionate as Sara. He put his hands in his pockets and looked away reminding himself that he had no right getting involved between siblings.

"We protect witches," Max reminded her.

"But...she is a witch! I know it," she looked from Max to Tom. "Alright, I know I'm not part of your *alliance*. I may not have the knowledge that you have, but you've taught me to be aware of certain feelings and sensations and to trust my gut."

Max nodded, "Yes and you've learned well. She is a witch."

"But, then why does Ivan..."

"Sara...," he said, letting out an exasperated breath.

"I know what you're known for in the alliance," she said quietly, taking a step away from him. "Hired Gun Gunther; cold, methodical, detached. Whenever Ivan needs someone eliminated, intimidated, or frightened he calls you." The step she'd taken away from him was as painful as if she'd slapped him and he looked away from the petite blonde as she continued her rebuke. "I don't ask questions. I know this is your work and it's what you do, but Astrid...she's a good person, Max. I know she is. She did save you from those men. How can you even think of...?" Max stood with his shoulders back and his head up rigid as a flagpole. His eyes looked off into the distance. Tom watched Sara's face as the tears welled in her eyes and her brow furrowed and he turned back to Max waiting for him to offer her some assurances, but he offered none. He could all but feel the ache in Sara's heart as she whispered, "Can you really be that detached?" Confused and hurt by her brother's silence, Sara hurried over to her car, giving one last look at her brother, and sped off down the drive.

Running a frustrated hand through his hair Tom said, "Max...," but before he could say anything else, Max got into his car and drove in the opposite direction. A quick gaze at his watch reminded Tom he was due for his shift at the hospital, but he couldn't get his mind off of Sara. Years of the same routine told him that she was probably sitting just a few miles down on the side of the road having a good cry. He looked at his watch again as he got into his car and tapped his thumb on the steering wheel. Although the hospital was to the left, he turned right, the same direction Sara had gone. Calling the doctor on duty he explained that he'd be a little late just as he located Sara's car. Slowly he pulled up behind her and walked up to her door lightly tapping on the window. Her head was resting on the steering wheel, but she looked up appearing neither startled nor surprised to find him standing there. The desolate look on her face made him immediately go to his knees as she lowered the window. "Sara," he said reaching out to take her hand. "Don't worry about Astrid."

"Why would Ivan want her dead? I don't understand."

When her big blue eyes looked up at Tom, he suddenly felt like the biggest waste of space and oxygen on the planet. Bending his head down a moment he said, "I'm sorry, Sara, but I don't know."

She reached down and grabbed a tissue. "I've thought, all this time...I mean...I know Max carries a gun and he's come home before with injuries, but I thought you all *protected* not..."

"Sara, we do protect," he said earnestly. "Maybe there is something about Astrid that...well, others may need to be protected from. Regardless of the no doubt exaggerated stories you've heard about Max, he's a good man. He's just...secretive, temperamental, and stubborn...ornery, feisty, and demanding...controlling, pushy, and...," he breathed a heavy sigh making her giggle, "And basically...he's a good man, but...there are times when he has tough decisions to make."

"Decisions involving killing people," she said looking him right in the eyes. He didn't want to answer and soon realized he didn't need to; she could see the answer on his face. Daintily blowing her nose she said, "Speaking of good men...aren't you supposed to be at the hospital?"

He stood up and slipped his hands into his pockets, "Yeah, I've got plenty of time. I can't let you go off getting in a car accident upset about your bone-headed brother. The other bone-headed brother would kill me!" Looking into her eyes, his heart cried out to tell her the truth, but his head just couldn't manage it and the words didn't come.

"Well, I've kept my date waiting long enough," she said suddenly. "We're meeting at Running Aces!"

"The casino?" he asked.

Sara turned away and shrugged her shoulders, "His wife is out of town for only a few days so we have to make the most of them!"

Tom stepped back to her car, "Sara, wait a minute..."

"Yes?" Tom shuffled his feet in the dirt and ran a hand through his hair.

"I ..."

"Yes? You what?"

"I don't think Max would like...,"

"Gotta go," she said letting out a breath she'd been holding, "I'm running late."

As he watched her car speed off down the road, Tom kicked the ground hard and the wind sent the sand and gravel back his direction; all over his pants legs. *Little Sara...at a casino...with a married man...a two-timer who doesn't even have the decency to pick her up,* he thought angrily as he pulled the keys out of his pocket and stalked back to his car.

♣

"I put her in the closet," Jackson said to Max's inquiry about Astrid when he returned.

"What?" Max yelled racing to unlock the closet doors. He'd just come from a nasty confrontation with Ivan Bronius about him beating the hell out of his own agents and now this. "Why would you do that?"

Jackson scratched his head watching Max explode. It had seemed like a good idea at the time. "I did it so she wouldn't leave. You said to make sure she didn't leave."

Taking deep breath, Max said, "I meant for you to just let her know she'd be safe here and we'd be back soon." Looking in, Max couldn't see Astrid. It was a deep closet and she'd pushed herself back behind the winter gear. He could just make out her feet peeping from under a long black coat. "Hey, Astrid. It's alright honey. You can come on out." He reached toward her and she smacked the back of his hand with a shoe. Quickly recoiling his hand, he glanced at Jackson with a look that told him he was in danger of being throttled at any moment. Jackson wiped his hand over his face and moved away from Max before his brother acted on the expression that was on his face. Speaking as he would to a frightened child, Max said, "I'm going to leave the doors open and back away. You come out whenever you're ready." Max went to sit in the living room.

Jackson tentatively approached Max. "Sorry," he said simply not really knowing what else he could say to fix his mistake.

"If you weren't my brother…"

"I know, I know. I'd be on the floor right now." Max made no further comment.

Twenty minutes later Astrid emerged from the closet. Sara had arrived and the three siblings were sitting in the living room talking quietly.

Max stood up and walked toward her, but before he could speak, Jackson came up beside him and spoke first. "I'm sorry about the closet. Max asked me to make sure you didn't leave while they went out this morning. I guess I got carried away."

Astrid glanced at him and said quietly, "You could have just asked me."

It was so simply said and such an obvious thing he should have considered, that he felt even more like an idiot than he had a moment ago. "You're right. I should have. I guess I figured you'd argue or refuse or demand answers that I couldn't give. I'm afraid the craziness of yesterday just kind of got to me." As he shifted his weight from one leg to the other and back again, he shook his head saying, "Anyway, it was stupid. I'm sorry."

He looked up into Astrid's face and was surprised when she said, "It's alright, Jackson. It must be difficult to be his younger brother."

Max frowned and Jackson grinned. "Yes, it can be very difficult," he said wondering how she knew. Living in Max Gunther's shadow was difficult to say the least, but it was the first time anyone seemed to notice the difficulty.

"Does someone want to fill me in on what that's supposed to mean?" Max said looking from one to the other.

Astrid didn't answer him. She looked up into his crystal blue eyes and said softly, "I'm sorry about your hand, Mr. Gunther."

He winced at the formality of his name, but the way her soft blue-green eyes searched his face, he was unable to fuss about it. "Don't worry about my hand. It's fine."

"I was just frightened."

"Having a virtual stranger suddenly lock you in a closet, it's understandable you'd be frightened," he said glaring at Jackson once again.

"No, it wasn't that," she said. "I've been locked in a closet many times," she admitted with a chuckle, "it's just…no one ever came in before. It just startled me. I shouldn't have hit you. I'm sorry."

Detesting subservience in any form, Max said, "I'll forgive you instantly…if you'll stop calling me sir and Mr. Gunther…permanently."

"I'm sorry…Maxim," she said softly, looking up into his eyes.

Max stared at her unprepared for the way his name sounded on her lips. He hadn't been called Maxim for a really long time, not since his mother was alive and even then…it didn't sound the way it just did when Astrid said it. As a tear slowly left her eye and rolled down her cheek, Max reached out and wiped it away with his thumb. "Really, Astrid," he said in a gentle tone his brother and sister had never heard him use before, "don't give it another thought. It's fine."

"Hardly a killing offense," Sara said with a smirk, breaking the quiet moment, "eh, Max?"

Max gave her a cold stare. Suddenly feeling as if he needed something to do, Jackson said, "Would anyone like some coffee?" and made his way to the kitchen to perform the task. Astrid looked from Max to Sara and felt a definite tension between them, but knowing how things could be between siblings, she decided not to ask questions.

They all sat down in the small living room and an uncomfortable silence descended until a few moments later when Jackson arrived with coffee and a few cookies on a tray. Max picked up a cookie and gave him a frown before placing it back down where he'd gotten it. "This isn't Sweden," Jackson said, "You want pastry, bring your own."

"So how do your ribs feel today?" Astrid asked frowning down at her cup of coffee. Max gave her a sympathizing nod to her frown. The coffee was terrible.

Seeing their frowns at his brew, Jackson quipped, "Don't worry about Max, Astrid. He's used to pain. How many hours did you spend on that rack, Little Fella?"

Jackson had always enjoyed being taller than his *big* brother and whenever he felt ill-used it was his first choice of brotherly jab. To his frustration it was usually ignored. "What rack?" Astrid asked.

"Ignore him. People who can't make decent coffee often look for inadequacies in others."

"I don't see any inadequacies," Astrid said innocently, but Sara couldn't hold back a giggle.

"Thank you," Max said with a twinkle in his eye.

Jackson laughed, but said, "He is short though."

"I'll have you know that five foot nine in considered average for a man…in this country."

"Well, from my six foot three vantage point, you're short."

Unable to finish the less than palatable coffee, Astrid set it down asking, "You said, rack. What kind of rack?"

Max picked up Astrid's coffee cup along with his own and said, "Come, before we leave we'll see if we can figure out if the problem with this coffee is the beans, the machine, or the man who made it." He glanced over at Jackson with a low voiced, "*uppföra sig.*" Jackson glared at his older brother for his suggestion to behave, but said no more.

Before going to the kitchen, Astrid walked over to Jackson, "Thank you for letting me stay here last night."

The light touch on his arm as she looked in his eyes completely dissolved the frustration he'd felt with his brother over his coffee comment. "You're entirely welcome, Astrid. Again, I'm sorry about the closet." They smiled at each other long enough for Max to feel the need to clear his throat before going into the kitchen to make a fresh pot of coffee and force the memories of the rack, back where they belonged; the far corners of his mind.

CHAPTER 4

"Thank you, for giving me a ride back to my car. I could have just taken the bus."

Max helped her out of his car. "It was no trouble to drive you. Are you sure you want to go back to your apartment all alone? We haven't figured out yet who was behind the attack." Max held her hand as they stood in the parking garage just a few feet away from where Ivan's idea of trying to frighten her into spilling all her information had failed. He'd convinced Ivan to back off a little bit, but he wouldn't wait long for the information they needed. A little more time with her and he thought he could get her to open up a bit.

"I don't believe that attack had anything to do with me. No offense, but…it was you they were beating up."

He couldn't help but smile at her chuckle. "Touché. However, I would like to remind you that the reason they were beating me up was because I was beating them up."

She held up her other hand in surrender, "Okay, okay. You were my hero."

He gently rubbed the top of her hand with his thumb and stepped closer to her, "No, you were the hero." He watched the smile fade from her face as he continued to move closer; close enough to smell the delicate floral scent of her perfume.

Before he had a chance to touch her, she stepped back and looked behind him and to the sides. "Max, I appreciate everything you've done for me," she said taking another step back. "I think I just need to get inside and have a little time to myself." She took her hand away from his comforting hold.

"I understand," Max said watching her. "I hope if you need anything you'll call me."

"I'm sure I'll be fine." She continued looking everywhere but at him and began rubbing her hands up and down her arms.

"I'd like to see you again. Can I give you a call?" She didn't answer right away. "Astrid, is there something wrong? You seem nervous all of a sudden." He smiled at her, "I don't make you nervous…do I?" Although he'd meant it as a joke, he soon realized he'd missed his mark.

"No…" she said quickly then looked back at him, "well, maybe…yes."

Max's smile faded, "I'm sorry, Astrid. I realize things have been a little…well, what's the word?" Clearing his throat and smirking he said, "Well, crazy I guess, but…," he suddenly got very serious and gently stroked a single finger down her cheek saying softly, "Please, don't be afraid of me."

Astrid felt mesmerized by the gentle tone, the soft touch, and his crystal blue eyes. "I didn't mean nervous as in afraid...exactly," she said softly making the back of his neck tingle. As he stepped toward her, she backed up putting up a hand to hold him away. "I'm fine, really. I just want to get to my apartment and you know...be in my own little space for a while."

Max wasn't convinced that was all that was wrong, but decided to let it go. "Okay, go on, but I will be calling you."

She gave him one last smile and he watched her hurry into her car. Once she was safely tucked away inside, he got in his car and headed home. It was nice of his brother to allow him to recuperate at his place last night, but this morning he really missed his coffee. He was obviously going to need to talk to his sibling about what kind of beans he's grinding up. It couldn't have been coffee beans.

He had only gotten halfway home when something started telling him to turn around. He pulled his car onto the side of the road and paused a moment trying to understand what was bothering him. *Astrid.* Maybe he should just drive past her apartment and make sure everything was as it should be. Usually when he had a nagging feeling about something...it meant something. He'd learned through the years not to ignore the feeling. He whipped his Jaguar around and headed to her apartment. Not bothering to park in a parking space, he checked the notepad on his phone for her apartment number and bolted. There were no other people milling about and as he approached he noticed the door to her apartment was partially open. Max pulled out his gun and slowly pushed the door open farther. "Astrid?" he called softly. Noticing the spray painted writing on the wall and a chair and couch ripped open with the stuffing pulled out, Max called louder, "Astrid, are you in here? It's Max."

"Max?" he heard her soft as cashmere call from one of the other rooms.

He hurried into what appeared to be her bedroom. More writing was on the walls. *Evil, Wicked, Burn the Witch.* The same words that had been in the living room. Printed pages torn from a book were strewn about the room. It looked as if blood was spilled all over her bed. Astrid turned to him holding something in her hands. Tracks of tears were evident on her cheeks, but they had begun to dry up. Putting his gun away, he looked at her hands to see what she held and she answered his questioning look, "It belonged to my grandmother." She held out the figurine. It was a very delicate, spun glass pink grand piano. In that moment she seemed as fragile as the figurine when she said sadly, "At least they didn't break it. It's all I have that…that really mattered."

"I'm glad it's alright, but try not to touch anything else. We've got to call the police. They'll want to dust for fingerprints." He tried motioning her back out into the living room, but she stopped.

"We don't need the police," she said, clutching the little piano to her heart with one hand and picking up some of the printed pages with the other. "I know who did this," she said letting out a sigh, then with the same sad tone as before added, "Why do you have a gun?"

"Never mind that," he said, although his mind was saying, *because of people like this.* "Who did this?" Max asked her.

"It's watered down paint," she said watching him investigating the red liquid spilled all over her bed. "They always use watered down paint."

Max frowned and asked gently, "Who is *they*, Cashmere?"

She walked over to a shelf and gently placed the piano on it then started around the room picking up more pages and stacking them neatly on her dresser. "My two brothers and my sister." She shook her head and sighed again, "If you look in my closet there is probably a stuffed animal hanging by a noose."

Max went to the closet and didn't bother to let her know she was correct. Trying to keep his well-known temper in check, Max asked what was foremost on his mind, "Why would they do this to you?"

"It doesn't matter," she said.

"The hell it doesn't matter!" Max said as she started picking up more of the pages from the living room floor. He caught her arm and stood her upright. "Are these the same people that used to put you in a closet?"

She pulled away from him and went into the kitchen coming out moments later with a sponge and a bottle of cleanser. She sprayed and scrubbed, but the paint didn't budge off the wall.

"Astrid," he said watching her. It was good to see that she was more angry than sad about all of this. It helped to take away some of the bastards power over her, but he knew what she was doing was an exercise in futility. "Honey, that's not going to come off with any sort of cleaner. It'll have to be primed and repainted."

"I know," she said softly, "I've been down this road three times now, but scrubbing at it…," she laughed at herself, "scrubbing at it makes me feel better."

"They've done this to you three times? Why haven't you called the police?" Max picked up a few of the pages and noticed they'd been ripped out of a bible.

"The police aren't necessary. They aren't hurting me."

"Astrid," he walked to her and took her hand, "I saw your face when I first came in. They're hurting you." She didn't say anything, but he was glad when she didn't pull her hand away. "Why don't you move so that they can't find you?"

"They're my family. I have to let them know where I am."

"Why?" Max asked exasperated. "If they're going to do this kind of thing to you, why would you tell them where you are?"

"Well, they're my family." Astrid frowned at him. "What if there was some kind of an emergency? If something happened to Mama or if I needed someone."

"I can't answer about your mother, but if you needed someone these people don't seem like the type that would help you."

Astrid gave him a pathetic nod and walked into the bedroom, he assumed she'd started gathering the sheets off the bed. Instead she started putting toiletry items in a little overnight bag. She glanced up at him as he walked in. "Would you mind giving me a ride back to the hotel? If I stay here tonight, they'll come by and…," she paused what she was doing, closed her eyes, and sat down on the edge of the bed. "I'm so tired," she said, her voice breaking. Both hands came up to cover her face as fresh tears started. "I'm sorry."

"What for?"

"For falling apart."

Max knelt down in front of her and gently took her face in his hands. Her hands dropped and he saw the desolation on her face and his anger peaked anew. "You're not going to a hotel. You're coming to my house to let me take care of you." He pulled her in close to wrap his arms around her.

As she wrapped her arms around him, he noticed her hand feel the wrapping under his shirt. "I don't think a man with bruised ribs is in any shape to take care of anyone."

He chuckled lightly, "Come home with me, we'll take care of each other." She stood up and walked over to the small window looking out over the courtyard. "It's a big place, Astrid. You'll have your own suite. Plenty of privacy," he said.

"Alright, Max," she said turning back to him.

He watched her soft greenish-blue eyes looking up at him so trustingly. "It'll be alright, I'll keep you safe." As soon as the words were out of his mouth he wondered what had possessed him to utter them. He turned away and tried to remember his mission and that this woman was putting his people in danger to advance her own career. It was his mission and obligation to protect others from her, but his instinct was telling him there was something else going on. She nodded, but didn't answer him. "Astrid...why the bible pages?"

Astrid looked down at the floor and tucked a strand of hair behind her ear, "They think it will help chase away the evil."

"What evil?"

"Me," she said so softly he could barely hear her. He reached out to hold her, but she moved away grabbing her bag and heading out the door asking, "Do you always walk around with a gun?"

♣

As they neared Max's house, Astrid chuckled to herself and Max simply had to know why. "Come on, let me in on the joke."

"I was just thinking about when you asked about someone like you and someone like me. This is a prime example," she said pointed out of the window at the estates they were passing. "Linden Hills, huh? Far cry from my humble abode or should I say grubby little apartment."

"I don't really see why the location of our homes should mean anything."

"Come on, you're saying it's not weird that someone like you; handsome, successful, confident, and intelligent is befriending someone like me?"

"Someone like you?" Max scowled out of the windshield. "A beautiful, single woman whose intelligence and imagination have blossomed into a budding writing career. Yeah, man that is weird," he said sarcastically.

"I'm not…beautiful," she said quietly.

"After you've settled in, I'll make you an appointment with my optometrist." They pulled into his drive and Astrid was unable to speak further about anything. Clearly she wasn't really in need of an optometrist because her eyes were able to pick up every incredible sight of the mansion before her. The house was three stories with two second floor balconies overlooking the front lawn. The front door was tucked into a turret in the center of the building. She almost laughed to herself at how old world and Medieval it looked considering its owner was from Sweden and they probably had castles around every corner there. This small castle was a perfect fit for him. They walked up the curved front steps and she noticed the old world front door and huge iron sconces flanking the door. Stepping inside she admired the ornate tile floor in the circular foyer and the curved staircase leading to the second floor. Max carried her bag straight up the stairs and along the landing of the second floor overlooking the foyer. He went to the third door and motioned for her to enter. Dark blue carpet accented a dark four poster bed with a blue damask coverlet. "I hope this will be alright," he said quietly as she looked around the room. "It used to be my sister's room."

"It's lovely, thank you," she said reverently as he set her bag down. She couldn't help notice how shabby the bag looked in such an exquisite room.

"The bathroom is over there," he said motioning to his right, "and the closet is huge, after all…it was Sara's," he chuckled. "If you need anything just let me know. I'll get out of your way so you can…do whatever you need to." He smiled as he left and she gingerly sat down on the bed before taking a much needed deep breath.

Astrid spent the rest of the day in her room resting and trying to put the events of the last few days into place in her mind. Although she knew that Max and possibly someone else were in the house, they had left her alone to get herself acclimated to her new environment. The following morning she walked down the stairs and peeped into the room to her right. It was a warm, masculine…very masculine, sitting room. Deep leather chairs flanked either side of the fireplace and a tapestry sofa of muted autumnal colors sat behind them. A coffee table with a huge clock base joined the conversation area and the enchanting gnome creatures that sat upon it made her want to sit and get warmed by the fire. Noticing the fire, she also noticed the mantel and her grandmother's little blown glass piano that Max had adorned it with. She smiled appreciating his acknowledgement of its importance to her. Crystal vases on either side stood sentinel over it with the same lovely flowers she'd seen in her room and other places in the house. She wondered if there was a special meaning behind them or was it that they were simply in season. There were shelves on one small wall filled with books that were in a foreign language which she assumed was Swedish. On another larger wall, the shelves were filled with books in English. A large globe with a dark wooden base held center stage in the room and a desk in the same dark color sat near the wall opposite the entrance into the room. One flower stood alone in an unadorned bud vase on the desk. Astrid thought about the desk's owner and wrapped her arms around herself feeling oddly sad suddenly.

Walking into the kitchen she couldn't help exclaiming, "Good grief! Why do you have so much coffee?"

Max had just opened the cabinet reaching for the coffee grounds. "I have different coffees for different moods!" He smiled at her bewilderment. "In Sweden taking fika is a very serious avocation!"

"Fika?"

"Basically having coffee or taking a coffee break with a friend…and usually a pastry." The way he wiggled his eyebrows up and down as he said it made her giggle. "Unless you're at my brother's house and then you get a hard, crumbly poor excuse for a cookie." He was rewarded with a second giggle and was unable to stop his own chuckle. When it came to his coffee he was used to being laughed at. His siblings thought he was a bit of a nut about coffee. He had a cabinet specifically devoted to what he considered the elixir of the gods. The cabinet was full to the top of bags of various coffees; St. Helena, Blue Mountain, Café Jerusalem Kosher Coffee, and various others with of course the most prominent being Gevalia Kaffe, direct from Sweden. It was a colorful display and he looked just like a child in a toy shop. She couldn't help but to smile at his obvious enthusiasm. As he brewed her a cup of what he said was *one* of his favorites, he explained the importance of the stainless steel coffee spoon…to keep the clean taste of the grounds. The gold coffee filter was also essential to keeping the grounds from being contaminated by paper or other metals and most importantly you must never grind anything in the coffee grinder other than coffee beans. Astrid took all this information into her head and managed not to giggle…until she quite seriously asked, "Is there going to be a quiz?" At which time Max's look of surprise caused her little giggle to turn into genuine laughter. She pointed to the coffee maker, "That is without doubt the fanciest coffee maker I have ever seen."

"This thing? This is nothing. This just makes coffee. I've seen machines that can do lattes and espressos and some even do the laundry!" Astrid shook her head, "I don't go for the fancy stuff…just good old fashioned coffee."

"You call this 'old fashioned coffee'?"

Max placed a cup in front of her and poured the fresh brew, "Always use a china cup, it tastes better," he said seriously, then added a grin and Astrid saluted the coffee general as she sipped.

♣

The rest of the day had been her own as Max left right after breakfast and was gone the rest of the day. Astrid sat down in the sitting room with her pencil and spiral notebook and wrote down whatever thoughts popped into her head. Before realizing it, she'd fallen asleep in the cozy leather chair. When she awoke there was a blanket draped across her legs and someone had recently brought in a tray of coffee. She got up slowly and poured herself a cup then set out to find her coffee fairy. Hearing a shuffle of feet in the kitchen she walked in to find a lovely woman about her age shuffling through a box of recipes. "Hello," Astrid said softly trying not startle the woman.

Looking up with a smile on her face she said, "Hello. My name is Manette. Is there something I can get you?" she asked in a Swedish accent quite a bit more pronounced than Max's.

"Oh, no thank you. I just wanted to say thank you for the coffee. It was a wonderful thing to find waiting for me after my unexpected nap," Astrid said with a timid smile. "My name is Astrid Martin. I'm staying here for uh…a few days. Are you…Mrs. Gunther?"

Laughing heartily, the beautiful girl said, "Heavens no! I am just a *hembiträde*."

"Oh," Astrid said sounding confused and looking away.

The woman laughed again and said, "I am sorry. I am…the maid? I clean, cook, and do shopping. Maid…yes?"

Astrid smiled, "Maid, or housekeeper, or even domestic engineer."

"I will stick with maid. It is easier."

Watching the maid taking ingredients from the refrigerator she said, "Could I help you with something?"

"That is not necessary. I am just making some *Kladdkaka*." A huge smile went across her face as she took out a tin of unsweetened cocoa powder. "He loves a good *öken,* but this is his favorite."

"I'm sorry, what was that you said, o…oak…"

Manette laughed and said, "I am sorry. It is *ö-ken*," she said pronouncing it slowly. It means dessert in Swedish. What is that they say, *you can take the girl out of Sweden, but you cannot take the Sweden out of the girl!*" The two shared a laugh and Astrid went over to read the recipe card.

"*Kladdkaka*? Did I say that right?"

"Pretty good! It has slightly crisp outside and gooey inside. A little like a thin, corner slice of your American brownie. Very chocolatey like maybe…fudge."

Astrid's mouth began to water just thinking about it and imaging it being paired with a rich cup of coffee. "I'd love to help you or at least watch if that's okay. I…I don't want to get in your way or…mess anything up."

Manette smiled and handed her a spring form pan, "Do you cook?"

"Just for myself, but I…well, I don't bake. I'd love to learn."

"Then you will learn. Butter that pan for me while I prepare the eggs."

"Are you here every day?" Astrid asked as she worked at the task shew as given.

Manette laughed whisking the eggs with an expert hand, "No, he doesn't make enough mess! I come on Mondays and Thursdays mostly to change the bedsheets and see that his laundry gets to the dry cleaners. He really is not in need of me, but…" Astrid watched as Manette's gaze drifted out of the window for a moment then quickly came back to the butter she was melting at the stove. "How long will you stay?"

It suddenly occurred to her that by staying there she was making more work for the young woman and said, "I don't really know. I'll try not to be any trouble."

Manette smiled and continued her work saying, "I'm sure you will not."

"So…Mr. Gunther's got a sweet tooth?"

Astrid watched Manette's hand pause at her stirring and her eyes slowly glanced over at the door. "He likes many things," she said defensively, "but…," another glance toward the door, "but especially likes treats with his coffee." Manette quickly focused back on her cooking and Astrid decided to ask no further questions about the master of the house.

CHAPTER 5

When Max came home, Astrid was excited to show him the dessert she'd helped make, but when he came in the door with blood running down his arm her excitement died. "What happened to you?"

He looked down at his arm as if he didn't know he'd been wounded and shrugged his shoulders. "It's nothing, don't worry."

Jackson came in the door behind him and before he noticed Astrid in the room said, "Did he take the baby? What happened?"

"It's all taken care of," Max said, looking from his brother to Astrid, but Jackson didn't seem to notice the signal to stop talking.

"You better get to the hospital to get the bullet out."

Taking a patient breath, Max said with a forced smile, "There is no bullet. It only grazed me. It's fine," his jaw clenched in frustration, "*lagom,*" Jackson finally looked over and noticed what or rather who, Max was looking at.

"Oh, hi…uh, Astrid."

"Someone…took a baby?"

Max groaned at his brother, but smiled at Astrid, "Everything is fine. It was just a family misunderstanding."

Jackson snorted shaking his head. Astrid watched him and slowly came closer to Max. "You were shot at and you consider that just a misunderstanding? Are you sure you don't need a doctor?"

Max headed for the staircase to get cleaned up. "It's just a scratch and I can…," his phone rang, "Hello?" Astrid watched Max's expression turn from a calm, placid look to a stern glare at his brother. "That isn't necessary," he told the person on the phone, "There's no need for…I understand. That won't be necessary he's with me." He hung up the phone and told Jackson, "We're summoned."

"Why?"

Max headed up the stairs again, "I don't know he's summoned several of us. I think...," he looked briefly at Astrid, "Something may have happened."

"Alright, but...do you have the baby?"

Through clenched teeth Max told his brother, "I'll be right back down."

As he dashed up the stairs and Astrid asked Jackson, "Do you really think his arm is alright?"

Jackson smiled saying, "If anybody can take a hit and barely notice its Max; bullets, knives, even burns don't stop him!"

Astrid walked back toward the kitchen contemplating what Jackson had said and wondered why someone in the publishing business needed to be able to *take a hit* of bullets, knives, or burns in the first place.

♣

As soon as they arrived at Ivan's office they were ushered into the board room of the publishing house. Several familiar faces were seated at the long table; Tom among them. Max took a seat opposite of Agent Heiss, always feeling a little more comfortable having the man in front of him rather than beside or behind. He wasn't surprised to see the seat beside Ivan empty. The brother of his formidable employer had been out of sight for some time causing some to speculate a family rift. Having his own brother and knowing it was a relationship riddled with various issues, Max wasn't one of the ones speculating anything; it simply wasn't his business. "You're late," Ivan said making eye contact with Max, "but, I supposed we should just be glad you're here and not in the morgue. I was told you were shot."

"Only grazed," Max said with a shrug of his shoulders.

"I assume the wielder of the weapon is dead and the mother and child safely out of the state," Ivan said moving files around, eager to move on to the next case.

"No," Max said slowly, "no…on both counts."

Ivan stopped shuffling papers and looked at him. "Your orders were to get that witch and her child out of harm's way."

"I know, but there were complications," Max said.

Various sounds of feet shuffling and chair legs moving sounded in the room as Ivan continued his intense stare at Max. Stealing an opportunity to harass someone he considered his nemesis, Agent Heiss, with his thick Latvian accent, said, "Maybe when he was shot at he was so frightened he forgot his orders."

Max's head slowly turned toward the agent that spoke. "I don't think anyone here yanked on your chain," Max said glaring at him.

"Hired Gun," he chuckled at Max's nickname, "Hired gun who does not know when to pull trigger." A few snickers were heard from covered faces around the table.

"Believe me I know when to pull the trigger," Max said, "Lucky for you I know when not to pull it."

Agent Heiss snarled at him, "We do not need rogue agent with too much ego, is dangerous."

"Yes, I am!"

Heiss snorted and Ivan stood up, "You two want to take your little game outside and see if the swing set is available so the big men can have their meeting?" Most in the room laughed, but not Ivan. The glare he delivered along with his fists balled at his sides made the big red-head look as if he would gladly toss them out of the window into the yard if that was their desired destination. Glaring at Max, Ivan said, "Do I need to send someone in to clean up a mess you didn't handle?"

"No," Max said calming himself down, knowing that Heiss was just trying to goad him and had unfortunately succeeded. Looking only at Ivan he said, "The grandparents didn't really have a problem with their daughter-in-law practicing witchcraft. The real problem was because she was considering moving with the child to the other side of the country."

Ivan nodded, "So their son was killed in Iraq fighting for his country and she was taking the last piece of him away from them."

"Yes. She wasn't trying to keep them from their grandchild, she just needed support and they weren't giving it. Everyone has calmed down a bit now. They stopped pushing and she started listening...then they listened. She's going to stay put and they're going to help her out both financially and emotionally. Everything is settled just not...how originally intended."

"To thwart me or because it was in the best interest of all involved? Might be best not to answer that," Ivan said, picking up the file of the next case he wanted discussed. "Keep an eye on things, but from a distance." Max nodded. "Heiss, incident down town?"

"He is dead," the large man answered with no sign of emotion.

"Did you get a chance to discuss things with him first?" Ivan inquired and Max almost laughed. Everyone knew that Heiss didn't discuss.

"Was not time," he answered. Max looked at him wondering why it was that he had been in America for at least six years and yet he still looked and sounded as if he just got off the plane from Latvia. He was rigid as a pole, spoke like a robot, and seemed to be in a constant state of angry. At six foot six few people were ever going to go against him and yet he always looked as if he expected someone to jump out at him.

"Gunther! If you'd like to rejoin the conversation!"

As Ivan's fist came down on the table, Max realized he'd let his mind wander and it wasn't being appreciated. He turned to his employer with a smile, "Sorry, painkillers making my mind a little fuzzy," he said holding his injured arm.

Ivan shook his head as Jackson choked on his water trying to hold back his chuckle. "I doubt you've ever taken a painkiller in your life. Now back to business. The little witch that went to the hospital after you killed her pimp, Tom tells me she's been released from the hospital. The police think it was just a turf war between two pimps. She's confirmed the story and now I want her out of here. She's got a mother in Wisconsin, get her there." Max nodded remembering the horrible scene.

When he'd found her, the boyfriend slash pimp had a knife to her throat. Max had told him twice to put the knife down, but when he hadn't complied Max shot him in the head. The girl was considerably shaken. Just recently her powers had begun to manifest and she wanted to get out of prostitution and go back home. A few of the regular John's had recently started complaining that there was something strange about her, but of course her pimp wasn't going to let her go regardless of the complaints. He apparently thought he could beat the witch out of her. Although he'd given the guy fair warning, there was a part of Max that was delighted he hadn't taken the chance to get out of the situation alive. "I wish you would take care of your current case as efficiently as you handled the last one," Ivan said glaring at him.

"Doing my best," he said with a grin, but only received a scowl in return.

"Do better," Ivan spat out, "I've cut back on the books being distributed to the bookstores, but I'm still paying her so she doesn't get suspicious. It was bad enough when it was just a storybook, but now people are taking her ideas and putting them into practice. I've told her we'd publish another book in the series just to keep her from shopping around for another publisher, but we'll not be releasing it. We need to know where her information is coming from." Max was toying with his pencil and not looking in Ivan's direction giving the senior man the feeling he was being ignored, "Damn it all, Gunther," he shouted, getting Max's attention, "Get that information," Max dutifully nodded to his employer.

The meeting continued on into the evening as Ivan wanted a check on every witch in their watch area, Minnesota, Iowa, and Wisconsin accounted for. A threat had come from the Dakota's that could possibly be linked all the way back to Sweden and the alliance nationwide was taking the threat seriously.

When they were finally given their new orders and allowed to leave, Agent Heiss walked over to Max. He stood over him and looked down with a forced smile. "Small men should look out. When in the way, they can get stepped on," he said and gave Max's injured arm a not so friendly hard smack. Max looked up at him refusing to show any sign of pain. Watching the blood appear on Max's shirt sleeve, the man smiled as he chuckled and walked away.

As he glared at his foe's retreating figure, Jackson walked up to him. "Hey, you're bleeding again," he said pointing to Max's arm.

"No kidding," Max said raising an eyebrow. "One of these days that guy and I are going to meet somewhere dark and dangerous and only one of us will come out alive."

"Are you sure it would be you coming out?"

Max grinned, "No, but I've got too much ego to avoid the confrontation." Noticing his brother's smile he said, "What? No argument?"

Jackson shook his head, "None. Go home and rewrap that arm…it looks gross."

Max looked down. *Another dress shirt ruined from the same damn injury,* he thought and shook his head as they walked out of the office.

He drove home trying to reconcile the information Ivan had given the group with his own instincts. Several of the recent murders of witches across the country were beginning to somehow be associated with Astrid. The woman who, thus far, Ivan was unaware was living in his house. The description of Astrid was in complete odds with the woman he had been slowly getting to know. She wasn't calculating, deceptive, or cagey. She was innocent, seemingly unaware, and even compassionate. Regardless of Ivan's pushing, he would get to the bottom of things before making any moves.

♣

A few mornings later, Astrid walked into the kitchen in a pink and green blouse made out of some flowy fabric that Max thought made her look like a flower with pretty petals. Just looking at her made him feel good and he took a deep breath before saying, "Good morning."

"Good morning."

"Coffee?" He took out a small tin can, but continued to hold open the cabinet. "Your choice this morning."

He seemed to be holding his breath hoping she would join him in his amusement. "I wouldn't being to know how to choose."

"Well, if you're adventurous I can offer something different," he said with a mischievous grin that made her wonder what other adventures he might suggest given half a chance.

"I would love to try whatever you'd like to brew." She sat down at a little table thinking that she'd never actually seen a man moving around a kitchen before as if he knew exactly what he was doing. His confidence was apparent and she had to admit, very attractive. They hadn't spent much time together since she'd moved in. He'd respected her need for a little space and let her get comfortable in his home. It was quiet and comfortable. She knew Manette came in twice a week to tidy and now she understood why the maid said he didn't make enough mess to require her more often. Max was so methodical and organized there wasn't really ever much tidying to be done. Everything he did he seemed to know exactly what he was doing. Confidence was not Astrid's strong suit and she smiled watching him preparing the coffee maker and getting out cups and saucers.

He glanced at her with one eyebrow up, "two sugars, stir three times, right?"

"Yes," she frowned, "…yes, I guess I do usually do that. How'd you know?" she asked with a chuckle.

"I always notice how people take their coffee. I'm sure there is some lofty psychological reason why people stir or don't stir and how many times and which direction, but I don't know what it is. I just seem to notice who is doing what with their coffee!" He shrugged his shoulders and grinned, "Silly really, but take Sara for instance, she puts in equals measure of sugar and cream and then only fills her cup half full. Jackson…he puts cream in first, then sugar, but doesn't stir it! Tom…black; no cream, no sugar, doesn't even let it cool off, just downs it like he's taking medicine he must endure. My boss? The man can't make up his mind," he said chuckling, "He adds a little cream, a little sugar, and stirs once clockwise then repeats…without tasting stirring counterclockwise, does it one more time stirring clockwise, then drinks it." Max shook his head as if it was the most ridiculous routine he'd witnessed.

The boyish grin on his face, his hair still slightly damp from his morning shower, and the funny way he jerked his wrist now and then made for a very charming picture to Astrid's mind and she felt more at ease than she'd ever felt in someone else's kitchen. "Speaking of strange things people do...why do you do that?" she asked.

He looked at her curiously, "What?"

"Twitch your wrist like that." She demonstrated for him. "Why do you do that?" she asked wrinkling up her little nose and smiling.

Max looked down at his wrists, "I wasn't aware I did." He smiled sheepishly, "Sometimes the hair on my arms gets caught in the watchband, but mostly...I guess it's some sort of habit." Max was transfixed by the beautiful smile that lit up her face.

"I like it. Your watchband makes a tinkling sound and you always readjust your ring afterwards. You stick out your thumb and pinkie and give a little...twitch." She stopped talking and looked at him shyly feeling as if she'd just revealed a secret. "Sorry, I kind of get caught up in little things people do like that."

He simply didn't know what to say to her admission. He'd never noticed the action. For some reason the idea that she would pay attention to something so insignificant delighted him. Whether it was the comforting smell of the coffee brewing in the pot or the way her shy smile seemed to increase the slight slant to her eyes, he didn't know. He only knew as he walked toward her, that he needed to kiss her. Not a want, but a need, a desperate need. As he moved her direction with obvious intent in his eyes, she smiled tenderly and whispered, "Maxim." He stopped briefly to enjoy the delicious quiver that always over took him when she said his name that certain way.

As she sat in the little chair in his kitchen, Max took her face in his hands. He felt her slight quiver of anticipation and smiled softly at her just before pressing his lips to hers. She opened for him and he deepened the kiss.

The world spun and Max could feel her hands clutching his arms gently massaging the muscles beneath the shirt sleeves. The kiss was warm and tender and he didn't want it to end. *"Du är välsmakande,"* Max said softly letting his Swedish roll off his tongue unchecked. His thumb gently stroked her cheek then seeing the smile on her face, snuck back in for another quick nip that turned out to not be as quick as he'd intended. He was breathing as heavily as she was and he loved the feel of her breath against his cheek as he leaned his face against hers. *"Välsmakande,"* he said again. The coffee finished brewing and in that moment, Max realized he'd found something better than coffee first thing in the morning, Astrid's kisses.

"I'm assuming that's Swedish. What does it mean?" She asked dreamily.

"It means tasty and you are…very." He smiled at the shy smile she gave him then stepped away to grab the cups and fix her coffee. "Are you settled in alright? Find everything you've needed?"

"Yes. Thank you for giving me a few days to…to myself," she said taking the coffee he handed her.

"Well, I remembered when I dropped you off at your apartment that you were looking forward to a few days to yourself and of course after finding your apartment in the condition it was in, a few days to decompress seemed compulsory."

"You have a beautiful home and very, very organized. Everything seems to be exactly where you'd expect it," she chuckled as she said it making Max frown slightly.

"Why does that make you laugh? I would think that would be a good thing," Max said sipping his brew.

"It is. It's just…I'm not used to quite so much organization."

"Basically, you're saying I'm obsessive," he said moving to the cabinet to grab a cookie or two, but quickly turned back at the sad sound of her voice.

"I'm sorry, Max," she said quietly. "I didn't mean…I…"

Max placed his hand on hers smiling, "Astrid, its fine. I am obsessive," he said. "According to my siblings, I'm also considered temperamental, demanding, controlling, and stuck firmly in my ways! Now, have a cookie. I always think having something sweet along with the coffee is the real reason for our existence." His smile and silly theory were impossible to resist and Astrid smiled as he extended a raspberry jam filled cookie her direction.

"You really are a puzzle," she said. "I mean, you're everything you just said," He grinned and bowed to her accepting the description, "but you're also kind, patient, and something else I haven't quite figured out."

Those words had never been used to describe him before, at least not in his hearing. It gave him an uneasy feeling in his stomach when he considered the reason she was in his home in the first place. Deciding to avoid the kind and patient bit, he enquired about the *something else.* "What is left to figure out?"

"Well, for instance, the flowers," she said. She had noticed the lovely flowers all over the house the first day she'd arrived. They were in beautiful crystal vases in nearly every room he'd shown her. The first morning when she'd awoken in her room the sunlight had bounced off the crystal vase making the beautiful blooms almost glow. She'd never in her life indulged in something as frivolous as cut flowers in the bedroom, but decided in that moment that wherever she lived for the rest of her life, she would treat herself. It was a small thing to bring such pleasure. She didn't know what kind of flowers they were, but that didn't diminish the pleasure they gave.

"What's wrong with flowers?" he asked pouring each of them a little more coffee.

"Nothing, it just…surprises me. I guess I just thought flowers were a woman's thing." When he cut his eyes at her, she giggled and said, "You're not keeping a woman stashed around here somewhere are you?"

Max blinked a few times then said quietly, "Certainly not."

She wanted to ask about the significance which she knew they must have, but the way he slowly stirred his coffee and didn't look at her made her think maybe it wasn't something he felt comfortable discussing. Considering the fact that he carried a gun, the bloody arm he'd come in with yesterday, and the beating he took in the garage…obviously there was a lot she didn't quite understand about this man and perhaps a little caution would be a good thing. She washed out her empty cup and placed it on the drain board. "Well, I have some writing to do. May I use your desk?" he didn't seem to hear, "Max?"

Lost in thoughts he wished he wasn't having, Max suddenly realized she was talking to him. "What?" he said frowning, looking up at her.

"May I use your desk, please? I have some writing to do." she said feeling a sudden nervousness at the change of energies in the room.

Between the thoughts that had just been plaguing his mind and her submissive attitude, his frown deepened. "You do not have to ask to use a piece of furniture in this house. You live here, at least for the moment, and contrary to popular opinion I am not a tyrant!" He walked out of the room leaving his half-filled coffee cup still sitting on the kitchen table. Just as Astrid finished washing it and placing it on the drain board, Max walked back into the kitchen. "I'm sorry for my outburst, Astrid," he said with a grimace. "I'm afraid my quick temper is legendary. Please feel free to use anything you need. There is another desk in the sitting room I set up for you yesterday. The computer on it is for your use or if you prefer there is also a manual typewriter or if you really want to suffer for your art," he gave her a little grin, "there are pencils and paper." She nodded as he walked back out.

No sooner had he gotten in his car than Tom called. "I think…I think we have a problem. Something…needs to be said…or done."

Max frowned at Tom's nervousness. When it came to the alliance, Tom was an excellent guardian. When it came to being a doctor, Max considered no one more capable. When it came to his sister, Tom turned into a shy, stumbling, nervous wreck. "Is she alright?"

"Well, I don't really know, I…how do you know who I'm talking about?"

"Is Sara alright?" Max asked again.

Tom had already told Max about her going to the casino with a married man and now he had more that was worrying him. "She just came by with some low-life with dirty clothes, slurred speech, and two huge knives on his waist that set off the alarms at the hospital entrance! Security called me down there to ask me if I knew her!"

"Why was she at the hospital?" Max asked, already knowing the answer.

Tom took a deep breath before saying dismissively, "Oh, she just wanted to bring a book by that she knew I'd been wanting about WW2 aircraft."

"That was kind of her."

"Well, you know Sara," he said then paused a moment and his voice softened, "She'd do anything for anyone." There was silence a moment, then he fired up again, "You need to keep an eye on her! She shouldn't be…I mean…this guy isn't the type for her." He breathed heavily into the phone and Max shook his head with a smirk on his face. Softly, Tom said, "Max, just…keep an eye on her."

"Okay, Tom," Max said, then hung up the phone and called his sister. Unfortunately for Max he got exactly what he'd expected. Sara was angry that Tom had called Max. If he'd had a problem with her behavior why hadn't he said something himself? When Max had no answer for her, she'd gotten angry and told him to stay out of her personal life. He was her brother, not her nanny and she'd do as she pleased. Max hung up the phone wondering when the two would finally figure each other out and anxious to get home to a cup of coffee.

CHAPTER 6

Thursday morning Astrid awoke to Manette in her room taking the flowers out of the vase and replacing them with fresh blooms. "Oh, don't throw them away yet. They'll last at least another day or two."

"I must change them before they fade," she said quietly, "I'm sorry to have woken you."

Astrid looked at the little clock on her nightstand. "You didn't. I know it's strange, but I always wake up a few moments before the alarm goes off." She got out of bed and walked over to the dresser the flowers graced, "Really, they still look lovely," she said reaching into the trash can to retrieve one of the pink flowers.

"They mustn't be allowed to droop or turn brown," she said adamantly then she paused her actions a moment and smiled at Astrid, "Would you like me to fix you some breakfast?"

"No, don't bother," Astrid said as Manette put all the spent blooms in the trash can and began to carry it out of the room with her. "Manette,"

"Yes."

"What kind of flowers are they?"

Astrid frowned as the woman paused at the open bedroom door and looked out of it before saying quietly, "Lilies"

Astrid gently turned the vase of new flowers and with a slight frown said, "They are so beautiful. I thought lilies were used at funerals to put on top of coffins and things."

"Some thoughts may be better left unsaid," the maid said as she quickly left the room.

A half hour later Astrid came downstairs to find no trace of Manette, but Max was in the kitchen engrossed in his favorite task of preparing coffee. She'd already begun to notice how the taste, the smell, even sometimes the act of preparing it could alter the energies around him. Boca Java turned out to be her favorite and every time he'd reach for the dark brown package he'd look over his shoulder at her and wink. This morning as he looked over his shoulder his gaze travelled down to her hand carrying the lily she'd retrieved from the trash can and he frowned walking quickly toward her. "Where did you get that?" he asked tersely then without waiting for an answer shouted, "Manette?"

Stunned from his sudden shout, Astrid didn't move. When the maid returned pale, tears spilling down her cheeks, Astrid began to tremble slightly.

Manette tried to clear her throat and hold her shoulders back as she looked up at Max. "Yes?"

"Max, it's not her fault," Astrid said immediately frightened for her, "I took it out of the trash can when she was changing the flowers."

"Come," Max said taking Manette by the elbow and ushering her into the next room.

Astrid couldn't stop her feet from moving toward the door any more than she could stop her ears from straining to hear what was going on, on the other side of it. Their voices were muffled and moments later she heard the front door open and close. As Max came back into the kitchen she asked, "Is...is she alright?"

Max looked at her a moment then slowly said, "Of course she is," he walked back to the counter to finish the coffee, "she'll be back tomorrow," he saved a hand her direction, "She needed a little time to herself today. *Lagom,*" he said dismissively.

Astrid took a steadying breath thinking that if she was coming back tomorrow obviously he hadn't fired her, but he was definitely agitated about something. She'd certainly not forget the look on his face when he'd seen the spent flower in her hand, which she'd concealed under some newspapers in the kitchen trash can before he came back in.

It seemed to be a mutual agreement not to discuss the matter any further and each went back to what had become their usual routine; he made the coffee, she took out the cups, he put the cream and sugar on the table, she set out napkins and spoons. Noticing the way they seemed to go on automatic pilot, Max frowned wondering when it had started. Feeling edgy, disconcerted and like he was beginning to be the bug under the microscope, Max was determined to try to get some answers for Ivan as soon as possible.

"Okay, just one thing. Answer me just one thing," Astrid said suddenly. Max turned to her surprised by her tone and braced himself for whatever she was about to ask. "That word...lagom," she said sarcastically, knowing she wasn't giving it the right accent and not caring. "What does it mean? You say it like...all the time. What does it mean?"

Max let out the breath he'd been holding and grinned. "Sorry," he said trying to look repentant. "I didn't realize I was saying it that much."

"Well, not that much it's just...," he smiled more finding her pout adorable, "it's a little annoying when you don't know what something means."

"Yes it is," he said, "It means...," he both chuckled and frowned at the same time, "I've never really thought about that before. Well, I guess it's sort of...sort of like saying alright. How's the weather? *Lagom.* Did you get enough to eat? *Lagom.* Okay if I turn up the heat? *Lagom.* Get it?"

"*Lagom,*" she said with a grin. "I get it."

The front door slammed hard making them both jump. Setting down their coffees, they went through to the foyer only to find it empty. Looking into the sitting room they found Tom clutching his hands together sitting in a chair in front of the fire with his head bent down nearly to his knees. "Tom?" Tom didn't look up to Max's inquiry, but he unclenched his hands only to drive them into his hair gripping his skull.

Concerned for Tom, but also whatever information he had to give, Max turned to Astrid, "Would you mind…"

"Of course not," she said gently, "I hope…I hope everything is alright."

When she was safely out of ear shot, Max walked closer to Tom and sat in the chair opposite. "Whenever you're ready," he said quietly. "I'm assuming I don't need to verify the safety of my brother and sister?"

"No," Tom whispered, "It's…nothing to do with them." His hands shook as he brought them back down to his lap and clenched them turning his knuckles white. The deep breaths he took didn't seem to help as with tear filled eyes he looked at Max and asked, "When is it murder and when is it just an accident? Where are the lines between accident, suicide, and a vicious push to death?"

Leaving the men to their discussion, Astrid went back into the kitchen to clean up from their morning coffee. Several minutes had passed when she heard the front door again and walked out to find Sara heading for the sitting room. "Oh, I don't think you should go in there right now."

Sara smiled, "Why not?" Her smile died looking at the worried expression on Astrid's face. "What's going on?"

"I don't really know. Tom came over a little while ago and is very upset about something. Max is talking with him right now."

Not waiting another moment, Sara walked right into the sitting room without knocking and charged up to them. "What's happened?"

When she had first opened the door, Tom had looked to see who was coming in, but as soon as he saw who it was he'd turned away. Max stood up and said, "Sara, everything is alright. It's just business."

"Obviously everything is not alright or Tom wouldn't be sitting there like that," she walked closer to him and gently placed a hand on his shoulder. "Please tell me what's happened," she said softly, "I want to help."

"Tom, I leave that to your discretion," Max said and then grabbed his car keys off of his desk, "I'm going to see about the situation myself."

"Ivan's been in a meeting," Tom's voice was soft and shaky, nothing like his usual tone. "I…I tried…reaching him."

Seething, Max said, "With or without Ivan I will deal with this."

"If you speak to Ivan," Tom said with a sniffle, tried to pull himself together, "tell him I'm sorry I failed."

Max scowled and walked back to the man still hunched in front of the fire, "I will not tell him that because you did not fail," he said angrily, "You will not take the blame for this, Tom. I won't allow it from you or from anyone else." Max reached into the left-hand drawer of his desk and retrieved his gun, checked the bullets, and put it in the holster behind his back. As he did so, he looked up to see Astrid watching him. Her eyes were wide and her face looked pale. He didn't know what she'd seen when she'd looked into his face, but without a word she dashed up the staircase and to her room. Walking toward the door he said to Tom, "When I know…you'll know."

As Max walked out the door, Sara knelt down in front of Tom, "I know you always try to shield me from things, but if you need…"

Tom shook his head and wiped his nose with his handkerchief. "I'm fine."

"No, you're not," she said softly, "You seem like you need a friend and…I know I'm just the Gunther brothers' little sister, but.... through the years you've always been there to dry my tears." She took out of his shirt pocket the blue cotton handkerchief she'd given him for Christmas years ago and gently wiped his cheek. "This time let me dry yours."

For the first time since she'd come in, he looked into her eyes and her own filled with tears seeing such sadness on his face. He cleared his throat and said, "One of my patients died today," he looked down at his hands, "I've had patients die before of course, but this one…she was special. It…it shouldn't have happened."

"I'm sorry. What happened?"

"That isn't important," he lied, unwilling to taint such a tender and benevolent soul with the uglier side of the world. "Thank you," he said standing up and reaching out a hand to help her to rise.

She stood up, the concern obvious on her face, "Tom, can't you talk to me about it," she asked as he walked to the door.

"I don't want to," he said with his back to her unaware of the hurt his words caused. "She was a beautiful, talented, and loving person that shouldn't have...," he looked up at the ceiling and took a deep breath, but tears once again came to his eyes, "She was special. I tried to tell her, but...," he stopped as he opened the door.

"I'm sorry," Sara whispered.

He stood at the door clenching the doorknob to prevent himself from wrapping his arms around her and taking the compassion she offered. He couldn't accept comfort from such an open heart, not with the anger and frustration that was churning in his own. Without another word, he left.

Sara watched him leave then got into her car and let her tears flow; tears for Tom, the patient he'd lost, and for herself. It was physically painful to see him so shattered and if she were honest with herself, it was painful to hear him speak about another woman being so special to him. So special in fact that he couldn't even speak about her. Her tears quickly dried up thinking about all the secrets that he and Jackson and Max were always keeping from her; always protecting little Sara. Tom was a good man, she believed that with all her heart. Whatever business they were doing with Ivan...maybe it's too much for him...*Tom isn't like Max and Jackson. He's...,* she paused in her thought, *maybe I don't know what he is. I didn't even know he had someone special in his life.* The tears slowly returned as she started her car and headed for home.

♣

Later that evening as soon as Max came in, Astrid met him in the foyer to ask, "Is Tom alright?"

"He's fine," he said smiling, "Don't worry. He lost a patient and it hit him pretty hard, but he'll bounce back." He walked toward the kitchen, "Have you eaten?"

"No, I...," she chuckled, "I guess my mind was on other things. I didn't realize how late it was."

He browsed through the refrigerator, "Manette left some turkey slices in here. Care for a sandwich?"

"Turkey with mayonnaise is my favorite sandwich," she said with a smile.

"Excellent," he said, but quickly turned away from her engaging smile. It made him uneasy how comfortable things seemed to be getting. He needed to stick to the business of getting the answers Ivan was expecting. When Astrid was relaxed and sitting at the little kitchen table enjoying her dinner, he began what he hoped would be a fruitful discussion. "You know you don't really seem like the 'paranormal mystery' type to me."

"Why? What is the 'paranormal mystery' type like?"

"Oh, I don't know; creepy, wearing black all the time, lots of piercings I guess; heavy eye makeup and speaking only when necessary to give the illusion of holding secrets." He smiled as Astrid's laughter rang out throughout the kitchen. "Well, I don't know."

"I thought you were in the publishing business, you said when we met you worked for my publisher, Iron Press. How can you be in the business and still have such antiquated notions?"

Max hesitated realizing he'd cornered himself. He had told her he worked for her publisher, but he hadn't exactly told her in what capacity. She was smiling at him and that always made thinking up lies difficult. "I do work for your boss, but not the actual publishing company. I work personally for Ivan Bronius." He took their empty plates to the sink and rinsed them off before placing them in the dishwasher.

"What do you do then?"

Max watched her face closely, "I get information...protect things, or people. Different things he needs at different times."

The atmosphere in the room changed marginally as she looked at him. Her gaze went from his wide shoulders to his shapely biceps and well-formed forearms. His hand twitched slightly at her study of him and she looked back up into his face. The slight slant of her green eyes became more pronounced as she said, "So in other words…you're his muscle. That's why you go around carrying a gun."

"Well, I wouldn't put it quite like that," he answered with a slight frown and slowly turning the lynx ring on his right hand.

"You intimidate, threaten, or punish people that don't behave the way you or Mr. Bronius think they should."

Somehow his occupation sounded worse through her lips and he could almost hear the wheels in her mind working, thinking about all the things she'd seen since she'd known him. He tried a casual tone, "I just keep an eye on things. I didn't want to frighten you before, but he's gotten some information that someone may be trying to steal the next installment of your series."

Astrid stood up from the kitchen stool. "Why would someone want to do that?" Her voice was so soft he barely heard her and she seemed to either not want or not able to look him in the eyes.

He took her hand in his and it trembled slightly. "Book one was a great story, someone may just want to steal it out of an obsession to find out how it continues or they may want to claim it as their own work. It's hard to say."

She took her hand from his and started to walk away. "Sometimes I think I should have never tried to get published in the first place."

"Why would you say that? Your book has been quite successful from what I understand," he asked halting her movement with a hand on her arm.

"There have been so many strange things happening since I first sent it to Iron Press."

"Come," he said motioning toward the sitting room and guiding her to sit on the sofa next to him. "What strange things have happened?"

"Well," she said grabbing a throw pillow to hold against her chest, "for starters, a few days after I sent it to Iron Press I got fired. I'd worked at that book store for ten years. I'd never been reprimanded or been given any kind of disciplinary action...nothing. Suddenly my boss just tells me there had been lots of complaints and it was time they let me go. He wouldn't even tell me what the complaints were." Max watched the tears well in her eyes and had to glance away. "I know you're thinking it was just a job and you'd be right, but...it paid the bills. Without another job or the sale of my book...," Max glanced back at her as she picked up a tissue and blotted her face. "It's important for me to be independent."

"Believe me, Cashmere, seeing how your family is treating you I can see why being independent is important." Getting her fired had been Ivan's handiwork. After reading her manuscript he wanted her to be desperate to accept his offer before she tried sending it to another publisher. He'd called her boss and threatened the man's family if he didn't do as he was told. Naturally, he'd complied. "It is odd how quickly they fired you, but I don't think its reason enough to give up doing what you love. Where do you get the ideas to write about?"

Max watched her eyes to see if she'd get evasive or put up some kind of barrier to her thoughts. "I don't know really. They just sort of come into my head and I can't really think of anything else until I get them written down."

"You must have something that inspires you though. Something that triggers certain scenes or thought processes of your characters."

She suddenly giggled and put a hand in front of her face in an embarrassed gesture. "Well, there is one thing, but you'll think I'm crazy."

"Not a chance." He couldn't stop a smile feeling as if he was about to be let in on some wonderful secret.

"I take baths."

He frowned at the cryptic information. "I'm a shower person."

"No. I mean, I take baths and I get ideas." He continued to frown so she tried explaining further. "I lie in the bathtub with the water as hot as I can stand it. I lean my head back and just soak and after a few minutes scenes start playing in my head like little movies. It doesn't happen every time I bathe, just sometimes. I told you you'd think I was crazy!"

65

"I don't think you're crazy. Water is a great conductor of energies. It only stands to reason that you'd be getting ideas from the spirit world that way. They searched for someone to tell their story to and found a witch able and willing to hear them."

Her jaw dropped and her smile was quickly replaced by a frown as she whispered softly, "Why did you call me that?" Huge, frightened eyes looked from side to side as if expecting someone to come out of nowhere. She wrapped her arms tightly around herself whispering, "I'm not that. I'm not what you called me."

"You needn't be frightened, Astrid."

"Says the man carrying the gun," she said with a tremble in her voice.

He'd expected a little evasion or a little side stepping, not fear.

"You said you worked for Ivan as some type of bodyguard. Am I what you're guarding?" Her voice was rising and her breathing becoming more rapid. "Is that why you asked me to move in with you so that you could keep an eye on me?"

Max wasn't exactly sure how to answer the last question. He couldn't say yes and yet he didn't really want to lie. "Astrid, look…"

"You think I'm going to do something bad don't you?"

"No," Max said trying to sound convincing, but having a feeling she saw right through him. "No one is going to hurt you," he said cautiously. Darting her eyes around the room, she held herself tightly and he reached a hand out to her.

"Don't touch me," she said in a panic jumping off the sofa to get away from him. Max was surprised at how much her words hurt him and he backed off. "You are guarding me…I can see the way your jaw is clenching. I can see something in your eyes… there's something you aren't telling me."

"You don't understand…" he said as she continued to back away from him. "I have given you no reason to be afraid of me," he said, trying to convey sincerity and silently damning himself for having the same cold eyes as his father.

Ducking her head she said formally, "May I go to my room? Please?"

There it was again, that submissive and almost servile behavior. Regardless of needing to get information, he wasn't going to let her feel subordinate to him and he said brusquely, "You never have to ask that." She didn't respond and he tried to reign-in his temper, "Look at me." Eyes that reminded him so much of Ermina slowly looked up at him. "You are free to come and go as you please. Either inside this house or out of it." As she seemed to relax a little, he took a deep breath slowly walked toward her. "I'm sorry I upset you. It wasn't my intention. Being a witch is a good thing, a positive thing." As he approached, she took a step back and he frowned, "Please," he said and hearing his own desperation paused to take a little breath. "Do not be afraid of me," he whispered remembering when another set of eyes much like hers had looked up at him with fear. Astrid didn't say anything more as she practically ran up the staircase. Just as she got to the top Max's phone rang. He bent his head and sighed answering Ivan's call. "Yes," he answered impatiently, but his tone quickly changed, "When did it happen? Yes…yes…*lagom*."

With his brow furrowed and jaw clenching his anger was obvious. Although she didn't know who he was talking to or what it was about, it was clear he was not happy with whatever information he was getting.

"This is what you pay me for isn't it?"

She could hear Max checking the bullets in his gun and peered over the banister. He put his gun in the holster behind his back and pulled a hand through his hair. "Don't worry," he said with his jaw clenched, "he won't get away with it." The tone of his voice frightened her and she drew back farther from the railing not wanting him to see that she'd witnessed his discussion. The front door slammed as he grabbed his jacket and rushed through it. Astrid walked slowly to her room and with a trembling hand locked her door.

CHAPTER 7

With bad directions and bad traffic, it took Max a couple of hours just to find the elementary school where the young witch taught third grade. One of her students was being bullied by a high school kid and she was trying to help him.

The bully had taken her while she was walking home. With the help of another agent on the phone and two good citizens, Max had finally found her in an alley. Bruised and beaten, the small woman was sitting behind a dumpster.

Jeremy Beerman pulled into the alley and saw a man bending over someone on the ground; a woman, with a bright green dress on. Seething with rage, he jumped out of the car, grabbed the man and threw him across the alley. His chin and hand scraped against the concrete, but he quickly recovered enough to stand and reach one hand behind his back. The other hand he held up in surrender. "Okay, hold on."

Taking a gun out of his pocket and pointing it at Max, Jeremy said, "Stay away from her."

Max slowly wiped the blood dripping off of his chin and noticed the blood on the back of his hand. "Look, my name is…"

"I don't give a damn what your name is. Step away or you'll get a few new holes in you."

"I'm guessing you're her husband…Jeremy, right? I only want to…"

The man waved the gun around and came closer, "Shut up. We're going to do this my way. Some bastard has just stolen my wife and if I find out you had any part in it we're going to end this right here. Now are you going to step back or am I just going to assume and get on with it?"

Still holding his hand up and looking the man right in the eyes Max calmly said, "I have seven reasons to comply, one in the chamber and six in the magazine…and I'd like them to stay there."

Hearing a scuffling noise, Jeremy turned his attention a moment to the dumpster and saw his wife slowly trying to stand up. "Jeremy," she said softly.

He started toward her then looked back at Max, "Stay put."

"I won't move. Go to her," Max said.

Jeremy hesitated only a moment before deciding his wife was more important and put his gun away to take her into his arms. Her skin was cold and she was shaking badly. "He's a guardian, Jeremy. He's not the one. He'd never hurt me," she said, her soft voice quivering slightly.

"Guardian? Of what?" He glanced back at Max who hadn't moved a step.

"Of me because…because I'm a witch," she said nervously.

With the other man's gun put away, Max let go of his own weapon and stood waiting to see the man's reaction to his wife's admission.

Giving Max another look up and down, he picked her up into his arms saying, "Well, first and foremost you're my wife." He carried her to his car and quickly assessed that her injuries were not substantial. She was dirty, cold, and frightened with a few small scrapes and bruises, but mostly she was okay and he took a deep breath. "Just a minute and I'll get you home," he said giving her a kiss on her forehead and shutting the passenger door. He looked at Max, "I'm not altogether sure what's going on, but I need to get her home and then I've got somebody to hunt down."

"You can't do that."

"The hell I can't," he said snatching his arm away when Max tried to grab it to stop him. "I'm not letting some piece of shit get away with this."

"I understand what you're saying and agree with you, but it would be better for everyone if you let me handle this." Max watched the big man shake his head and walk over to the driver's side door. "Let me follow you home and after you've tended to her needs we'll discuss this calmly," Max said.

Seeing the obvious concern on the stranger's face and appreciating the fact that the man had stayed put when he'd been asked, Jeremy relented and nodded his head getting into his car.

Once they were home, he carried his wife upstairs leaving the door open for the stranger who had followed him home. He went through the bedroom and to the bathroom to gently set her down on the toilet seat while he prepared her bath. With her eyes downcast he examined the bruises on her face. A cut near her left eye had stopped bleeding, but was bruised and swollen and her lip was torn. As he put the bath salts in the tub he noticed her knee was bleeding and her ankle bone was scraped pretty badly. Her eyes never met his and she didn't speak as he undressed her. The only sound she made was a slight gasp when he picked her up to set her in the tub. When he put her down he saw a nasty bruise under her arm and along her back as if she'd fallen onto something. "I'm sorry, love," he said softly for causing her more pain. He used the bath sponge to gently wash her and his slow and careful ministrations worked to stop her trembling and gradually the frightened look faded from her face. Next he washed her hair to remove the bits of leaves and mud. As he rubbed her head and ran his fingers through her hair, her eyes closed. After he helped her out of the tub and wrapped a towel around her, he got the first aid kit out of the medicine cabinet and applied ointment and bandages where they were needed. He carried her to the bed and tucked the blanket around her. "I'll fix some coffee and a sandwich for you."

"I'm not hungry," she whispered.

"You should try to eat something," he said softly, "You'll need some medicine to help you rest, but it would be better if you ate something first." She nodded. "Rest and I'll go talk to our friend downstairs," he said, bothered by the fact that she had yet to actually look at him.

"Jeremy."

"Yes," he said as he moved toward the bedroom door.

"I love you," she said with tears in her eyes, "I'm sorry about all this."

"I love you, too," he said coming back to her and bending down to gently kiss her lips. "There is nothing for you to be sorry for. You did the right thing trying to help that child and as for the other thing," he held her face as he looked into her eyes, "When we married I promised to take care of you no matter what. I'll not break that promise and whatever you are; witch, fairy, or painter," he said with a grin, "I would not change a thing about you."

Jeremy entered the sitting room and noticed Max perusing his shelf of model cars. "Just makes you want to take it off the shelf and give it a spin doesn't it?"

"Indeed," Max said smiling, "You build them yourself?"

"Yes, tends to be therapeutic after a long day of installing cable. I'm either crawling under houses or climbing up ladders and sometimes it feels good when I get home to just sit on my…uh…well, you get the idea." They enjoyed a chuckle, but the levity didn't last long as each was anxious to put the evening to rest. "Sorry to have kept you waiting so long. Have a seat." Max's hand and chin had stopped bleeding, but Jeremy handed him a damp towel to try to clean up a little.

Nodding his thanks, Max sat down on the hunter green sofa as Jeremy sat down opposite him on a plaid chair. While he'd been waiting, he had casually wandered around the cozy room appreciating the little pieces of each of the occupant's personalities. The model cars, several miniature clocks in a glass case near the door, and a basket full of colorful yarn with knitting needles resting on the table next to it. He hadn't minded waiting, in fact he'd appreciated the fact that the husband was more concerned with his wife's comfort than dealing with the monster that had hurt her or the stranger downstairs who knew more about his wife than he did. "I didn't mind waiting," Max said sincerely, "How's Maggie?"

"Resting," he said tersely. "Look, I don't know how you know her, but…"

"I'll be glad to explain." Jeremy regarded Max a moment, then sat back in his chair ready to listen. "My name is Max Gunther. I am part of an organization called the Witches Guardian's Alliance. It's pretty much what the name suggests, we watch over witches when we find them."

"The idea that we have such a group is somewhat disturbing and quite honestly…sounds a bit medieval. This isn't Salem for God's sake. In this modern age we don't burn people at the stake for witchcraft."

"Believe it or not there are still witch haters out there; people who associate them with the devil, omens, and anything negative that comes along. We were established in 1677 after the Torsaker Witch Trials when the authorities definitively decided that the witch hunt that took place from 1668-1676 had expelled all the witches from Sweden. The worst day in Sweden's history to my mind; seventy one souls, sixty five women and six men were beheaded, stripped and burned."

"Dear God, were they…were they all witches?"

"No, but regardless of whether or not they actually were, we protect anyone who stands accused and in need of our protection."

"Well, she's not Swedish."

"A Swede," Max corrected, then acknowledge, "But that doesn't matter. She's human and therefore deserves our protection. Consider it Sweden's atonement."

Jeremy frowned, "From what I've heard of Sweden, at least these days, it's a very liberal country striving for fairness and equality almost to the extreme."

"Yes, it is, but like all countries it's had its dark time. Your wife is not an actively practicing witch which is why we've only recently discovered her. I assume you heard about the child at school that she was assisting?"

"Yes, she has a tender heart and couldn't help but intervene. Who would have thought teaching third grade could be dangerous?" He shook his head in bewilderment and Max nodded agreeing with him. "How did that fella even find out that she was a witch?"

"There is a new book out that is making a few suggestions of how to find a witch and things to…well, let's just say that although your wife was kidnapped, beaten, and left terrified and alone, she has fared better than others."

"I guess in your business you have to sort out the big bastards from the little bastards."

Max cleared his throat, "Yeah, something like that."

Jeremy fixed Max with a steely gaze, "It sounds to me like you need to focus on getting this author to draw back a little on his or her storytelling."

"We're uh…working on it. In the meantime getting people to understand what witchcraft is and isn't is important." Max looked at Jeremy closely, "There is no reason to be afraid of or mistrust someone simply because they have a special ability."

Knowing he was being assessed, Jeremy quickly said, "I don't care that she's a witch. To me it's no different than someone having any other kind of gift or talent."

"I'm glad to know you don't hold any grudge against her for not telling you."

"We all have secrets of some kind or another; things we don't even tell the ones we love for fear of losing that love. My wife is a beautiful, compassionate, and thoughtful woman and I wouldn't change one damn thing about her…even her being a witch. I consider it part of her charm," he said with a smile.

Max watched the glow of pride on the man's face and couldn't resist a smile of his own. Not only was this man not angry about her carefully guarded secret, but he was proud of who and what she was. "I think you should consider joining our alliance," he said sincerely.

"Are there really that many women out there being mistreated for being witches?"

"You'd be surprised," Max's droll tone causing Jeremy further anxiety.

"I guess I should apologize for your injuries, but hell, I'd do the same thing again. I didn't know who you were and at the time…I didn't much care."

Max appreciated his honesty. "There is no apology needed. Trust me," he grinned looking down at his hand, "I've had a lot worse and I understand your motivation behind it. I can also understand your motivation to go after this guy, but it's not a good idea. The chances are that the police will eventually get involved. Either from him killing you or you killing him or just the two of you causing a scene. Let us handle it. It's what we do."

Jeremy stood up and walked over to the glass case of clocks. "Mr. Gunther,"

"Max, please."

"Max," he turned back toward him, "You're asking me to put aside my general manly, husbandly, and let's face it…high testosterone tendency and allow another man to defend my wife." Unable to keep still, he walked over to his shelf of model cars and then paced back to the case of clocks.

"I do understand your impulse. I've seen a lot of behavior that honestly made me want to do a lot more than just *get someone under control,* but you can't always act on your impulse."

"Are you married?" Jeremy raised an eyebrow almost in challenge.

"No, no I'm not. However, I do have women in my life who are important to me and if someone did this to them…well, I can only hope that one of my friends would talk me out of doing what you're wanting to do right now."

The two men enjoyed a companionable grin before Jeremy sighed deeply and walked back to his chair. "It would not be good for her if I got arrested or hurt because of all this. The silly woman already feels guilty," he said sitting down. "Since I don't even know how to find him my first thought would be to contact the police and report her being assaulted."

"Please don't do that," Max said standing up and handing back to borrowed towel, "it will only bring more attention to the fact that she's a witch and could provoke others to copy him or at least defend his behavior. I know how to find him. There are more than one thousand agents in North America alone. We've gotten very adept at finding people like him."

"When you do find him," Jeremy asked looking Max squarely in the eyes, "What do you intend to do?"

Max walked to the front door, "You just worry about making Maggie feel better. I'll take care of him. The less you know about all this the better."

Jeremy got up and opened the door for him with obvious uncertainty still playing across his face. "One more thing if you don't mind."

"Certainly,"

"In the alley…why didn't you pull out that weapon holstered in your back?"

Max smiled noting to himself that along with his other attributes the man was also observant. "Although you were angry when you stepped out of the car, the most obvious emotion you exhibited was concern. Concern for what was happening. That pegged you for the husband. Why would I threaten a husband for being worried about his wife?"

"I could have shot you. I could have killed you."

Max shook his head, "No, you were too steady. You were going to find out what was really going on before you acting on anything. That's another reason you should consider the alliance. I deal with monsters regularly and it's an ongoing struggle not to become one. Tamping down emotion and maintaining perspective is essential. You've been calm, cool, and unexpectedly logical throughout this whole thing. We could use more men like you."

Jeremy held out his hand and Max shook it. "I'll give it some thought."

"Good, I'll call with an update as soon as I have one so that you two can rest easier. Have a good night."

Jeremy closed the door behind him and turned toward the kitchen to make his wife some coffee and a sandwich contemplating his new friend's suggestion.

Max went home hoping he could talk to Astrid and get things straightened out. Just as he pulled in the driveway, Sara came out of the house and straight toward him with disapproving look she frequently gave him. Taking a deep breath to gear up for battle, he got out of the car and tried a smile, but it failed as Sara pounced. "Why is she here?" Sara asked just as he stepped out. He saw her slight frown looking at his bloodied chin, but she didn't mention it so he wouldn't.

"Nice to see you, Sara," he answered walking up the front steps.

"Max," she stopped him placing a hand on his arm, "Is she one of your one night stands?"

Max paused in the act of opening the front door. "I don't really see how that's any of your business."

"If you've brought an innocent woman here to kill her I consider it my business. Human life is valuable to some of us," she said making him all too aware of what she really thought of him.

Sighing deeply, Max said, "I did not bring her here to harm her," he could not bring himself to look into her eyes. He opened the door and she followed him in.

"Do you always act so hospitable to your victims?"

"Victims? Really? Is this my sex life you're describing or my work?"

"I guess both," she said putting her hands on her hips and shaking her head sadly, "I should have known, but…it's still sad to hear you say it."

"Say what?"

"That for you it would be your sex-life not your love-life."

"Why are you even here?" He asked when it suddenly occurred to him that they were in his house and she was there uninvited; not that she normally needed to be invited, but he was aggravated with being scrutinized.

"I came by to talk to you, but obviously you have your hands full…of what I can only imagine! The poor girl has locked herself in her room apparently terrified of you and I'm not so sure she's not got a reason to be."

Max's head jerked up and he whispered, "Sara?" and for a moment neither of them spoke.

The minute she'd said it her stomach clenched. She'd hurt them both, but she tried to keep her face from showing it. "I just meant…be careful…with your decisions."

In the same calm, brotherly tone he'd always had with her he said, "If you need to talk to me…I am always available to you," he bent his head down and turned away from her.

Sara wrapped her arms around herself as tears sprang to her eyes, "I should go. It feels like winter in the Lapland in this house. I'm surprised the lilies survive."

The front door slammed indicated Sara's departure. Hearing a door upstairs softly close, he knew Astrid must have heard all or part of their conversation and closed his eyes on a weary sigh. Any hope of getting things smoothed out with Astrid left and he slowly walked into the sitting room to check on his e-mails. *All these years,* he thought to himself, *all these years, I've worked so hard to create this persona,"* he shook his head with a self-deprecating grin, *now the persona is bigger than I am.* He looked at his computer and tried to get the sight of Sara's worried face out of his mind; her worry and if he wasn't mistaken…her disgust.

CHAPTER 8

The next morning Astrid sat in the window seat in her bedroom overlooking the front of the house dreamily jotting down notes in her notebook of a new scene she was thinking of. It was just before sunrise and she loved watching the day waken; the soft rays of the new sun shining on the dew of the flowers making them glimmer, the birds waking up and waking each other up, and the squirrels beginning to chatter over their breakfast. The smile spread across her face watching the lovely scene slowly melted away as she thought about the house she was in, why she was there, and the man living there that she couldn't quite get figured out. As if he knew he was being thought about, Max came out of the house and walked to his car. Astrid put aside her notebook and couldn't stop staring at him. He was wearing dirty jeans with holes in the knees, an old faded t-shirt, sneakers that had seen much better days, and a dirty baseball cap. Except for the confident walk and the fact that he'd just come out of the house and went straight to his Jaguar, the figure she watched didn't seem a thing like the Max she was acquainted with. She watched on as he slowly backed his car up to the side of the house and opened the trunk. She could see the edge of a bright blue tarpaulin as Max set inside the trunk a shovel, some gloves, and what looked like a pick axe. Picking up the edge of the tarpaulin and carefully putting it over whatever else was in the trunk, he shut it and drove away. Astrid sat back on the seat and her mind raced. *He has new injuries,* she realized, *His hand is bandaged and his chin is scraped.* She frowned and doodled a flower on her notebook, thinking, *Why would a man who works security and normally dresses like he stepped out of a magazine, suddenly dress like that and need a shovel? What...what could he possibly have in that trunk?* Astrid doodled for a solid hour contemplating and then contemplating all over again, what could possibly have been going on.

♣

"She's afraid of being labelled a witch. I believe someone has made her afraid. Naturally it's made her hesitant to speak much about the information in the book," Max told Ivan. Of course he didn't tell him that a few hours ago when he'd gone home to shower and change, she was still locked away from him in her room. Ivan didn't need to know that, so he continued, "I think perhaps she doesn't realize…"

"Kill her and be done with it."

Max stared at him. "You don't understand…I think someone has frightened her; tormented her."

"Perhaps you don't understand. You were given your orders in that file. Damn it, Gunther! For once do your job the way it's meant to be done. If you need to assuage your physical need do it, then get rid of her."

"This isn't about that," Max said frustrated that once again his sex life was coming up in conversation.

Ivan's fist slammed down on the desk, "Really? According to my sources you're playing house with her." Max flinched wondering how he'd found out, then his question was answered, "Men enjoy a good gossip as much as women do, unfortunately. I've heard for years about all your one-nighters in all the local hotel rooms. Normally, from what I understand, you keep them at a distance. Why is it that when there is a woman you're supposed to dispose of, you take her into your home instead? If this was a man the deed would be done already."

Max clenched his jaw, "I don't think my personal life is any of…"

"No, it isn't any of my business and I'd be glad to not know any of it! However, when you're given a direct order and you defy it, it becomes my business." He walked over to his liquor cabinet and poured himself a whiskey. Max watched him as he came toward him. Although Max was only five foot nine inches, he was well muscled with wide shoulders and impressive biceps. Ivan was six feet, and well-muscled from shoulder to waist, an impressive shape for his age. The men sized each other up a moment before Ivan said, "Sometimes I feel you thwart my orders intentionally." Max didn't answer him. "You might want to make sure I never discover that is the case." Ivan went back to his desk. "Now, back to this woman. I don't give a damn what you do with her as long as she's dead before any more information gets out about our people."

"Damn it, Ivan. She is our people; a witch. The very ones we're supposed to protect."

"You are sworn to protect *witches* plural. It is better to lose one treacherous witch than to lose a hundred loyal to themselves and their craft. This one is dangerous to her kind."

"I understand your position, Ivan," Max said quietly, "I have a little brother, too."

Though the words were said quietly their meaning was as if he'd shouted. Ivan slammed down his glass with so much force Max was surprised it didn't shatter. Not too long ago, Ivan's brother was tricked and severely injured by a witch in Ivan's protection, but it was a subject no one had thus far had the backbone to bring up in front of the fierce head of the alliance. Max tried to steady his heartbeat as Ivan glared into his eyes with deadly intensity. "She was a venal witch and if this Astrid Martin is as well then she deserves no protection."

"She isn't," Max said clenching his fists and jamming them into his trouser pockets.

"You haven't proven that to me yet. You've only proven that you're not objective. *This* woman was one of the kind we are sworn to protect," he said holding up a newspaper from his desk. On the front page was the face of a lovely woman with the words *satanic murder* written under her picture. "She was murdered by someone using information from Ms. Martin's book. They took her ideas of death to a witch by use of the elements, did a little research on their own, and killed this woman. ONE OF OURS!"

Ivan's roar made Max's ears ring, but he shook his head in protest. "Astrid Martin wouldn't…"

Ivan slammed the newspaper back down and glared at Max, "A guardian aware of her presence in the area was also killed when he tried to interfere in the ritual."

"He should have been aware that the ritual…"

"Do not *dare* to blame a guardian for giving his life to the promise of this alliance. Maybe the other agents mean nothing to you, but I can assure you they mean something to me!"

"I didn't mean to imply…"

"Enough!" Max looked down at the carpet. The lives of the other agents did mean something to him, but at the moment he didn't think Ivan would believe him if he told him. Clenching his jaw to keep silent, he looked up as Ivan continued, "He made the same commitment you did to the Witches' Guardians Alliance of Oskarshamn. While you dally with that woman her body count rises." He paused a moment and Max wondered briefly if he was expected to speak, but decided Ivan was probably just trying to figure out if Max had gotten the message or not. He wasn't about to tell him that he had. Instead, he looked him in the eyes and waited. "You *will* find out where her information comes from so that we can deal with it. Then you *will* put an end to A.R. Martin." Ivan turned to the side and started working on his computer then said angrily, "You're dismissed."

Max would consider it an insult to compare Ivan Bronius with his father…but there were moments. He walked out of the man's office feeling like a ten year old boy who'd failed his arithmetic test and been thoroughly thrashed for it.

♣

Astrid hadn't stepped a foot out of her room since she'd asked to be excused, too many questions plagued her mind. After falling asleep in the window seat she was awakened by a knock on her door. "Astrid, is

81

Manette, may I come?" Astrid unlocked the door and gave her a hesitant smile. The lovely blonde maid walked in carrying a tray with coffee, some sandwiches, and a pastry. Aware that Max was probably responsible for the pastry, Astrid couldn't help a small smile at the thought. Seeming to understand, Manette gently laid a hand on her arm and said, "Is there anything else I can get?"

"No, I'm…I'm fine."

"You do not seem fine," Manette said softly as she poured a cup of coffee.

"I don't want to cause you a problem with Mr. Gunther. I know you're afraid of him and it's certainly understandable. I wouldn't want you to say anything that might make it hard for you."

Manette handed her the coffee cup and stood up straight to say, "I have never and will never be afraid of *Mr. Gunther*, which I will tell you now, he hates to be called that."

"Yes, he…he did ask me not to call him that, but…the other day when we were talking," Astrid set down her coffee cup and rubbed her temple, "you were nervous about saying too much. I could tell you were uneasy talking to me. You were crying and when he saw that flower in my hand…I thought…I was afraid he was going to fire you or…or I don't know what."

"I…I was un-easy to talk to you." Manette smiled briefly. "That was…not because of Max. That was because of you."

Astrid's heart started pounding in her chest and she backed away from the housekeeper who seemed to have gone from kind to cautious in mere moments. "You're afraid of me?" She leaned against the window and wrapped her arms around herself. "He told you that I'm a witch?"

Seeing her obvious distress, Manette relaxed a little and sat down on the edge of the bed. "I am not afraid of Astrid the witch hurting me. I am worried about Astrid the woman hurting Max." At Astrid's confused expression she continued gently, "My tears were for the memories of my past…my past with Max that your questions brought up. When I went into the kitchen and saw his face…," tears quickly filled her eyes, "his face when he saw that flower, wilted and dying. He cannot bear it you see. To see them withered, broken, and no longer beautiful." Manette got up to get a tissue and blew her nose daintily before turning back to Astrid. "Fire me?" she laughed, "I could break every dish, ruin all his clothes, and dump all his coffee in the trash and he still…still would just calmly ask me if I needed a little time to myself. When he took me out of the kitchen, he held me in his arms and asked about my tears. I told him and he laughed at me and suggested I take the rest of the day off." Taking a deep breath she said, "The things I was not sure to tell you before…well, they are things that…if you wanted…you could use to hurt him."

"I wouldn't…"

"You say you wouldn't, but yet you sit in here away from him…afraid or…not trusting him…or…I don't know, but Max has had to learn the hard way that when someone knows a weakness…they will use it."

"I can't even imagine Max having a weakness," Astrid said with a faint smile.

The pretty maid nodded her head in understanding, "He is strong and tough and would never back down from a fight, but…" Pausing, Manette smiled and patted the bed for Astrid to have a seat beside her. Once she'd made herself comfortable she said, "You wanted to know about the flowers?" She waited for Astrid's nod. "They are special because his mother's name was Lily. She was fragile like a flower," Manette's voice softened as she turned her mind back to a day in Sweden when she'd met Max's mother. "She was beautiful and kind, but somehow it seemed…too fragile for this…this hard world. I only met her once, but I will never forget. We were teenagers and…well, my family had thrown me out of the house because I was pregnant. I was just sitting on a bench down by the harbor crying as a storm started coming across the water. Max saw me and remembering me from school, insisted I come home with him until my family and I could work things out. I walked into the house and there she sat in a chair by the fire with a blanket over her knees. She had the look of something uh…like heaven…about her?" Her brow furrowed trying to find the right words. "Like…Angel?" Astrid shook her head understanding and Manette continued, "For a moment it…not frighten, but like…startle me. She almost did not look real." Manette smiled shyly and went over to get Astrid's coffee cup and hand it to her. "Try a sandwich," she said and Astrid went over and took two off of the tray. "You are right in thinking the pastry was Max's idea," she said and wondering how the housekeeper had been able to read her mind so easily, Astrid added the pastry to her plate. "His mother's voice was so weak I had to get up close to hear her as she introduced herself and held out her hand to me. I took it gently because it seemed so small and…delicate. She was very beautiful with bold blue eyes like the twins and long golden hair the same color as Max's. I told her my name just as his father came into the room. Lily quickly pulled her hand back and looked to the floor. Max came to stand in front of me. It was obvious that they were both afraid of what was going to happen and…," Manette chuckled, "it made me a bit afraid watching them. When Mr. Gunther asked who I was and what I was doing there, Max explained that I needed a place to stay. His father wanted to know why I couldn't go home and he told him that I was pregnant and that my family needed time to get used to it. His father practically roared that he would not house some other family's cast off and he would be damned if he would take on his son's bastard child. I tried to explain and took a step away from Max because I didn't want to cause trouble for him." Manette's voice faltered and she quickly got a tissue from the bedside table to dab at her eyes. "His father came toward me and shoved me to the floor. Max yelled and stepped in front of him, shouting at him that he would hurt the baby. The laugh that came out of him was so…I don't know how to say, but…it was not a nice laugh. It made me frightened. His eyes," she closed her eyes and shuddered, "so cold and…hard…unfeeling. He tried to shove Max out of the way, but he stood his ground and then…," she blew her nose in the tissue and Astrid handed her another one gently putting her arm around her shoulders. "The baby was not Max's child. We were never a couple. I was only a friend he was trying to help." She blew her nose again. "The beating he took that day…oh, blood spurted from his lip, his nose…one of his eyes was so swollen he could not see out of it. I was screaming for his father to stop, but he just kept going. He just…just kept hitting him. When I looked over at Lily for help…," Manette shook her head and took a deep breath. "Huge tears rolled down her cheeks, but she said nothing. She watched on as her son was on his knees swaying like a drunk and his father hit him again and again. He wore his hair longer back then, but you couldn't even tell it was blonde as it clung to his face with…with so much blood in it. Finally he collapsed unmoving on the floor and his father looked at me and said to get the hell out of his house. I tried to help Max up, but his father told me to leave him and go. I said no. I told him I would not leave without Max, but coughing and blood dripping from his lip, Max quietly asked me to please go. At first I refused, but he looked at me with the only eye he could open and said if I were to be hurt it would hurt him more and I…I could not refuse after that. I left with him still lying on the floor." Cleaning her face, Manette pointed at Astrid's cup and plate, "Try to eat. I do not know why you are here. I don't know why you have locked yourself up in this room, but if it is you are…afraid of him…I can only ask that you try to understand him. Think of this, he has the key to this room in his desk drawer, yet he hasn't used it. Has he even tried to coerce you into coming out, beaten on the door, or demanded anything of you?" She dried her bright blue eyes and smiled wistfully. "Those flowers are like a piece of his mother. Although she had said nothing as he was beaten, I saw him look over at her. He knew she was there and that alone brought him comfort. The flowers bring him comfort and so I make sure that they are always there watching over him. I try to never let him see them withered and broken like she was."

As she headed for the door, Astrid wiped her eyes and said, "Manette, did you have a boy or a girl," she enquired trying to find something more positive to help the young woman's emotions.

"I don't know what it would have been," she said sadly, "I miscarried three months later…the same day his mother died," she left the room closing the door behind her.

♣

85

Max sat at his desk with his head in his hands. He'd spent the last few hours looking up every aspect he could think of about Astrid and her life before he'd met her. When Ivan broke into her apartment the night she stayed in the hotel, they discovered that she didn't have a computer so social media was useless. She typed her stories on an old fashioned typewriter. She had no cellphone, no tablet, or any other electronic gadgets. He was searching her old employer's information looking for someone, anyone she may be in contact with who could be her informant. When a knock sounded from the doorway, Max looked up and smiled softly. "Hey, how are you feeling?"

"A little...uncertain."

"Would you like to talk about it?"

Her smile indicated she was more than willing, "Coffee *and* talk?" she asked sheepishly.

"You know you're talking my language." He turned off his computer and started past her toward the kitchen when she slowly took his hand.

"Max, are...are *we* okay? It's just that...I enjoy this...whatever it is, but...I'm uncertain about so many things. If I've..."

"You've done nothing," he quickly reassured her. His warm hand reached up to cradle her cheek and she briefly closed her eyes enjoying the sensation. His crystal blue eyes looked at her and the tender expression made her heart flutter. "We are definitely, okay. *Lagom,*" he said making her smile, "I'm enjoying my time with you, too."

They walked into the kitchen together and Max opened the coffee cabinet with a flourish making her smile. "What will it be? I just got this one in yesterday its Camilina, from the Finca La Aurora Farm near the border of Costa Rica." he said wiggling his eyebrows and obviously hoping she'd pick it. Astrid couldn't resist him and nodded with a smile. As he brewed she took out the necessary cups, saucers, and spoons. Max grabbed the sugar and cream and placed everything on a tray. "According to the experts this is supposed to have a slight Jasmine aroma with a hint of citrus and berries."

"You know, since I've been here you've told me things about these coffees that I'm supposed to taste…but I confess that I never do. Fruits, florals, and all the spices that are in there…," she shook her head.

Max smiled broadly surprising her, "I don't taste them either," her mouth fell open and he chuckled, "All I know is whether I like the taste or not!" Astrid stared at the handsome man in the kitchen who had the ability to seem as a complete expert regarding his favorite beverage and yet in reality he was nothing but a fraud. As she laughed, he said, "Really how important is all that anyway? I mean…," he looked off in the distance finding the right words then looked back at her, "isn't the important thing…how a particular cup of coffee makes you feel or the memories that a particular brew conjures up? I can smell the grounds and remember the last time I had it or who I had it with. Some smells are uplifting and some are transportive." As he spoke the coffee finished and he put it on the tray carrying it into the sitting room.

He fixed hers the way she liked it and fixed his own. They sat in the quiet sipping, smelling, and creating a memory. Astrid watched him thinking about what he'd said before about how other people drink their coffee and smiled knowing she already knew his routine; first a little sugar, then a little cream, and then slowly stir a figure eight over and over watching the cream alter the color of the coffee. His strong hands wrapped around the cup as if they needed warming with the handle pointing out opposite of his lips. She watched his eyes close and nostrils flare as he breathed in the aroma. The whole process, she noticed, brought him comfort. It seemed silly to think he needed comfort, a man like him; strong, brave, and in control. As she watched him sipping however, her mind simply wouldn't let go of the idea. For him, it was a hug, a kind word, and a friendly presence. Max looked up and noticed her watching him and gave her a curious look. "It just occurred to me that I've never seen you drink coffee from anything but a china cup. I thought coffee lovers usually went everywhere with those refillable, thermal things."

Max made a face clearly indicating his dislike of the said articles, "Can't warm my hands if it's thermal and somehow the aroma doesn't seem the same. Kind of ruins the whole experience." Pointing to her cup he asked, "How do you like it?"

Her shy smile warmed him as much as the coffee had. "It's very good. I love the scent."

"So do I," he whispered as he set down his cup and moved a little closer to her on the sofa. Seeing her slight blush and the way her eyes glanced at his lips, he said, "Don't be afraid of me...or of this," and leaned in to place a kiss lightly on her lips. When he leaned back to look at her, she gave him a timid smile and he kissed her again. It felt like a hurdle had been jumped when she didn't back away from him, but afraid to push his luck, Max backed away giving her a little space.

The coffee, the fire, and the devastatingly handsome man kissing her so tenderly had the effect of a warm, safe cocoon. She felt safe to start the discussion. "So you said I am a witch," she said quietly.

"Mmhmm," he said casually.

"How do you know?"

"For one thing, I can feel the energy you radiate. For another thing I am very adept at recognizing a witch and lastly...," he paused deciding how much he wanted to say. "Lastly, only a witch could write the stories you write...unless of course you were writing the stories for someone else. You, know...like a ghost writer."

"So you've met other witches?"

It wasn't really the thread he was hoping she'd grab ahold of, but he smiled slightly and said, "I've met many. It's my job."

"I thought you worked for Iron Press." Before he could answer she remembered, "Oh, yes. You said you worked more with Ivan personally."

"That's right." He poured her some more coffee. "You see, I am part of a group of men called witches' guardians."

"Witches' guardians?" Her chuckle was unexpected and Max looked at her curiously. "If someone was a witch than they'd have powers; something they could do that humans couldn't. They could hurt people whenever they wanted." She'd gone from a fragile smile to near frantic in seconds and Max struggled to keep pace with her mind. "They could do spells and make bad things happen. Why in the heck would they need guards?" She set her coffee cup down noisily on the saucer and clenched her hands tightly together. "Seems to me the humans are the ones who need guarding from the witches!"

CHAPTER 9

Suddenly Astrid jumped up from the sofa and walked to the window to stare out at the dark night.

"Astrid?" Max walked up behind her.

She spun around and grabbed a hold of him. Naturally as breathing, his arms came around to hold her. Her body quivered slightly, tears began cascading down her cheeks and she buried her face in his shoulder sobbing. "Please, just for a minute. Don't push me away."

The desperate plea wrung his heart and he tightened his hold. "My darling girl, I have no intention of pushing you away." The timbre of his voice softened and deepened as he said, "I would never push you away."

After a few moments her sobs quieted, but Max continued to hold on until her breathing slowed and she began to move away from him. "You must think I'm a complete mess," she said with a chuckle.

"Of course I don't," he said watching her closely, "I think you're just like everybody else who tries to come to grips with their past and present and figure out their future."

Remembering what Manette had told her about Max's past and the struggles he must have also gone through, she smiled appreciatively. "All my life my siblings have used the word witch to hurt me. If I did something they thought was weird or different, they would say it was because I was a witch. My mother said my father left us because of me…because of my…my evil." She dabbed at her eyes with the handkerchief Max offered her.

"You talked once of a grandmother you were fond of. Was that your father's mother?"

"Yes."

"Her name was Ingmar?"

Astrid looked up at him frowning and said, "Yes, how did you know that," she chuckled, "It's not exactly a common name."

"The other day…when I frightened you, I looked up all the information I could find on you and your family." Max turned away from the frown and suspicion in her eyes to walk over to his desk. "You talk of her as if you...as if you knew her."

"I did," she said walking up to his desk. "She was very dear to me."

Max turned to face her saying, "Astrid, you were just a toddler when she died. How can you remember?" Astrid shook her head and Max picked up a paper he'd copied from the computer. Her grandmother and father had both been killed in Sweden when Astrid was only two years old. With a shaky hand, she took the paper and studied it. Watching her mouth hanging open and the lines deepening on her brow, Max knew it wasn't an act, it wasn't that she was intentionally being evasive, she was truly shocked at what she was reading. Ingmar Martin, a known witch from Idre, and her son were visiting friends when an explosion occurred leveling the apartment building.

Astrid slowly shook her head. "Max, this isn't right. I knew her. I…I saw her, spoke to her." Tears threatened as she gazed into his crystal blue eyes pleading for some kind of explanation. "I felt her arms around me. My family believes affections make you weak and never held me, but…but she did. She held me, Max."

Unable to bear her tears, Max wrapped his arms around her and cradled her. "I believe you," he whispered. "I believe she held you and talked to you, but she wasn't alive." Still wrapped in his arms, Astrid shook her head. "She was gone when you were two, but she came back to you in spirit to watch over you."

"Do you hear what you're saying?" She asked pushing away from him.

"Yes. I'm saying you're a witch, just like she was and you can hear her and speak to her and feel her presence. It's called necromancy and you're very accomplished."

"I felt her arms around me. I…I did Max."

"I know you did. Some lucky people do get that sense of being held by someone they loved."

"You mean *witch* people."

Max looked steadily into her eyes and said gently, "She knows you needed her so she's with you; supporting you, loving you, helping you to not feel alone."

She backed away shaking her head again. "Not anymore," she whispered sadly. "When my mother said she died…I never saw her again." She took a deep breath and said, "That's when she died. I wasn't two. I was seventeen when she died."

"No, Cashmere," he said softly. "You stopped feeling her then, because of what your mother said. She must have known you could sense your grandmother and she wanted to put an end to it. You believed her so you stopped trying to feel her presence."

"She…she did know," Astrid said frowning and gazing into the fireplace. "She was always telling me…*don't listen to Granna, she's crazy.* According to her, my grandmother had lost her mind years earlier and didn't know what she was saying anymore." She wrapped her arms around herself and sat back down on the couch still gazing at the fire; casting her mind back to when she was young. Max walked over to her and wrapped a blanket around her shoulders. The room was warm, but Astrid was shivering coming to terms with her past. "When mother came to me to tell me of Granna's death," she whispered, not looking at Max as he sat down next to her. "She said there would be no funeral, because witches were evil and it was a time to rejoice when one died, but Max," her blue-green eyes looked at him so trustingly, he reached out and took her hand. "Max, she was so kind to me. I don't believe…"

"What?" he saw the answer in her eyes, "say it, Cashmere. Words have power, use them with that in mind."

"I don't believe…She wasn't evil. I don't really understand much about it, but she was kind to me and I loved her," she swallowed hard and looked into the crystal eyes that seemed to emit some rare and wonderful comfort to her, "I know she was a good person with a kind and loving soul. When some people have touched me they've felt bad, weird…whatever, but I never meant for them to. I never tried to hurt anyone," her hand came up to gently caress his cheek, "I don't want to hurt you. Do you believe me?"

"Of course, I believe you. I have felt nothing but comfort from your touch." He leaned forward and kissed her gently. "There is nothing evil about you, Cashmere." She clung to him as if by holding him it made it true.

Snuggled together in front of the fire, she whispered, "Max, why do you call me Cashmere?"

"Have you ever slid on a Cashmere sweater and felt the soft, almost sensual glide of the fabric over your skin?" She slowly nodded her head caught up in his warm tone and comforting embrace. "That's what your voice feels like to my soul. I especially like the way you say Maxim. I imagine it's one of your powers like most witches; to comfort and soothe."

"Doesn't it bother you or…or worry you that I'm using a power over you?"

Max chuckled. "Is it really all that different than any other woman having a power over a man? I've known men to spend an entire week's pay on a single piece of jewelry for the woman in their life who wasn't a witch! The way I see it, there's a little witch in every woman…and I like it," he said with a mischievous grin that she couldn't help smiling back at.

"You know," she said softly, snuggling into his arms, "sometimes I feel like *you're* the witch putting *me* under a spell." Max smiled and gave her a slow, lingering kiss.

♣

The next morning when Astrid came downstairs the house was empty. Even though it was Manette's day to work, she was nowhere to be found. Astrid went into the kitchen already so used to having fresh coffee in the mornings now that she couldn't resist brewing some for herself. Foreseeing her need, Max had placed a new bag of coffee on the counter with a pastry in a little white box and a note, 'This coffee is one of my favorites, enjoy! Max.' Both the coffee and the strawberry topped pastry were indeed delicious and she felt so good when she'd finished, that she went in search of her spiral notebook to write a little about a story she was working on, but also…a little bit about the man occupying her thoughts. As she started up the stairs the door opened and wearing black suits, Jackson, Max and Tom walked in the front door accompanied by Manette and Sara both wearing black dresses. "It was kind of you to pay for her funeral, Tom," Manette said dabbing her eyes with a tissue.

"There wouldn't have been a funeral if she hadn't been trying to be something she wasn't," Jackson said.

"So you're blaming her?"

The quiet tone to Max's voice was a warning most heeded, but not his brother, "Yes," Jackson said unapologetically, "the boyfriend was a monster, but she gave him the ammunition. We are what we are. You can't just up and decide you want to be something else for a change."

"She was just trying to find her way," Tom said softly. Sara looked up into his face and the expression there tugged at her tender heart. It was obviously still causing him a great deal of pain and yet he wouldn't share it with her; causing her to ache for both of them. "He took advantage of a beautiful, loving soul that..,"

"That didn't know what she was doing!"

"Jackson," Max admonished him, "You can't blame someone for wanting something better than what they have."

"It wasn't making things better…it was making them worse!"

Tom's pain turned to anger, "That creep maimed her and drove her to that overdose!"

"Rather than trying to be a witch she should have tried getting off the drugs!"

"She was trying," Max argued.

"If she was trying then why did she go back to him?"

Tom shuffled his feet, the feelings of guilt about the situation surging back up again, "She didn't know what he'd done. She had already nearly overdosed. We were afraid…she couldn't see without a mirror so we thought...I bandaged it and told her to keep the bandage on or it would get infected. We were planning to tell her when things calmed down and her head was clearer."

Jackson shook his head at him, "We? You and that witch?"

"Yeah," Toms said miserably and Sara's heart ached for him.

"Keeping secrets never works. Perhaps if you had told her right then she wouldn't have gone back to him. Maybe if she'd seen it when you were there to comfort her rather than her seeing it while she was with him…drugged up, maybe she'd have reacted differently. You didn't give her that chance."

"Damn it, Jackson. Don't put the blame for this on him. He was doing what he thought was best. It was a bad situation," Max said angrily.

"Being another one that likes to keep secrets," Jackson said with a sneer, "I don't think you can really understand the situation."

"Oh, stop it," Manette yelled, "I can't bear listening to you tear each other apart!"

"Manette, wait," Jackson called out to her as she started for the door. "I'm sorry, I…" He reach out to grab her arm before she made it out the door, but he missed and knocked into Max in the process. Max stumbled backwards and hit the round table in the middle of the foyer. Jackson grabbed his arm to help steady him, but it was too late. The crystal vase holding the lilies crashed onto the table, breaking and spilling its contents onto the floor. With Sara's sharp intake of breath, all eyes slowly looked down at the pool of water and flowers as if time suddenly stopped. For a moment no one spoke, no one moved; as if a tragedy had suddenly struck and no one was capable of any reaction. What had moments ago been a noisy room of arguing and rustling of shoes and coats, was now completely silent except for the soft sound of the water still dripping off the table. Astrid watched on as in unison, all eyes then turned to Max who stood with his gaze transfixed to the floor. The way his eyes looked at the spilled flowers it was as if he was seeing something no one else could see and the expression on his face was painful for everyone seeing it. He seemed incapable of movement and even his chest didn't look to be moving to bring air to his lungs. Astrid didn't know what to expect, but it wasn't the dead silent that overtook the entire assembly.

After several anguish filled moments of inaction on everyone's part, Jackson spoke in a hushed and reverent tone, "I'm sorry, Max." He looked down at the floor, unable to bear the devastation on his brother's face.

"I'll clean it up," Sara said in the same mournful tone as Jackson, but Tom held her back silently shaking his head; Max was not ready. Tears welled in her eyes and she trembled slightly so he put his arm around her shoulders.

"Jackson," Max whispered somewhat shakily, going down on his haunches and delicately picking up a flower whose stem was broken. The water dripping from the table grew quieter and slower, mimicking Sara and Astrid's tears. Jackson leaned down putting a hand on his brother shoulder and Max murmured something to him in Swedish. Jackson nodded and gave the strong shoulder beneath his head a gentle squeeze.

Standing back up, Jackson turned to Sara and Tom. Sara had heard the request and seeing the tears already making trails down her cheeks, Jackson smiled at her saying softly, "It'll be alright. He just wants to be left alone for a little while," she nodded and Tom turned to walk out with her. Jackson looked up at Astrid still standing on the staircase. Casting one last look at Max, she quickly left to go to her room.

♣

When she came down two hours later Jackson was sitting alone in the sitting room with a little wooden box in his hands. As she walked in, he opened the box and turned the key winding it. A beautiful song emerged with an old fashioned tinkling sound and she smiled. "That's lovely," she said softly.

Jackson stared at the box and smiled sadly. "It was what Max always played for Sara and I when....For some reason right now it just seemed fitting to play it."

Astrid sat down in the chair opposite of him. "That was kind of him to play it for you," she said hesitantly, "he seems a bit like a doting brother."

Jackson closed the box saying, "He was always trying to make up for...our lack of good parentage. He's a fool."

Astrid smiled at him, "There wasn't the least amount of sincerity in that insult." Jackson didn't respond. "Where is he?"

"Out," he said shrugging his shoulders and shaking his head. "He asked me to leave, but...I just...couldn't. Not with him like that. I came in here out of his way and waited. He was just...still for a while. I don't know where his thoughts had taken him," as he cleared his throat it was obvious to Astrid how much the incident upset him. "Eventually he cleaned everything up and just...calmly walked out the door."

"Jackson, the funeral you went to today...who was it?"

Jackson looked at her, "Someone Tom was looking after. A witch that knew Tom brought her to the hospital one day. She'd nearly overdosed and while she'd been unconscious, her boyfriend had carved an upside down pentacle into her shoulder-blade."

"Why upside down?"

"Well, you know the pentacle is a symbol for witchcraft," Astrid nodded, "upside down it's a symbol for devil worship. She wanted to be a witch like her friend and was studying spells and things to try to be one. The boyfriend told her she was wicked and going to hell. He told her the devil was watching her and while she was doped up the bastard played a cruel joke carving it into her. She was weak mentally and he played on it. Freaking her out and such. Tom...I know he's a good guy. I know he was trying to do the right thing," he let out a breath, "but secrets get out and people…can only be what they are not something else. Secrets, lies, deceptions…sometimes I feel like…"

"What?"

Jackson shook his head, "Nothing. Anyway, she went missing for a few days and when Tom and his friend finally found her the bandage was ripped off, a mirror was beside her, and she was dead of a drug overdose just lying on the side of the road. It was ruled suicide, but…we're not really sure."

"Poor Tom," Astrid said quietly.

"This young girl who had no family and felt all alone in the world. I wonder what she would think if she knew how many lives were affected by hers; Tom, the witch that tried to befriend her, Sara because she cares so much for Tom, Manette because she had her own turbulent teen years, and now Max and I as it serves as another bone of contention between us."

"Why has it come between you and Max?"

"Because everything does. I wish…"

"What, Jackson," she asked softly, placing a comforting hand on his knee.

He closed his eyes briefly wanting the comfort she offered, but unable to bring himself to let it in. Swallowing the lump in his throat he said, "I wish I wasn't…" he let out a sigh and bent his head down.

"What?"

"Just his little brother," he said with a thread of anger in his voice and carefully set the musical box on the coffee table taking a deep breath and clearing his throat.

"There is nothing wrong with being a little brother," she said smiling.

"There is when that's all you are," he said, his anger rising, "Not a friend, not an ally, not even a comrade in arms…just a baby brother."

"Jackson, I don't believe that's all you are."

He shook his head looking at her, "Think you understand the beast do you?"

"Certainly not. I feel like a yo-yo going back and forth unsure of every thought and feeling I have about him. One minute I'm afraid of him and the next minute I want to wrap my arms around him." Jackson snorted and nodded his head as if he understood the feeling. "One thing I know for sure is that you and Sara mean a great deal to him." Jackson's only response to that was a grunt.

After a few moments of thought he said, "You know, at work they have nicknames for all of us."

Astrid smiled, "What's yours?"

"Lynx," he said quietly, frowning down at the fire in the hearth.

"That's funny, the ring Max wears…"

"I know," he said as eyes that had gone from angry to sad turned to look at her, "that's why they call me that.

"I don't understand."

"They call me that because I'm just an accessory hanging on his finger," he said softly. "He's got it all together you see. Life just seems to work out exactly as he wants it to like he has this magic ability to make the pieces fall into place. He knows exactly who he is, what he wants, and how to get it."

"I don't think he would agree with that," Astrid said. Although Max exuded a certain confidence in his manner, she'd witnessed a few chinks in his armor. "Why did he play the music box for you and Sara? Was it a special gift from someone or something?"

Sitting up in the chair, Jackson smiled slightly, "Special? No. It was to drown out Mother's crying.," he balled his fists in his together, "I never knew what it was all about, but when Sara and I were very young, Mother cried a lot. We weren't close to her…or to Father for that matter, but Sara is such a softy, hearing mother cry would make her cry. It never failed, Max always seemed to know to come see us and he'd wind up the music box." Jackson chuckled and picked up the box again. "He'd play it over and over again until I was nearly sick of it, but…for some reason," he bent his head down remembering, "for some reason, I would ask him to play it just one more time. We'd sit on the floor and he'd read to us, usually Findus and Pettson," he smiled looking at Astrid and asked, "Have you ever read those?"

Shaking her head Astrid asked, "Do you still have them," she looked around the room at all the bookshelves hopefully.

Jackson's smile faded slightly, "No. One night there was a fire in Max's room. All his books were burned except for his favorite, Pancake Pie. When he left Sweden, all he took out of the house was that book. I've looked on all these shelves and never found it." Astrid thought back to when she'd seen Max without his shirt when he'd been beaten in the hotel parking garage. She'd seen large burn marks on his skin and couldn't help wondering if that was when they'd occurred. Staring into the fire, Jackson smiled, "You know he's hated fires ever since, which is why this fireplace is gas with a remote control so that he doesn't have to actually get near it! I don't know why he has it at all...unless...," he chuckled saying, "Knowing Max it's probably just to prove to the fire that he's tougher than it is and damn it...he'd be right!" Jackson got up to leave, "I'm sure he'll be back before long, but I can stay if you don't want to be alone."

"No, I'm...I'm fine, Jackson. Thank you." He walked out and Astrid walked into the foyer; the vase of flowers were conspicuous by their absence. Quickly she raced up stairs to retrieve the vase and flowers from her room to put on the table before Max got home.

♣

The day before had been a bit of a disaster; the funeral, the flowers, spending the entire night and into the morning looking for a witch and mother of two small children that had seemingly disappeared, and then having to spend what was left of the morning explaining to Ivan that he'd been unable to find her, but that he suspected it was a marital dispute rather than anything relating to her being a witch. Max was exhausted, hungry, and irritable. He hadn't stepped foot in the house since he'd cleaned up the flowers, but as he entered and saw the vase from Astrid's room adorning the foyer table. He couldn't help but smile; a sad and tired smile, but a smile. It was comforting to know she'd done it for him, so that he wouldn't see the empty table. In pursuit of a cup of coffee and something sweet, gooey, and preferably covered in strawberry preserves, if he had his choice, Max entered the kitchen. "It's not your day," he said to Manette, "However, since you are here, fika...please," his boyish begging earned him a smile and she pointed to the coffee pot already brewing. "Which?" He asked already feeling better.

"Gevalia Kaffe of course," she said with a bright smile. Being that it was considered the coffee of Sweden it was Manette's favorite. Anytime Max didn't specifically request a certain brew, it was the one she chose. "I have *gräddtårta med jordgubbar!*" Max smiled at the thought of the Strawberry Cream Cake; delicious layers of cake with custard and lots of fresh strawberries and cream. "I'm giving you a raise," he said warmly.

"Oh no you're not. You already pay me too much for just two days a week tidying." She poured his coffee saying with a grin, "besides, this is a bribe." He raised his eyebrow and she continued, "Yesterday was my day, but with the funeral and all...so I came in today, only...I have a date tonight and I want to leave early to get the full treatment at the salon!"

"Date with whom?" Manette laughed at the big brother tone matching the expression on his face. "Bring him here first," he said walking back to the kitchen door.

"I'll do no such thing. Where are you going?"

"To see if Astrid would like to take fika."

"She isn't here," the pretty maid said as she wiped the countertop.

Max stilled her hand, "What do you mean? Where is she?"

"Well, she...she said she was going out. What's wrong?" Max walked out not answering and leaving his coffee and cake untouched. "Max?" He took his phone out of his pocket and tried calling Astrid. "What's wrong?"

Taking a deep breath, he looked up at her. "Nothing is wrong...I mean, probably nothing. It's just...," he paused a moment to gather his thoughts as Astrid didn't answer his call and he prepared to send a text. "We've had some...threats recently and...," he smiled, "I'm probably just over reacting."

"One day there is going to be something or someone you can't control...maybe it is her!"

Max gave her a look of mock annoyance before saying, "Enjoy your date, but…I will meet him at some point."

Manette shook her head laughing as she walked away. Max sent Astrid a text asking her to call him right away. As soon as he found out that she didn't have a cell phone he'd gotten her one, but he knew that she'd barely taken any notice of it. He stood staring at his phone a few minutes as if he expected it to ring at any second. Realizing the futility of what he was doing, he went back to the kitchen to retrieve his coffee and cake and sit at his desk in the sitting room. It occurred to him that she may have left a note on her desk and he walked to it quickly noticing a letter to her editor, 'Dear Penny, here is another scene I was considering using. Since Mr. Bronius wants everything to go through you first, I thought you should go ahead and read it before I set it into the book.' Max took the pages back to his desk and read through the scene. It was the story of Blakulla, the place of the devil in Nordic tales. The poor souls who were burned in the Torsaker witch trials were accused of working with the devil and kidnapping children; taking them to the place where the devil held banquet and hell could be seen through a hole in the wall. The tale was dark and scary and her version made it out as if witches everywhere were in league with the devil. She went on to describe the sacred stones on the island that make up a labyrinth that is known to have been there for hundreds of years. People have been warned for centuries not to take the stones. There is documented evidence of terrible things happening to people who disregarded the warning; bad enough that they often mailed the stones back to the city official asking him to replace the stone. Astrid's story was actually encouraging taking the stones home as souvenirs. Mentally exhausted, Max's head slowly lowered to the top of the desk as he tried to understand why the woman he knew to be compassionate and kind was writing in such opposition with her character. It was as if…they were two different…

CHAPTER 10

Hours later the front door opened and Max jumped up and staggered to the foyer wondering when he'd fallen asleep. Seeing who came in, he said testily, "Where have you been?" At her bewildered expression, he looked at his watch realizing he'd been sitting at his desk for the last five hours; three of them sleeping. "Didn't you get my text," he asked a little more angrily than he meant to as he was trying to get his brain to wake up.

Astrid stared at him a moment before answering, "I forgot to take the phone with me, but..." she frowned as she hung up her coat and handbag, "you did say I could come and go as I pleased. Isn't that true?"

When she stepped back away from him as he attempted to help her with her coat, he realized his mistake and took a deep breath. "I did...yes...you are certainly allowed to go where you please." He smiled at her and bowed slightly, "I'm sorry. I was worried...obviously unnecessarily because I can see you are perfectly fine." She continued to scowl so he thought to change the subject, "Did you enjoy your outing?"

"Yes and I bought you something," she said holding out a bag, but still keeping her distance from him. When he opened the bag and looked at her with an odd mix of a frown and a smile, she finally offered a smile of her own. "It's called Tiny Footprint Coffee. It's the American Swedish Institute's special roast; made just for them."

"You went to the American Swedish Institute? Why?" He took the coffee out of the bag, always ready to try a new brew.

"You never tell me anything about yourself," she said shyly, "I thought I'd learn a little about where you come from; the language, the culture, anything." Max pointed toward the sitting room and they made their way to the sofa. A bright smile appeared on her face as she described her adventure. "I toured the mansion, oh...," she clapped her hands together, "Turnblad Mansion! It was breathtaking...the wood carvings and tiles...have you been there?"

"No," he said with a chuckle.

Her eyebrows shot up as she said, "Why ever not? It's your heritage."

With a shrug of his shoulders he said, "I guess because...being a Swede, I already know about my culture."

"Well, I see what you mean, but...this is celebrating you!" Max couldn't hold back a smile of her obvious enthusiasm. "They even named the café Fika! I didn't have time to try the food though; there was too much to see. The mansion has thirty three rooms to look at and there are exhibits and the loveliest courtyard. I loved it," she said smiling at him.

"Since you haven't had a snack I can recommend Manette's latest offering. It's Strawberry Cream Cake and it's delicious. The coffee is a few hours old, but we'll try the Institute's blend."

"Sounds wonderful, uh...about when I came in...,"

Max held out a hand to help her up from the sofa and was pleased when she didn't shy away from it. "As I said, I was just worried. You may as well know...I'm a hot head and a control freak, but...I'm harmless."

"Oh, I don't believe that for a second," she said allowing him to continue holding her hand into the kitchen. "But, uh...you did say once that you *weren't* a tyrant."

Max slowly looked up at her looking like a naughty little boy, "Maybe...slightly tyrannical?"

Astrid smiled, "It's nice to know someone cares enough to be…slightly tyrannical," she said. "No one has ever been worried about me before."

Setting the new coffee on the counter he said softly, "Speaking of being worried about…thank you for putting the flowers on the table in the foyer. It was very thoughtful and I appreciated it when I came home."

"You're very welcome," she said softly and he leaned in to give her a quick little kiss, but she reached up and held his face looking into his eyes long enough that he felt the need to give her a bigger kiss and then another.

Tearing himself away from her, he opened the refrigerator to get her a piece of cake then realized what time it was. "Hey, it's dinner time. What do you say to some leftover soup then cake?"

"I say, you warm up the soup and I'll set the table!" Feeling as if on a cloud, Astrid went into the dining room to set the table. Seeing the candles on the sideboard, she added them to the table and lit them. Leftovers or not, why not be romantic?

An hour and a half later, they were relaxing in the sitting room, both attempting to work. "What are you thinking about looking at me that way?" Max asked Astrid from across the room. He'd been watching her for a few minutes expecting her to say something. She hadn't moved, she'd just kept staring at him or not exactly him, but rather his hand. When he'd first noticed, he'd put down his pencil and joined his hands together to see if she'd follow the movement, which she had. His curiosity finally got the better of him and he had to know what was on her mind.

She fluttered her eyelashes a bit as if she was surprised he was there, which was ridiculous of course because she'd been staring at him for ten minutes. Still not adjusting her gaze she said softly, "I was thinking about your hands."

Max noticed that whenever she used that tone, a warmth seemed to wash over him. It made his blood stir in the most intimate way. Keeping his voice as soft as hers, he asked, "What about them?" He didn't move. She was looking at him; studying him, but not in an intrusive way. It was more like, appreciating. No one in his experience had ever looked at him so intimately before and he discovered he liked it.

"I was thinking about how different your hands are from mine. The wide, masculine palms are always so warm when they touch me. Your long slender fingers, so gentle when they stroke the back of my hand in that comforting gesture you do. It's amazing the way your hands can be strong and protective when they need to be and at other times touch me so softly they make me feel like I'm made of porcelain or something else fragile and delicate. Sometimes just the idea of them dancing along my skin gives me the most delicious shivers." Her eyes suddenly moved to look into his face and she grimaced looking away. "I'm sorry. I tend to ramble sometimes."

Max stood up and walked over to where she sat next to the fire. Bending down close to her beautiful face he said tenderly, "I like the way you ramble." He kissed her softly placing the hand she so admired against her warm cheek. In his mind she was like porcelain; precious and rare.

♣

A few days later it was Sunday night and as was their usual, Sara and Jackson arrived for dinner. Astrid enjoyed Sundays and listening to the siblings, who obvious were very fond of each other, banter back and forth; having had such a different experience with her own siblings. Max sat, ushering them all to the table with a strange grin aimed at his sister. "I must say, Sara, I'm surprised you came tonight."

"We always invade your privacy on Sunday night," she said smiling.

"Yes, I know, but according to Tom you've been hanging out with some musician at a club called, *The Booby Trap.*" As he said it, Jackson choked on his iced tea and doubled up laughing.

"Does he come to you with everything?" she asked angrily.

"Unfortunately, yes. I would appreciate his informing me... if it was true, but since I know you're filling his head with nonsense," he looked at her raising an eyebrow, but she turned away, "since it is nonsense, it's annoying."

"Why would you tell him that?" Jackson asked, still chuckling.

Sara frowned and practically snatched the plate of dinner Max offered her. "Oh, stay out of my business, Jackson." She turned to Astrid. "So, not to change the subject, but to change the subject," she gave Astrid a grin, "Does Max still insist Manette make soup on Thursdays?"

"Yes," Astrid said then leaned closer to Sara, "He hasn't told me why though."

"My guess would be he hasn't told you much of anything!"

"Sara," Max said under his breath.

Sara just looked at him smiling though it wasn't a genuine smile. She was irritated that he'd seen right through her stories to Tom and now Jackson was in on what he seemed to think was a joke or at least something to be laughed about. "Max has soup every Thursday because he's a Swede."

"But...aren't you and Jackson as well?"

"We adapted to American life and now eat whatever we choose on Thursdays. Max is much more...stuck," she said with a giggle as Max glared at her.

"It's probably his age. Hey, at least when we're here on Sundays he doesn't require us to speak Swedish, which even the Swedes don't seem to want to speak anymore or worse Elfdalian," Jackson said laughing.

"What is that?"

Sara giggled, "Sounds like some made up movie language, doesn't it!"

"Well it isn't," Max said seriously, "It's a very ancient and noble Viking language."

"Which no one speaks anymore," Jackson said behind his hand.

"That's not true," Max said turning in his seat to his little brother, "In Älvadalen they continue to speak *Älvdaska*."

Astrid frowned trying to keep up with the conversation. Seeing this, Sara said, Elfdalen to us Americans.

Without looking up from his dinner, Max said, "Swedes."

"Swedish-American then," Sara said exasperated.

"I like soup," Max said innocently, "Why not have it on Thursdays? You have something against soup on a particular day of the week?"

Sara shook her head and lifted her fork, "These meatballs I suppose just wouldn't be the same without a side of lingonberries?"

"You and Jackson are so quick to put aside your heritage. Sunday dinner is my day to place it back in front of you," Max said raising an eyebrow.

"You cook one day a week and only Swedish food," Sara said then turned to Astrid when she heard her giggle. "It's okay, Astrid. You can admit he's strange. He won't *kill* you just for that," she said sarcastically glancing at Max. "You won't...will you, Max? Kill her...just for that?"

"The dinner is delicious," Astrid said with a smile, ignoring the looks going on from brother to sister, "I think it's wonderful the way he embraces his Swedish heritage even though he's in America." Max smiled at her and offered her a salute with his fork.

"Even though Sweden brought him the most horrendous moments of his life?"

"Sweden didn't do it, Jackson. Our father did," Max said staring at him.

"Fader, Moder, Manette and don't forget Ermina." Sara dropped her fork suddenly and Jackson turned to look at her. The expression on her face made him seem to think better of what he'd said and he became fascinated by the embroidery on his dinner napkin as he mumbled, "Max, I didn't mean to..."

"I never forget Ermina," Max said quietly without looking up from his plate, "Mother and Manette have never done anything to cause me to view the association with them as a negative."

"What?" Jackson said with undisguised astonishment. "How can you say that? They are the reason that..."

"You cannot blame them for the actions that happened around them."

"I don't know how you can separate them."

"Because, Jackson, I will not allow one closed minded, abusive, and heartless monster to cloud my feelings for my beloved country or the

108

people who have been a part of my life. I will not give him that power," he said slamming his fist onto the table. Realizing he'd revealed more than he'd intended, Max looked down at his meal taking a deep breath. "I'm sorry, ladies," he looked up at Astrid and tried a smile, but it didn't reach his eyes, "Forgive my outburst."

She smiled at him and nodded wishing she could ask about Ermina, but knew it wasn't the time. Giving Max time to compose himself, she turned to Sara, "How old were you when you came to America?"

"Eighteen. In fact, it was the day after our eighteenth birthday," Sara answered softly. "Max came and got us and we've never returned."

"Max came and got you? So he was already in America?"

"Uh, well…," Sara looked at Max unsure how much he'd want her to say. What at first seemed like harmless sibling teasing rapidly turned into much more than she'd expected.

Understanding her hesitation and noticing the sad look on her face, Max whispered, "*Lagom*." She looked at him and smiled when he gave her hand a little pat. "I'm seven years older than the twins. I came here when I turned eighteen," he said to Astrid.

"So, the one time you went back was to get them?" Max nodded, remembering that he'd admitted at their first dinner that he'd returned once. Cautiously, not wanting to bring up old wounds, she said, "Your father didn't come to American then?"

"Father," Jackson said bitterly, "Father didn't want anything to do with America. He didn't want anything to do with us."

"Jackson," Sara admonished him then turned a smile on Astrid. "In the seven years Max was here before us, he bought this lovely house. When we were of age, he invited us to live with him. We stayed here until we…well, needed to sprout our own wings." There was obvious affection in her voice as she looked at Max.

"That was kind of you," Astrid said softly to him, but he shook his head making her frown. "Why are you shaking your head, no?" He didn't answer and wouldn't look at her. "Max?" the sadness in her tone prompted him to look into her face.

Her compassionate expression was impossible for him to resist. "It would have been kinder to get them out sooner. I tried, but...failed," again he shook his head and looked down at the table.

Jackson snorted, "That master manipulator just used us against you. Just like he always used Mother against you. You always fell for her sad, pitiful look."

Max didn't look up and Sara frowned. "Max, you tried," Sara said gently placing a hand on his arm. Feeling the need to defend the brother who wouldn't defend himself, Sara said, "Father knew that Max wanted us to come live with him, but he refused to let us go. I still remember the day you left," her voice dropped to nearly a whisper, "You gave me the music box and wound it up for me. Watching you walk out the door I honestly thought...," she sniffled and he reached out to take her hand, "I thought I'd never see you again."

She tried a chuckle, but the sound was so pathetic Max squeezed her hand and whispered, "I'm sorry, Sara."

"The new maid Clara told me that you said to call if we were ever injured in any way or if we needed anything. She told me that you called every Sunday to check on us." Her chin quivered as she said softly, "For seven years, every Sunday." Max bent his head down and she turned to Astrid. "That's why we always descend on him on Sundays," she told her. "Manette was struggling a bit at the time so Max brought her over as well."

"Yes, she told me," Astrid said. He looked at her, but to her surprise he didn't ask what they'd discussed. "I had been asking her about the lilies," she said quietly. No one spoke for a while as dinner was consumed and everyone sat contemplating their own thoughts.

After the siblings left things quieted down into what seemed to be a usual routine. Max went to his desk to work and Astrid sat usually on the floor or the sofa in front of the fire to write in her notebook.

When he hadn't heard her pencil scratching along for several minutes, Max looked up to see her staring into the fire with the eraser end of her pencil poised on her bottom lip. For a few moments he stared at her as the firelight glimmered off of her black hair and as her eyes glazed over looking at the fire he knew she wasn't really seeing it. She was day dreaming, or playing out some little scene going on in her head. Knowing he was getting no work done, he turned off his computer and walked over to sit on the floor next to her. She glanced at him and smiled rather mischievously. "I was just thinking about you," she said with a giggle.

"Were you?" he said intrigued remembering the glowing look she'd had on her face as he watched her. "What were you thinking?"

She bent her head down and doodled a flower on her paper. "I...I'm not sure I should tell you."

"Why not?"

His tone was so warm and gentle she felt her insides tingle. "I don't know how you'd feel about it. I don't like it when people are angry with me or disappointed. Usually I'm not even sure what I've done." She tried a little laugh, but it wasn't very convincing. Max knew this was no laughing matter.

"Cashmere, I cannot imagine myself ever disappointed in you for any reason." He tilted her chin up with his finger as he spoke to her. "As far as angry, well I do have a temper. However, I can promise not to get angry right now about whatever you tell me." Maybe this was the moment she was finally going to reveal her sources. At last he could get Ivan off of his back.

"Well, you know how when you got beaten up, you said you weren't sure if they were after me or you..."

"Yes," he said encouraging her.

"Well, I actually didn't...," Astrid doodled another flower on her paper and then frowned and scribbled over it. Max gently laid his hand on hers to stop her movement.

His phone rang and he let out an audible sigh at the bad timing, "Yes," he practically yelled into the phone. It was Ivan.

"Don't take my head off you insolent pup!"

"What can I do for you, kind sir?" Max said sweetly causing Astrid to giggle.

"You asked me to look into Ms. Martin's family."

"Well,"

"Nothing doin'. My office...the usual time," Ivan said hanging up the phone. Max stared down at the carpet. Whenever Ivan refused to discuss things on the phone and got cryptic over times and places, it was bad.

"Max, everything alright?"

"Well, I guess I'm not sure," he said quietly with a chuckle.

"Is it alright if I finish telling you what I wanted to say? I think...I think I need to tell you," she said.

He looked up and noticed her bottom lip between her teeth and gently removed it. "Tell me," he said giving the abused lip a little kiss.

"Max, I didn't say yes to stay with you because I was afraid." She glanced at him and then back down at the carpet. She whispered, "I wanted to be with you. I...," she tucked her head down, "I've been a little afraid, but still...I wanted to stay with you."

Max couldn't stop the slight grin and said gently. "I didn't want you here just because I was worried about your safety. I wanted you with me."

Astrid looked into his eyes and smiled, "You did?"

"I did. I do." It wasn't the big reveal he was hoping for, but for some reason he couldn't bring himself to be disappointed.

"Maxim," she said making the back of his neck tingle, "I wasn't trying to pry when I asked Manette about the flowers." Taking a deep breath he turned slightly away from her and she gently touched his chin to make him turn back to her. "I only wanted to know about them. I didn't know it was so personal. You promised not to be angry with me, but...I don't want you to be hurt either. Please believe that it was never to hurt you."

"I do," he said bringing the smile back to his face. "I've just never discussed it with anyone before." He frowned suddenly and a feeling of pain and regret washed over him. "I loved my mother very much."

"Did she love you?"

To some it would have seemed an odd question, but Max understood why she would ask and said, "Although Father tried to prevent her from telling me or showing me…I always felt it in her eyes when she looked at me. When she died…I felt it keenly," he said softly looking down at the carpet.

"I'm sorry. Were you with her when she died?"

"Yes, she was in bed and I held her hand until she was gone and then I went to the twins rooms and told them."

Astrid frowned, "Why didn't your father tell them?"

"He was in France with his current mistress at the time. I called him and said, 'she's dead', and hung up the phone. I didn't want to hear whatever nonsense he might try to say. He managed to get back the day before her funeral. Two years later I was eighteen and moved to America."

Gently caressing the side of his face she said, "I'm glad. I'm glad you came here…so that we could meet."

Appreciating her wanting to help change the mood, Max looked at her and smiled, "I'm glad, too."

She set down her pencil and stroked the top of his hand. "I like touching you."

"That's good. I like you touching me."

"When…," she stopped and looked down at the ground and frowned.

"When what?"

"Nothing, it doesn't matter."

"It matters, because you matter. You matter to me." Max leaned down and kissed her softly on the tip of her nose realizing he meant what he said. She mattered to him and he wasn't sure how he felt about that.

He'd shared something of himself, so she felt maybe it was time to share a little of herself as well. Taking a steady breath she looked into his eyes then looked away again afraid she may see censure. "Well, one time when my oldest brother Jimmy had locked me in the closet," her voice was quiet and timid and Max stayed motionless feeling whatever was about to be said was painful for her. "I heard him talking to one of his buddies about taking five dollars to let the boy kiss me. Well, Jimmy unlocked the closet and told me to come out and then left. The boy kissed me a few times and then…I don't know what happened…he shoved me away from him and looked at me funny. He went outside and I heard him yelling at Jimmy that there was something wrong with me and he wanted his money back. Jimmy came in really angry and..."

Max had a feeling the five dollars was for a lot more than just a kiss, but he wasn't about to tell Astrid. One day he'd get a hold of her brother Jimmy and he planned to beat a whole lot more than five dollars' worth out of him. "Astrid, did you want the boy to kiss you?"

She stopped her fingers that had been softly tracing the muscles on Max's arm. He saw a tear glistening on her lashes, "No," she said softly, "I didn't. I didn't know him and..."

"And what?"

When her eyes met his, his gut clenched at the fear in them, "I didn't like the way he was holding on to me. He...he hurt me." Instinctively, she rubbed the arm the boy had held too tightly.

The tear fell and he wiped it away with the pad of his thumb and smiled softly at her. "There was nothing wrong with you. There was something wrong with him. His own negative energies. You defended yourself against him doing what you didn't want him to. You're a very powerful witch and you had backup." When she frowned he explained, "Your grandmother was there with you giving you her strength." He chuckled suddenly and said, "I knew a witch once that made her attacker vomit uncontrollably."

"What happened to her?"

"It doesn't matter," he said sobering.

"I think...it does matter." Astrid grinned. "It matters because you matter." He returned her smile recognizing that she'd just thrown his own words in his face.

"Cashmere, what did Jimmy do when he came back in?" The smile melted off of her face and she turned away looking down at the carpet. "Cashmere?"

A tear slid down her cheek, "Maxim, I don't...I don't want to answer. I don't want to talk about it."

"I understand, but...can you just answer one thing?" He cupped her cheek with his hand and his thumb gently stroked. "Is that when you found out about taking shallow breaths with damaged ribs?" She nodded her head and he brought her forehead to his closing his eyes a moment against the anger that rose up within him.

When he pulled back, she looked down at her hand as it softly stroked his arm. "It seems odd and…I don't understand why, I hardly know you, but…you make me feel safe," she said shyly.

Using his finger to tilt her head up at him, Max looked into her eyes and said, "Good," and gave her a peck on her nose. "You said you've been afraid and…I understand that, but I would never hurt you, Cashmere."

"I believe you," she said breathily. "Since I've never felt that way before, it's very…," she looked at him and he just raised his eyebrow in question, "…it's very alluring," she whispered. "Max,"

"Yes?"

"Could I…?"

"Yes?" he encouraged gently watching her gaze down at his hand and then slowly back to his face.

"Would you mind if…if I…?"

Max waited patiently as she searched his crystal blue eyes then gazed down at his mouth. She brought her hand up and grazed her thumb along his warm bottom lip. Her tongue peeped out in anticipation. Max thought if she didn't make her request soon he was going to burst into flames. She was watching him with such a mixture of desire and curiosity he didn't think he'd be strong enough to take it much longer.

She leaned close to him, close enough that he could feel her breath on his cheek. "Maxim, I want to touch more of you. I want to know how your body looks, how it feels, how it tastes. Everything."

Max's entire body began to burn with anticipation. When she leaned back Max held her gaze. She was so beautiful and so innocent. How could a woman be such a seductress and have no idea? It didn't seem possible. With a herculean effort not to ravish her, he said, "You can touch me anywhere and in any way that you want to." His hand caressed her cheek and he waited for her to come to him.

CHAPTER 11

Astrid leaned in and kissed him tentatively at first and then moved in closer and closed her eyes with a sigh. If there was anything more alluring than a woman discovering passion for the first time, he couldn't imagine what it was. Her soft little moan against his mouth made him have to start counting backwards just to keep control. Her lips were soft and warm and they glided along his lips soft as a feather over and over again before landing and pressing against him. Although he wanted to crush her against him, he kept still and let her set the pace.

Slowly pulling away, she glanced into his face and reached for the buttons on his shirt. He made no move to take her hands away so she continued to unbutton him. "I don't...I don't want to do anything wrong," she said with an uncertain chuckle.

"There is no right and wrong to being intimate. It's only a matter of whether or not we're both enjoying it." She looked into his eyes and he smiled broadly, "I'm definitely enjoying it. I want you, Astrid. I want your touch."

Returning his smile, she tentatively laid her hands on his abdomen and moved up feeling his ribs and chest, biting her bottom lip as she slowly caressed his shoulders. "Sometimes...when you're holding me...kissing me...the only thought in my head is...more."

"Good," he said huskily, "because that's exactly what my head is saying right now."

Max watched her face as she closed her eyes briefly at the sensations touching him created within her. "Your skin is so soft and yet your muscles are so hard," she said. Her hands reached over his shoulders

116

brushing his shirt down his arms. "So warm. It's like…it's like I can't get close enough to you," she murmured as she brought her mouth to his neck and kissed him. Her roving hands made their way down to his belt and she glanced up at him before moving them back up. Bestowing open mouth kisses to his shoulders and back to his neck and giving significant attention to the hollow between them, she whispered, "Maxim?"

"Hhmm?" he answered.

"Can we take everything off?"

In answer, he took his shirt the rest of the way off and then reached for the hem of her shirt. "Your turn," he said pulling it over her head and taking her lips for a long and passionate kiss. He kissed her neck and shoulders just as she had done to him then turned his attention to removing her bra. He nuzzled her neck and caressed her breast making her quiver.

She touched and tasted and allowed him to touch and taste then stopping long enough to look directly into his eyes she said huskily, "I want more," and reached for his belt buckle.

Max smiled at her and pulled the blanket from the couch as he gently guided her to lie back onto the carpet in front of the fire. "I have more," he softly replied. It was hours before he needed to meet with Ivan. There was no point in stewing about whatever was going to be said when he could be enjoying the moment. With all his skill as an experienced lover, Max showed Astrid the many ways of bringing sweet torture to your partner. She'd said she wanted to learn how his body looks, feels, and tastes and he let her do as she pleased knowing her every touch was pleasing him as well.

Lying on his back with Astrid's warm arm draped across his chest, Max stared up at the ceiling trying to understand the strange thoughts plaguing his mind. After showing her all the delights of sharing your body with another, he'd taken her up to his room. He'd never taken a woman to his home before let alone his bed. Before, with other women, it had always been hotel rooms where it was easy to leave when the moment was over. He'd never laid in a peaceful and silent haze satisfied with simply holding and being held by the woman he'd just had sex with.

As her soft hand lazily drifted over his nipple and onto the patch of curls on his chest he couldn't resist a small smile finding it strange how truly wonderful it felt; not necessarily arousing just...nice. He was unable to recall the last time he'd felt so relaxed and yet he knew he had no reason to be so calm. In a few hours he'd meet with Ivan to argue yet again about what needed to be done about the little witch he was currently caressing. Slowly he drifted his eyes closed wanting to savor the moment for as long as he could.

♣

"You asked me to delve deeper into her family than what you were able to uncover and I think we've stirred up a hornet's nest." Max frowned and sat down in front of Ivan's desk. "Those damn brothers of hers have been investigated several times by the FBI for sabotage, arson, stalking, and harassment. Her mother was investigated by the CIA for that explosion that killed her husband and mother-in-law in Sweden."

Max shook his head and said, "I knew there was something more going on. She needs us to protect her...not assume she's the enemy."

"Don't be so quick," Ivan practically growled, "I haven't finished. The Swedish Guardians have also been investigating the entire family for a series of murders that have taken place over the last decade. Three guardians have been found dead and the circumstances all suggest a connection to witchcraft."

"That doesn't mean that Astrid had anything to do with..."

"You presume to know more than the FBI, the CIA, and the Swedish Alliance? They haven't declared her innocence!"

"I do not presume to know more of these facts than they do, but I know Astrid. She's already told me that she's never been outside of Minnesota."

"Then she's already lied to you." Tossing a file at Max, he continued, "They have proof that her entire family has made several trips to Sweden over the last ten years coinciding with the deaths. These people do know what they're doing." Max quickly looked in the file trying to find the evidence that she'd lied to him about her traveling. It listed that her mother had traveled with two young men and two young girls she claimed were her children. A picture accompanied the report, but it didn't show the faces of the two young girls very clearly. To Max it still wasn't enough proof that she'd lied to him. The form didn't actually identify Astrid, but he hung his head worried that he was now inventing explanations to convince himself of her innocence. Ivan stood up and leaned over the desk toward Max, "I'll admit that getting personal had never been your problem before, but obviously that's the problem with this case. The slight pink tinge to your complexion gives me the impression you've considered the same thing." Ivan sat back down and began shuffling papers on his desk. "I'm removing you from this case and I would advise you to get that woman out of your house it will only makes things messier."

"This is my case," Max said quickly as his chest tightened.

Ivan didn't bother to look up until he found the paper he'd been searching for. "We'll try to keep her death as low key as possible, but I don't want any of my agents associated with it so get her out." He picked up his phone and said, "Call Agent Heiss and tell him to come to my office at once I have a new case for him. What?"

As Ivan continued talking with his secretary Max glared at the man sitting at the large walnut desk. He sometimes wondered what had ever possessed him to join the alliance. Of course, he was always able to remember. He could never forget the little girl that died in his arms after being stoned to death for being a witch. Little Ermina had only been ten when she'd exposed herself as a witch, accidentally. A well respected man from the village had attacked her in back of the school. As he tore at her clothes she was crying and her little dog came running to her rescue. The man had kicked the dog making it whimper. Ermina had gotten angry and before he could understand what was happening her powers manifested. His head began to throb mercilessly, his nose began to bleed, and he began throwing up. He looked at Ermina and noticed the strange stare she was giving him. He twisted the story around making himself to be the victim of her witchcraft. The next day after school some of the villagers threw stones at her calling her evil. His father watched on from

119

a distance, refusing to intervene. By the time Max, only thirteen at the time himself, got to her, it was too late. She looked up into his eyes and smiled and then her breathing stopped and the hand he held in his let go. He'd held her in his arms and let the tears silently roll down his face until a policeman came and took her from him. Later that night Ermina had called to him and led him to the Isle of Jungfrun. In the center of a labyrinth she stood holding a hand out to him and smiling. It had helped to mend his heart a bit to see her again even though it was only her spirit he was seeing. She'd told him the secret of the labyrinth and once he was on the other side the alliance approached him and welcomed him. He bowed his head now thinking of her and the promises he'd made. Ivan wanted to sacrifice this witch to save others, Max simply couldn't and wouldn't do it. When he saw Astrid, he saw Ermina and he couldn't go through that again. He'd just have to find a way. Crossing Ivan Bronius wasn't a step to be taken lightly. As soon as Ivan put down the phone, Max said, "We've got time. She's starting to open up to me and…"

"*Starting* to open up to you? She sent a copy of some of the pages to me because she's under the belief I'm her editor. She's named names, boy! Names!"

He hadn't been called a boy in quite some time and if he remembered correctly he didn't like it then either. Keeping his formidable temper in check, knowing that Ivan was intentionally goading him, Max concentrated on twirling he gold lynx ring. He hadn't seen Astrid working much lately and had hoped she'd been preoccupied. It was somewhat surprising to hear she'd been writing right under his nose. Trying to appear calm he asked, "What names?"

"Names of the twenty four men on the Royal Norland Witchcraft Commission that were responsible for the witch trials! She's trying to put them in the damn book. I want to know where in the hell she got those names from. Someone has got to be feeding her information and damn it all I want to know who. I want the name of her informant and then I want them both dead before any more innocents are harmed. If this case has gotten too touchy for you because you're thinking with the wrong part of your anatomy or because she's got you under a spell, I'll send in someone else to handle the job."

"No. I will get the information, keep your thugs out of it, Ivan." Max's eyes bore down on the other man challenging him to argue. Lesser men would have cowered under the intense gaze, but not Ivan Bronius of the Vanir Clan of Sweden. Max hadn't really expected him to. He'd built his reputation and his empire by never cowering to anyone. The two men were well matched in stature as well as ego and it created a mutual respect as well as tension between them. The two of them going head to head would be a fight not to be missed, however they both knew it and neither one was interested in the battle scars it would produce. They were, after all, supposed to be on the same side. "She is a witch, she is one we're sworn to protect. We cannot kill a woman for doing something she doesn't even realize she's doing."

Ivan stared into Max's eyes intently, "You've never been squeamish about killing before."

Max didn't let Ivan see him flinch, but it took a formidable effort. His jaw clenched down on the words he wanted to say and chose not to jump at Ivan's bait. "You may request, but the decision lies with me."

"We cannot allow one witch to threaten the safety of thousands of others."

"The *safety* of others or the *punishment* of others? Isn't that what you're really worried about? That those names being leaked out will give the descendants a heads up to their fate?"

Ivan took a fresh cigar out of the antique box on his desk and sat back in his chair sniffing the pungent aroma of a well-made product. A slight grin appeared briefly on his face. "I know who they are and that's enough. I don't want the descendants of those bastards knowing their being looked for. If they don't know they are the descendants of those assassins that beheaded and burned innocent people, that's their tough luck."

Max almost choked. *Tough luck? Being hunted down and killed for being the great, however many removed, grandson of someone you don't know and know nothing about. Yeah, that's pretty tough,* thought Max.

"The universe has invested in us the power and responsibility to protect these women. It has been this way for centuries and it will continue to be our responsibility to protect the Isle of Jungfrun. You know that." Max glared down at Ivan. He understood full well his destiny and didn't feel he needed it spelled out. Ivan glared back at Max raising an eyebrow. The buzzer on Ivan's phone sounded, "You know better than to disturb me in a meeting, what is it?"

"I'm sorry, sir, but Ms. Vette is here to see you," his secretary informed him.

"Oh," Ivan looked at his watch frowning at the late hour. "Is she alright?" His suddenly quiet and concerned tone surprised Max.

"She's fine, sir, just wants to speak with you."

"Tell my cousin I'll be finished in a minute."

"Yes, sir."

Ivan sat staring at his phone for a moment as if in contemplation. "We'll do it your way," he said leaning back in his chair, "For now." The room was quiet as the men continued to watch each other. Max couldn't but wonder at the change in Ivan's tone. This cousin seemed to have an interesting effect. She might be worth getting to know. On the other hand, knowing Ivan the way he did, sticking his nose where it didn't belong could also prove fatal. He watched interestedly as the man's brow furrowed, smoothed, and then furrowed again until finally he said, "But, I'll have the information soon, or I'll find other means starting with taking you out of the equation and calling in Agent Heiss. Now get out." Max stared at Ivan a moment at the mention of Agent Heiss, taken a little off guard at the mention of that particular agent. Max went out the door hoping to get a glimpse of the cousin, but was disappointed to find no one outside the door, not even Ivan's secretary.

Max went over and over everything as he drove toward home. If he didn't find out what he needed soon Ivan was going to call in someone else. He knew the kind of men the man would send as a last resort, thugs. Men who didn't have any problem with killing, torturing, destroying any and everything in their path to get what they were paid to get. The agent Ivan had mentioned calling was, in Max's opinion, the most dangerous in the alliance. Never ask question, never alter the plan, and never stop until the job's done; that was Heiss. Part of the reason he and Ivan didn't always get along was that Max always asked questions and made his own decisions about what needed to be done. It was imperative that he come up with some way to get the information from Astrid that she was holding back. Could it possibly be that she did have him under some kind of spell? The notion was ridiculous. Astrid Martin was sweet, innocent, even at times a little detached or could it be that was what she wanted him to think? Ivan's own brother had been duped, it wasn't beyond their capabilities to mess with a man's head. *Ridiculous!* He thought, *now I'm starting to sound like those heretics that hunted them down in the first place.* It doesn't take witchcraft to mess with a man's head, just a woman.

When Max got home Astrid was no longer in his bed. Apparently she'd woken up in the night, realized she was alone and went to her own room. He couldn't bring himself to be disappointed. Not with all the confusing information he'd just gotten from Ivan. It was two o'clock in the morning and all he really wanted to do was go to sleep and shut his mind off.

♣

Max changed his clothes and stepped out of the men's locker room heading straight for the universal machine. When he'd gotten into his bed last night he hadn't counted on the pillow smelling like Astrid's perfume. Nor had he expected to find her sky blue panties under the sheet. It hadn't helped settle his mind and he wasn't sure he'd actually ever gotten any sleep at all. As soon as the sun came up he'd given up on sleep, bolted from his bed and had breakfast out. After a few phone calls to touch base with a few witches in the area per Ivan's request, he'd headed for the gym. His mind felt overworked and nothing helped relaxing it like getting physical. Of course there was always sex, but right now that wasn't the best option. For one thing, Astrid was what was foremost on his mind so having sex with her wouldn't solve the problem. For another thing, sex with someone else didn't really hold any appeal and that thought only added more concern to his already overburdened brain. He continued working his muscles, pushing them to their limits as the sweat gathered on his brow and ran down the sides of his face. "Hey Max, don't break my new machine man. I'm still not convinced it wasn't you that wore out the old one!"

Max grinned as Pete, the owner of the gym approached. "If I break it, I'll buy it," he said stopping to get up, shake hands, and accept the bottle of water he was offered. Just as the bottle got to his lips, their attention was drawn to the door of the gym. Three uniformed officers filed in and stood looking around a moment before coming straight to Max.

Pete greeted them cordially assuming they were potential new clients. "Welcome fellas," he said holding out his hand, "I'm Pete Lang the owner here. Are you looking for a new gym?"

"No, son," the biggest of them said, "We just want to ask this uh...gentleman some questions."

Pete turned to Max, who wiped the sweat off his face with a towel and said, "Yes officer? What can I do for you?"

"Have you got any witnesses that can verify your whereabouts at seven thirty this morning?"

Max looked down at the floor a moment running his morning thus far through his head, "No, I would have been in my car about that time, alone."

The man turned to the other two officers with a smirk and then back to Max. "Well then...," he set his hand on his gun holstered on his hip, "I'm going to need you to come down to the station with me."

"Why?"

He frowned at Max, "Well son, simply put, because I said so." Max just stared at him.

"Uh...officer has something happened?"

The first officer and Max continued to watch each other, but the other two officers turned to Pete and one answered his question, "Someone tried to kidnap a little girl this morning on her way to school.

The girl and another witness have described him and this guy here matches the description. We need him to come in for a lineup."

"I've known this gentleman for several years and I can tell you he would never…"

"I'm afraid your word for his character isn't going to be enough," the first officer said.

Max raised an eyebrow at the officer, "Do I look like a child kidnapper," Max asked with a smirk.

"As a matter of fact…yes." The officer looked at the scar on Max's neck and pointed at it saying, "Close call on that one." He noticed the other scars exposed by Max's tank top. "Get in a lot of fights, don't you?" Max looked at the officer without answering. "You're a dead ringer for the witness' description; average height, built like a brawler with the bruises and scars to prove it, hard expression and eyes that would frighten a corpse."

"Officer, I can assure you…"

"He's coming in…the hard way or the easy way, but he's coming in."

Max set down his towel and water bottle. "It's alright," he told his friend then looked back to the officers. "As I've done nothing wrong I have no problem coming in to aid in your investigation," Max said gritting his teeth. Embarrassed at the very idea that he fit such a description, Max glanced at his friend, "Don't worry, Pete," he said as he was escorted out and placed in the backseat of the patrol car.

CHAPTER 12

"Another two for the kidnapping," one of the officers told the desk clerk as they entered the police station. The desk clerk sneered at Max and he turned away. Apparently everyone being brought in was considered guilty first and innocent only after the witness dismissed them. The car ride had been a true test of Max's patience. They'd made several other stops looking for other potential, scuzballs, as they were described by the youngest officer. Naturally every stop they made had people peering in to see who was in the backseat. Refusing to sit lower in the seat, Max had put up with their snickering and pointing and frowns of outrage when they found out what he was being taken to the police station for. The officers picked up a man from an alleyway that smelled as if he hadn't showered in at least a week, had spit at the officers, and used every profanity in the English language. The thought that this person sitting next to him in the back of the police car was someone he was being compared to was revolting. When they'd finally reached the station, some two hours after he'd been picked up at the gym, they were requested to sit down on a bench with several other men and told to wait. Max looked over at his companions and cringed. Although the others weren't in gym clothes, other things stood out as being just like him...a side of him he hadn't paid much attention to before; meaty, scarred hands that were obviously used to abuse, various other bruises and scars on their faces and arms. Their faces more commonly held expressions of distrust, tension, and anger than expressions of happiness and kindness. Their jaws flexed and fists tightened and Max realized he was doing the same thing. One of them on that bench was possibly the bastard that tried to take that child and it made him sick to think he was in their company. Sitting on the bench with six street thugs was both humbling and humiliating and Max was grateful no one he knew was there to witness it. An hour later, an officer stood next to the bench and they were escorted into the lineup room. They stood, turned when told, turned again, stood facing the mirror they all knew was a window where someone on the other side was evaluating them, judging them, and holding their future in their hands. One by one they were being dismissed until only Max and one other man were still in the room. Although it was a mere two minutes it seemed as if it dragged on forever. Knowing you're innocent isn't much consolation when you're standing there vulnerable to another's decision. His hands began to sweat, but he refrained from wiping them on his gym shorts and make his nervousness known as they awaited their fate. Finally they were both escorted out of the room and told they could go.

"Shit," the other man said under his breath as they walked out.

"I must say I agree with you," Max said quietly.

The other man, whose size and coloring was a match for Max, turned to him and said, "I didn't try to take no girl, but I just got out of jail three weeks ago and if my woman gets wind of this she's going to run off with my bastard of a cousin," he said shaking his head, "You know they pick on us, but we're the reason they got jobs in the first place. They ought to thank us for givin' 'em somethin' to do." The man smiled as he walked away, but Max just stood watching him. *Pick on us? Now I'm one of you? Oh, I don't think so,* he thought to himself and quickly left the police station deciding he'd rather walk back to the gym than receive one of their offered escorts.

Moments later he was thinking he'd have been better off to swallow his pride and take a ride. "As I live and breathe if it's not Max Gunther, Agent Extraordinaire." Max turned to his left and scowled at the man grinning at him from the seat of his motorcycle. "You know, without your suit I barely recognized you." Max didn't response and didn't stop walking, at least not until the motorcycle pulled up in front of him blocking his way. "Not only is the suit missing, but I'd be willing to bet the hardware that usually goes with it is missing as well." Max looked him in the eyes not acknowledging that yes, his Beretta was with his suit in the locker at the gym. "Where's your ride? You do look a little naked!"

Max felt naked, but he had mastered the art of hiding his feelings years ago from an opponent far worse than the street crud in front of him. "I'm sure there are other places you could be poisoning with your presence, Shawn." Max walked around the motorcycle and continued toward the gym.

Shawn Lasseter got off of his motorcycle, stepped in front of Max and gave him a shove. Shawn was slightly taller, but Max was heavier and the shove had little effect. "I haven't forgotten that you're the reason I got kicked out of my own home."

Although Max had no real interest in fighting the young man, the idea of getting physical and letting out a little frustration was appealing. "Shawn, you got thrown out of the house because you threatened your mother. I merely supported her decision."

Shawn shoved him again and Max raised an eyebrow in warning that his patience was getting thin. "I only hit her one time."

"There shouldn't have been even one time," Max said scowling at him, "You also threatened to expose her as a witch to her boss. The boss I might add that signs her paycheck. The paycheck she uses to pay for the rent and food for both of you."

Frustrated and embarrassed, Shawn yelled, "You turned her against me just so you could screw her!"

Max's patience was gone and he reared back and gave the young man a solid right to the jaw. Shawn scrambled up and grabbed Max at the waist and hauled him to the ground. He punched Max in the face and bloodied his nose before Max rolled them over and pinned his opponent to the ground. "Listen you little shit," Max said, sitting on his stomach and holding his arms down, "You got yourself into your situation. I never had sex with your mother. I was doing what you should have been doing...protecting her. Now, I'm bigger, stronger, and a hell of a lot more experienced at this than you are so this is only going to get worse for you." The young man had calmed down a bit so Max slowly got up. "Your mother still wants you in her life." Max watched as the young man went back to his bike, "Get your head screwed on straight and go see her, but if you hurt her again I'll know it and it won't end well." He looked up at Max and gave him the finger before he drove off. Max shook his head, dusted himself off, and resumed his walk.

Back at the gym, Max noticed the doors were locked. Since his phone, gun, and car keys were in the locker room it was important he get in. He tried the door again then walked around the building to see if there was a back door open. Pete's car wasn't in the back parking lot and Max rubbed his head in frustration. All the cops had let him grab before escorting him out was his wallet for identification purposes. He walked over to the gas station next door and asked to use the phone. The attendant looked at his face a moment then down at his hands. Max noticed his hands were filthy and the knuckles on his right hand were red then he noticed his shirt and shorts were covered in a nice layer of dirt clearly indicating he'd had some sort of altercation. The attendant offered him a paper napkin and pointed to Max's face. Reaching up he realized his nose had bled a little bit. He dabbed at the blood and offered a five dollar bill to the attendant to use the phone to call Pete and have him come unlock the gym. Getting a bottle of water and a snack, he headed back to the gym to wait. *Well Father, I guess it's a good thing you're still in Sweden so you don't have to see how the 'worthless runt' turned out,* he thought to himself, *hauled in by the cops, brawling in the street, not really one of my better days.* The little cake he'd purchased had a sell by date that was nearly a year away and he couldn't help but wonder how much preservatives must be in it to keep it fresh for so long. The thought of it made him frown, but since he'd not eaten all day, he ate the cake anyway. The texture was a new experience and what the wrapper referred to as cream didn't taste like any cream he'd ever had before. Still, it was food.

♣

The doorbell rang and Astrid opened the door surprised by the large, well-dressed man on the steps. "Astrid Martin," he said in a deep voice.

It was a statement rather than a question, but she still felt compelled to answer, "Yes."

"Agent Gunther hasn't been answering his phone for the last several hours and since it is known you are in his home our employer was concerned for his safety."

He had a heavy accent, but it wasn't the same as Max's and the look in his eyes wasn't nearly as reassuring. The man didn't smile or offer any sign of civility and by the way he looked at her, she had the feeling he knew what she was. "You uh...," she cleared her throat, "you work with Max...I mean...Mr. Gunther um...in the alliance?"

"When was the last time you saw him?"

He had to have heard her, but it was obvious he was there to ask questions not answer them. She cleared her throat again and scratched her head absently, "Uh...not since last night." She could feel herself blush thinking about the last time she'd seen him; she'd been lying naked in his arms, but she wasn't going to tell this menacing creature in front of her that. "Yes, it was...sometime last night."

He watched her as if he knew she was hiding something and said, "Was he well at that time?"

Caught off guard by the question, she stammered, "Well, yes...yes of course he was."

"It is perhaps good for you to know that many people are interested in this situation." He turned and walked back to his black suv and Astrid quickly closed the door. She stood there a moment with her hand braced on the door waiting to hear the man start up his vehicle and leave. She took several deep breaths and pushed back the tears in her eyes. It was difficult for her to decide why she was shaking. Fear obviously, but fear of what? For Max or for herself and the fact that people knew she was a witch and obvious considered she was a danger to him. Astrid frowned, *strange things have been happening and it seemed strange when I woke up and Max was gone, but what did he mean, situation?* She had to admit what frightened her the most was...*what if they're right? What if...I am a danger to him?*

♣

As he finished his water, Max stood up to stretch just as a police car pulled up. "Not thinking of doing anything foolish are you," the officer who got out of the car asked him. It was one of the same ones that had picked him up earlier and he was suddenly reminded of his comrade at the police lineup.

"No, officer. I'm just waiting for the owner."

The officer sneered, "Looks like you've already had a spot a trouble just since I saw you this mornin'."

"Just a friendly misunderstanding," Max said passively. It really was embarrassing the idea that he was actually brawling in the middle of the street like any other thug. He hung his head down with a small sigh. "I've called Pete and he's on his way down here to let me in to get my clothes. That's all," he said

"From what I hear on the street this fella's got his hands full right now with his wife and all so don't let me hear of you giving him any trouble. This gym's got new hours. Too much riff-raff around in the evenings," he looked at Max with a sneer as if to say he was one of them, "He's closing up earlier now so you just adjust your schedule."

Max was worried about what the officer could have meant about Pete's wife Kate, but he wasn't about to ask him. "I only recently got released from the police station," Max explained, "I'll get my things and be on my way."

"See that you are," he said then to Max's relief he got in his car and left.

Moments later Pete showed up and Max was quick to ask about Kate. Pete smiled, "Oh, it's not witch trouble. It's not really trouble at all. It's just...well, she's pregnant."

Max relaxed, "That's wonderful, but is everything alright?"

"Everything is fine she's just…," he wrinkled his nose, "she ain't really feelin' very well. Nearly everything she's tried to eat is making her feel sick. Doc says it's all normal, but I've changed the gym hours so I can be home earlier. Sorry about your stuff getting locked in."

"Don't worry about it," Max said cordially.

"Did they find that would-be kidnapper yet?"

"No, it was none of the ones they brought in."

Pete looked at the dried blood around Max's nose, "Nice way to spend an afternoon, huh?"

Max raised an eyebrow, "I hope I never have that experience again." Max glared at Pete's chuckle and carried his things out. As they got in their cars he said, "Go home and take care of your girl. Don't forget we're here if you need anything."

"Thanks, Max. Hope your evening gets better." Max just shook his head to Pete's grin.

Sitting in his car, he noticed he had several missed calls from Ivan, one from Jackson, and to his surprise one from Astrid. He was just about to listen to the message she left when the phone rang and upon answering heard Ivan's bellow, "Where the hell have you been and why haven't you returned any of my calls?"

"Really, you don't want to know," Max said sighing deeply.

"With all this mayhem going on right now and you holding that little witch in your house I need you checking in more often. Your brother tried to get a hold of you and when that failed I sent Heiss to your home to no avail. I…"

"Hold up," Max interrupted him, "You sent Agent Heiss to my house? Why the hell would you do that?"

Ivan did not appreciate being shouted at by his subordinate. "Because you were missing you reckless rogue! He was the closest one to your home, is an agent of the alliance, and sent to do a job which he did! I'm assuming, since you have the audacity to question my motives, that you are not dead or otherwise impaired! Which makes me ask again, why the hell you weren't answering your phone."

Max started his car and took a deep breath realizing that Ivan was right. He had no right to question his motives, things are dangerous for all of them right now, and he hadn't been answering his phone. "I was brought into the police station for a lineup," he said disgustedly.

Ivan slowly and quietly responded, "Oh, yes. Must be about that attempted kidnapping this morning. They're on a manhunt and more power to them. Brought you in did they?" Ivan's chuckle made Max frown as he turned his car toward home. "I guess you do match the description," another chuckle, "Well, obviously it wasn't you so cheer up old lad." Max grunted. "Back to business."

Max hung up the phone and listened to his voice mail. Astrid sounded frightened, "Max, I...I don't want to bother you with...whatever you're doing," she sniffled, "I just...a man was here looking for you and...I hope you're alright." Max pushed his Jaguar to go a little faster. Agent Heiss didn't trust Astrid any more than Ivan did and although he had no love for Max, Max knew he'd not put up with a fellow agent being harmed. Calling seemed silly since he was only moments from home so he just drove a little faster.

Moments later Astrid greeted him at the door. "Hi," she said cordially as he walked in. Seeing her standing there with a smile on her face, he let out a breath he didn't realize he'd been holding. "I'm glad you're alright." Her hand gently touched his arm. "People have been worried about you," she said softly.

"Yes," he said a bit disconcerted by how nice it was to see her when he came in the door. He scratched his head and walked toward his desk. "I'm sorry about your visitor."

"Well," she chuckled, "he was a bit..."

She didn't finish and he turned to look at her, "Yes, I know. Are you alright?"

"*Lagom,*" she said with a grin bringing out Max's grin.

Max stood looking at her wondering what she would think if she knew where he'd been. If she would agree with them that he fit the description provided by the witness. Did this beautiful, compassionate woman see him as a thug? He looked down at his bruised, scarred knuckles and was unaware of the frown that appeared on his face.

Astrid noticed and as he stood there she also noticed how tired his eyes looked. Although he offered her no explanation of where he'd been and why'd they'd been looking for him, she had the idea that it had not been a good day. "I might feel better...," she smiled and came closer to him, "with a nice cup of coffee."

Max smiled, brought out of his negative thoughts. Bringing her into his arms, mentally and physically exhausted, he welcoming the comfort she offered. "Coffee," he said quietly into her ear as he caressed her, "definitely." They walked arm and arm into the kitchen and the simple act of making coffee worked its magic on them both.

♣

The next morning Max drove toward Ivan's aggravated both with himself and the situation he currently found himself in. Getting Astrid to move in with him seemed like a good way to gain some insight about who she really was. Somehow it got turned around and now he felt like the one being probed. No one that had been in his house before had ever noticed the flowers or at least they'd never mentioned them. For some reason when Astrid mentioned them he found himself inundated with memories that had been long suppressed. His phone rang and he hit the hands free device on his console. "Hello," he said.

"Where are you?" Ivan asked in his usual, aggressive tone.

"On my way to your office, per your request," Max said.

"Well, belay that. I need you going over to Imelda's. Somebody vandalized her porch last night. She says she doesn't need our help, but she always says that. I'm sending over four other guys as well in big black suvs. I want to make a statement to the neighborhood and nobody makes a statement like you do," Ivan said almost laughing. "Go be scary."

"I'm on my way," Max said, thinking he was just in the mood. Turning his Jaguar in the necessary direction, he asked, "By the way, I'm assuming she wasn't hurt or anything."

"No, they just hung stuffed toy cats by their tails all along the porch roof and toilet papered the tree out in front, that kind of juvenile crap. That's why I'm thinking it was just some kids from the neighborhood."

"Alright, I'll take care of it." Max hung up and shook his head. They'd been trying to get Imelda to move out of that neighborhood for five years, but she wouldn't budge. She was known locally as 'the crazy cat lady' and if Max had to be honest, he understood why. He'd never encountered someone so enamored with their cat before. There were plenty of ladies out there that indulged in having several cats; sometimes even an entire house full of cats. They pampered them and baby talked to them and indulged in all kinds of spoiling, but Imelda out shined them all. She had only one cat, but that cat was treated like a little human. She dressed it every morning in little outfits she had especially made for it. Surprisingly it never pulled or tugged at its clothing. Max guessed it was probably because she'd been doing it since the thing was a kitten and didn't know it wasn't supposed to be dressed. She fed it at the table opposite her own place setting. As she would talk to it, the little thing would cock its head different ways making it look as if it actually understood. The most disconcerting for Max was when it seemed to meow after she'd ask it a question as if it were answering her. He pulled up in front of her house and noticed not only what Ivan had told him about, but the vandals had also dug up all the flowers she'd planted across the front of her property and replaced them with plastic black roses. They mounted a sign in the yard, 'Crazy Cat Lady Witchcraft, inquire within.' Max shook his head and pulled the wooden stake holding it out of the ground. The two suvs were there and the guys got out of their vehicles in black suits and dark sunglasses and walked up to him.

"What's the plan, boss man?" A tall and thin young man asked.

"You guys start getting those stupid flowers out of there and get the toilet paper out of the tree. I'll call a landscaper to come fix up her yard the way she wants it." He pointed to two other guys who'd gotten out of the other vehicle. "You guys take care of the porch. Any of those stuffed cats in decent shape we'll take down to the children's hospital, she'd like that. After I talk with her, we'll then go door to door to do a little...polite intimidation," he said smiling. The idea of going intimidating with Max Gunther had all of them working quickly at their tasks so they'd be ready when he was.

Max knocked on Imelda's door. "Come in, come in," she called happily.

Max stepped into the cozy little sitting room. "I hope you at least looked out the window and knew it was me before you said, come in."

Imelda came into the room with her usual big smile in place, "I knew it was you coming," she said with a twinkle in her eye as if she was trying to make him believe it was some kind of magic. Max just grinned as Odin came prancing up behind her. "Come up here my darling and say hello to Max," she said picking up the cat and setting him on the sofa. The cat looked at Max with his one eye and meowed.

"I assume it's a waste of breath to ask you about moving." Imelda looked at him raising an eyebrow and he took it for a 'yes'. "You could talk to her, you know," Max said to the huge gray and white tom cat. It was odd the way the cat never tried to remove the eye patch that was placed on his head after he'd lost his eye. No one knew how he'd lost it. He'd just come home one day with a scratch across his eye and when she'd taken him to the vet they told her the eye needed to be removed. Max sometimes wondered if it was simply because his name was Odin and he was living up to the part.

Imelda sat down on the sofa, her long purple caftan billowing about her. "I told Ivan I didn't need any help. It's just some children playing a prank."

Max looked around the room saying, "I suppose none of these cameras caught any of their faces."

"Max, you know those cameras are so I can watch my cutie-pootie when I'm away from home," she said giving the cat a scratch and an Eskimo kiss. Max did know and it never ceased to amaze him. She watched the cat through her smart phone. He'd even seen her watching it when she was just in the next room. There were framed pictures of the cat in every conceivable cat position littering the mantel, the coffee table, and the side tables. "I'm fine, the house is fine, and more importantly Odin is fine."

"Right now, you're fine. These things have a habit of escalating." She didn't try to argue that one and he was glad. She was a sweet, open hearted woman and he'd hate for her to find out the hard way that the world wasn't as innocent as she thought. "We're going to do a little talking to the neighbors and see if anyone saw anything. I'll have a landscaper come in tomorrow, be ready with anything and everything you want done. Make it the garden of your dreams," he smiled at her and gave her a wink, "you know Ivan would want it that way."

Imelda smiled and blushed. No one liked Ivan. Max didn't even think Ivan liked Ivan, but she did. One of the sweetest souls to ever live had a thing for Ivan the Terrible. Some things are just beyond human understanding. "I'll give it some thought, now…Oh!" she exclaimed suddenly, "doesn't he just look adorable," she said looking at Odin rolling on his back on the carpet back and forth. "Does baby-waby have a little itchy," she crooned making Max wince at the sugary sweetness to her tone. She practically jumped from the sofa, "You need some cream…that's what baby needs…a little bitty bit of cream." She looked at Max as if her behavior was completely normal and said calmly, "You go on now and tell Ivan everything was fine and I didn't need anything," and she walked into the kitchen.

Max took a deep breath and walked out. The men in black wearing sunglasses looked up at him waiting for instruction. He almost smiled, it was a cliché, but they did look intimidating. The five of them started making the rounds of going door to door getting the answers they knew they'd get with their questions; nobody knew anything, nobody saw anything. At one house they'd made a tall teenage boy extremely nervous, but he claimed to not know anything. He was lying of course, so they made a point of letting him know the neighborhood was being watched. One more house and they'd consider their job done. It was a run-down little house at the end of the street the same side Imelda lived on. Max and the others walked gingerly up the steps noticing several loose boards. The porch wasn't in any better condition and not wanting to cause further damage, Max suggest they stay on the steps and he approached the door alone. Max knocked and a pretty young brunette answered, "Yes?" she said nervously.

"Good afternoon. My name is Max Gunther. I'm a friend of the woman in the house down there with the blue shutters," he said pointing in the direction of Imelda's place. "She had some vandalism done to her home last night and I just wanted to come by and see if you or anyone living here may have seen or heard anything suspicious."

"Oh, well, I worked until ten o'clock last night and when I drove down the street everything was quiet," she said wiping her hand down the front of her dress. She had opened the door a little wider, which Max took as a good sign. Usually people with something to hide tried to keep the door closed as tightly as possible regardless of who they were speaking to.

Before Max could reply, a small boy came up behind her and said, "I know something, Mama." She moved to the side and took his hand in hers. "I was lookin' out of my window," he looked wide eyed at Max, "I was lookin' for the meteor shower teacher said we were s'posed to have."

Max smiled at him, "What did you see?"

The small boy looked down at the ground and said sadly, "I didn't see no shower. I saw someone going up to t' witch's house and watched that 'stead."

"Jefferson, I've told you not to call her that. It's not nice," she scolded gently.

"No, Mama. She told me she was a witch."

"You're not supposed to talk to strangers," she said kneeling down to be on eye level with him.

He reached a hand out to the frayed collar of her dress and lovingly stroked it. "You're talking to a stranger."

She smiled at him, "Yes, but one…I'm an adult, and two…well, someone did something not very nice and I'd like to help her if I could."

He leaned in closer to her, "I don't talk to mos' strangers, but I had to talk to her, Mama. She's the one that helped me t'other day."

"You mean, when you fell?"

He nodded his sandy blonde head and with that same wide eyed expression he had before looked up at Max. "I fell off my bike and she came out of her house and put stuff on my knee. Took the pain right off. She said she was a witch and it was magic potion. When she poured some stuff on my bloody knee," he leaned closer to Max and whispered, "It foamed up just like potion in a witch's pot." The mother looked up at Max and smiled both knowing that hydrogen peroxide had the same effect. The pain going away was probably do to his intrigue in watching the foam. "She gave me money for t'ice cream truck, too. She said ice cream was magic and could make you stop feeling like you wanted to cry." He looked away from Max and said, "I did cry, but just a little bit." His little head jerked up, "but t'ice cream worked!"

Max nodded, "I'm sure it did. Well, tell me, when you looked out the window and saw someone go up to her house, do you know who it was?"

"Yes, sir, I…"

"Wait, Jeff," his mother said nervously. She looked at Max and said quietly, "I want to help. She was kind to him and I've certainly no quarrel with who she is or how she lives, but…"

"But?" Max queried.

She looked down at the little boy who had wrapped his arm around her waist. He was a very small child and as he turned toward his mother, Max saw a small hearing aid in his ear. "Jeff is…well, he sometimes gets picked on himself…he's a little small for his age and…" she frowned uncertain how much she wanted to say in front of the child. "I don't want it to get worse if they find out he's said something." She frowned down at the ground, "I don't quite know what to do. I seem to want to help both of them and that doesn't seem possible." She ran a hand through her hair and looked into Max's eyes, "I'm just a single mom trying to make ends meet waiting tables. I have to look after mine first."

"You are not *just* a single mom and waitress. You're a loving mother, a good neighbor and obviously a thoughtful human being," Max said smiling. He crouched down at the boy, "I don't need you to tell me anything else. We don't really need names. We're just trying to let folks know we're watching. If anyone asks you, you didn't tell us anything. Alright?" The boy nodded and Max rubbed lightly on the top of his head. "And don't worry, I was little for my age, too."

The boy grinned, "You were?" It was difficult for him to believe the man in front of him was ever little. Average in height, Max knew he was still a formidable presence. He spent time in the gym several days a week to keep toned what he considered his most intimidating feature. Most of his colleagues knew it was the steely gaze in his crystal blue eyes that intimidated the most.

He gave the mother his card. "If you need anything or anyone gives you or Jeff any trouble, call me." She smiled and thanked him and all of the men left the neighborhood feeling they'd gotten their point across that the neighborhood witch was protected. Max called Ivan and let him know what had taken place and suggested they send a carpenter out to the little house at the end of the road to fix the steps. If his feeling was correct that it was just a rental, it was obvious the landlord wasn't going to fix anything.

Jackson greeted him at the front door and he glanced at him as he walked past him to sling his keys on his desk. Noticing his brother following him into the sitting room and looking disheveled, he breathed a heavy sigh. Sara was sitting in front of the fire and he joined her noticing she had the same bewildered look. "Someone call a family meeting?"

"Is she alright?" Sara asked quietly.

"Who?"

"Astrid," Jacksons said, "She...the...the kidnapping?"

"What?" Max's roar shook the windows and renewed the worry of both his siblings.

140

CHAPTER 13

Sara could sense that he was tired or frustrated, but they had to know. She watched Max dialing on his phone and running a hand through his hair. It was obvious he didn't want to talk, but she was resolute in at least finding out if the woman who'd become a friend was alright. Keeping her voice calm, she explained to her temperamental brother, "We're not trying to get into your business. We just want to know how it went and that she's okay." Seeing the look on his face she suddenly paled and placed a hand over her mouth. "Oh, no." She stood up and glanced at Jackson then back to Max. "It wasn't you was it? You weren't the one who…" The shock and panic on her face had Jackson hurrying over to wrap his arms around her.

"Max?" Jackson said waiting for some kind of explanation, "We thought it was you."

"Helvete!" Max bowed his head and said more venomously than the first time, *"Helvete."* He looked at his watch, the person on the other end wasn't picking up the phone and he dialed again.

"I came by and she seemed upset about something, so I asked her to go to the market with me to….you know…get her out of the house for a while. Some men came toward us in the parking lot and Astrid said they looked like the men from the hotel parking garage; the men that beat you up. As they came closer she told me to run away, but I wasn't going to leave her. One of them pushed me away and they took her," Sara's tears cascaded down her cheeks and Jackson took her hand. "They threw her into the trunk and raced off. I…I didn't call the police because I thought it was you or…or Ivan." Max again rubbed a hand through his hair and down his face as once again the person on the other end didn't answer his call.

"Max, was it you or…or was it Ivan or someone else?" Jackson asked frustrated. "Damn it, tell us what's happening!"

Max grabbed his keys and headed for the door still trying to get someone to answer his call. Jackson raced toward him and stopped him, grabbing his arm. Max looked up knowing he owed them an explanation. "I forgot about the kidnapping. I was dealing with Ivan and…" he looked down at the carpet furious with himself, "I'll make it right. I…*Jag måste gå. Jag måste gå,*" he said angrily.

"I get it, you have to go," Jackson said, knowing it was never a good sign when Max resorted to Swedish, "but they won't hurt her, right? You did tell them not to hurt her, didn't you?"

Max looked into Sara's frightened face and felt sick to his stomach knowing what she was thinking of him. Especially since he was thinking it of himself. "They're not supposed to harm her in any way, but…I gave the orders weeks ago. I don't know if Ivan may have changed those orders." He turned away from Jackson's aghast expression. "I have to make sure they don't get carried away," he said leaving, not wanting to waste another moment. Furious with himself, he took it out on his Jaguar pushing it to its limits. The disappointment, disgust, and horror on Sara and Jackson's face was one he'd never wanted to see. The kidnapping idea was just to rattle her cage a bit and he'd meant to call it off, but Ivan had been breathing down his neck. It wasn't like him to get distracted on a case, but it seemed every time he tried to discuss the book with her, she steered the conversation to something else. Whether it was intentional or not he wasn't quite sure. As he raced down the road his heart was beating rapidly and his palms were sweating. Keeping his cool in these situation was his trademark, but right now he didn't feel in control. He'd had cases before when information had to be extracted with force. He'd killed when it was necessary. It was his job to do whatever was necessary to protect their people, but this time it was different. This time it was Astrid and the thought of them hurting her in any way made him sick. The worst part was knowing, it would be his fault and she'd trusted him. *Why in the hell would anyone trust me,* Max thought driving faster.

Sara slowly took Max's vacated seat by the fire. "Jackson, what did he mean about them 'getting carried away'?"

Jackson sat down across from her and said, "I don't know, but I know Max. He'll take care of her. That's what he does. He takes care of things." As they sat looking into the fire, Jackson couldn't help thinking, *Max…forgot? Max never forgets…anything.*

The room was dark and cold. Astrid's arms were aching from being tied behind the chair. The ropes around her ankles were biting into her skin. She could taste blood on the corners of her mouth where the gag was tearing her lip. Wanting to make light of her situation she told herself that next time she was kidnapped she should wear a sweater. It almost caused her to smile, but her headache made her feel both dizzy and nauseous erasing any thought of a grin. She'd stopped her tears from flowing when they'd first shoved her into the trunk of the car, but she couldn't put a stop to the fear. With all the silly pranks her brothers and sisters had put her though over the years she'd never been as terrified as she was now. At least with them, she'd known who it was. All she knew about these men was that they were violent. She'd seen what they'd done to Max and she was nowhere near in the kind of shape he was in nor nearly as capable. He'd held them off and nearly won. She almost smiled thinking about how well he'd fought them, but it soon faded looking around a room she didn't recognize. At this moment, she didn't even know where any of them were. Aside from the cellphone one of them had left on a table that kept ringing, there was no sound at all in the room. They'd just tied her to the chair and left. Being alone was nothing, she'd spent most of her childhood alone. It was easier to be alone because alone, no one can mistreat you or make you think something is wrong with you. *If only I hadn't tried to get my stories published. If I had just stayed in my little apartment this wouldn't be happening,* she thought to herself. She was afraid of the real world and her current situation was just one reason why. *If I get out of this,* she told herself, *I'm going back to my apartment and tell the publisher thanks, but no thanks.*

Suddenly she could hear footsteps. A door somewhere behind her opened and light filtered in. She looked around at what appeared to be a hotel room. A man she didn't recognize stood in front of her and ripped the gag out of her mouth shouting at her, "Don't make no sound or you'll regret it." His breath smelled of alcohol and Astrid turned away from it.

Another man stood next to him grinning at her. Her skirt was just above her knee and the man reached out and ran his hand along her thigh. "Let's have some fun." Astrid refused to look up at the men and the door behind her opened again. The two men looked up as a third man came to stand next to them. She thought she'd heard more footsteps behind her, but she wasn't sure. No one seemed to acknowledge anyone else. The room was dark except for the lamp shining in front of her. "You're just in time, we're going to have some fun with her before we get down to business." Putting his hand on her knee he slowly moved it up her thigh until he reached the edge of her panties giving her a wink. It was all Astrid could do not to cringe at his touch, but she was afraid he'd like seeing her fear.

One of the other men was stroking her hair. "She's awful pretty. Which of us gets a go first?"

Astrid tried turning away and two of them laughed. She let her mind wander. In romance books there was always someone who came in and saved the day, some white knight that could come charging to the rescue. Where was a knight when you needed one? Forget mysteries, if she got through this, she was going to write romances. In romances there is always a guy that gets there in time to save the girl. There would always be a happy ending because in life...in life there wasn't. She couldn't stop herself from thinking of Max. Where was he? Did he even know she'd been kidnapped? What would he do if he knew?

Standing in the shadows behind her unbeknownst to anyone in the room; Max stood with his hands fisted, rigidly holding his arms to his sides. It took all his self-control to stand there in the dark waiting for these idiots to do their job and ask her about the book. If the fat one put his hand on her one more time it was over, Max knew he'd snap.

"We better take care of business first." The tall man said, "I don't fancy facin' down the boss." The fat one nodded his head and stepped back away from her. "Don't fret little lady, you'll have the pleasure of us soon enough!" She let out a breath she'd been holding and tried to relax, but her body was quivering both from cold and fear. "Where are you getting the information for that book of yours?"

Astrid frowned and shook her head slightly not understanding what they wanted. Taking her confusion for stalling another man yelled in her face. "Come on, answer the question. You like being tied up? We can keep you here for days and days, lady."

"Hey Jack, if she's going to be tied up a while, let's take her clothes off." The man grabbed the front of Astrid's blouse and pulled. The delicate pink fabric ripped and Astrid couldn't help a small cry of panic.

"Who are you?" The fear in her voice was painful to Max's ears and he struggled to maintain his position in the shadows.

"None of your business, bitch! Just answer the damn question," the man shouted getting up close to her face.

Max watched Astrid's head pull back trying to get away from the man. He heard her sniffle and knew she was crying. As his jaw clenched and his fist tightened, he held his breath willing her to just tell them what they wanted to know. He hadn't been able to get her to tell him and although he'd wanted to call this off, it was too late for that and he needed that information. If she would just tell them, it would all be over.

"Who gave you the information for your book? Who's tellin' you this stuff? Give us the name," the man who'd come in last said while holding a knife to her throat. He grinned and drifted the knife down between her breasts.

"I don't know what you mean! I don't know what you want! It's just a story. No one is telling me anything. Please let me go!"

"You're not going anywhere until the boss gets the answers he wants. Now, where did you get the names from?"

"What…what names?"

"The names of the bad guys in the story. Whatever you called 'em…the…the witch hunters. Boss wants to know who gave you those names." Max frowned, he'd not told them that information. Ivan must have known about the kidnapping and simply chose not to remind him of it. He'd make sure to discuss that with the bastard later.

Astrid could smell alcohol on the breath of the man leering down at her and the smell made her nauseas. The way the other men were smiling looking down at her breasts filled her with panic. "I just wrote a story. It's all fiction…it's not real. It's just a made up story." Tears were streaming down her cheeks as she realized they wanted something she couldn't give. She also realized that like any other bully whose victim wouldn't give…they were going to take. Knowing that…her tears began to dry.

Suddenly the feeling in the room began to change. It crackled with an energy Max soon recognized was Astrid. She was moving past her fear and into anger. Although he was glad she was feeling less fear, right now all her anger would do is fuel these idiots fire. The brute with the knife noticed the change on Astrid's face. "Hey, now. What's going on with you?" Looking into her eyes made him begin to feel sick to his stomach. His own negative energies making him nervous and uneasy. "There's something wrong with her," he said backing away a bit.

"What are you talking about?" The skinny man that had wanted to take her clothes off put his hands on her legs. "She looks good to me," he said then began frowning as he started getting a throbbing headache and he had a metallic taste in his mouth.

Seeing his friend rubbing his temple and fumbling away from her, the fat one said, "Whatever you're trying to do knock it off, bitch."

Max was about to give the signal to abort the mission, when the fat guy forgot their instructions and back handed her hard across the face knocking her and the chair she was in to the floor.

When Astrid opened her eyes, she saw one man on the floor and another man fighting the other two. She closed her eyes again and opened them when she felt someone trying to get the ropes off of her hands. It was Max. There was a small cut above his eye bleeding a bit and his knuckles were bruised. He was sweating and his breathing was rapid, but what got her attention the most was the look of rage on his face. Three men were lying on the floor not moving as he helped her to stand. "Let's get out of here," he said brusquely, quickly wrapping his coat around her and racing out the door.

Once in the car, Max called Tom and asked him to meet him at the house. Max stared at the road in front of him so angry with himself he couldn't think straight. Next to him, Astrid's smooth, soft voice cut through his thoughts. "Thank you for coming for me," she said, her blue-green eyes looking at him with so much gratitude he couldn't bear it. As quickly as he looked at her, he had to turn away knowing he had no right to her gratitude. Words to comfort her simply would not come to his mind. If he hadn't gotten to the hotel in time he didn't know what those fools would have done to her. As she sat next to him in silence holding his coat tightly around herself, Max felt sick to his stomach. He remembered giving the orders for the kidnapping and telling them the importance of getting the information. They weren't supposed to touch her, but he knew…guys like that…Regardless of their ineptness, the responsibility and the guilt lay with him. If she knew of his involvement…if she ever found out…Before, there had been moments when she was afraid of him. Now, how could she not be afraid? He glanced down at the raw knuckles gripping the steering wheel. *What would she say about the death of those three men?* He shook his head at his thoughts. *Even a damn stranger at the gym cheered when the cops took you away.*

"Max, I'm sorry for being so much trouble, I…"

"Don't," he said quickly. Relaxing his grip on the gear shift and taking a deep breath when he realized she'd misinterpreting his silence, he tried a little smile, "Astrid, you have nothing to be sorry for. I'm just," he glanced at her, "I'm glad you're safe."

When they arrived back at the house, Tom immediately sat Astrid down on the couch and began checking her injuries. He bandaged her wrists and asked about any pain she had anywhere else. "I'm fine, but

Max has a cut above his eye you should take a look at and...and his knuckles are scraped."

Tom smiled at her as he started bandaging her ankle. "I'll take a look. Whether he wants me to or not. I'll take a look just for you," he said with a wink and a grin.

Astrid tried smiling at all of them telling them she was fine and not to worry, but Max was there and he knew how terrified she'd been. Tom walked over to Max and whispered in his ear that she might have a slight concussion, between getting thrown into the car trunk and knocked on the floor she needed to be watched over night. "Now let's have a look at you, tough guy," he said aloud checking out the cut on Max's head.

Max noticed Astrid's look of concern for him and smiled. "I'm fine," he said softly. Astrid shook her head not convinced in the least.

"He's been through worse, honey," Jackson said. "Compared to the rack, the time he fell into the ocean, and all the times he's pissed people off," Jackson chuckled, "this is nothing!"

Sara handed Astrid a warm cup of coffee she'd just brewed before they came home then turned to scold her twin, "Jackson, really...that again?"

"I'm just saying, this is nothing. He likes pain, anyway."

"Do I?" Max had to ask.

"You're going to say you went through hell on that rack just to be taller? No way, you probably got some twisted enjoyment from the pain! That's why you work out at the gym so many times a week. Pain...your best friend."

"Jackson," Sara said frowning, "enough!"

Jackson watched as she dabbed at her eyes with a tissue. She handed a cup of coffee to Max and when she did he mouthed the words, 'it's all right' to her. Feeling left out of the conversation, Jackson said, "What's up with you two?"

"Nothing," Max said tasting his coffee and then standing up straighter and staring pointedly at his sister his tone changed dramatically, "Sara, dear,"

"Uh-oh," Jackson said with a grimace, "What'd you do?" he asked Sara.

She shrugged her shoulders looking at Max. He closed his eyes briefly then with a raised eyebrow stared at her asking, "Darling sister, what coffee did you brew?"

"Uh…the one in the pretty golden package." Max carefully set down his cup of coffee and bowed his head. "Max, what's…what's wrong," she asked coming toward him.

"It doesn't seem like anything is wrong to me. It tastes great," Tom said pouring himself another cup.

Max slowly raised his head to look at his old friend and then back to his little sister to say, "It should be great. This coffee is three hundred and fifty dollars a pound." Several coughs were heard in the room and several cups set down noisily on their saucers. Max looked around the room and picked his own cup back up, now that his hand was steady. "You may as well all enjoy it now…since it's already brewed," he said bringing his gaze back to his sister.

"Three hundred and fifty…for coffee?" Sara stared at Max as if he had three heads, "Why would you pay that for coffee?"

"Because it's very good coffee. It's grown at the base of guava trees on the slopes of Mount Barú in Panama," he said shrugging his shoulders and deciding he may as well enjoy it.

"Well, you should have that in a safe or something not just…just in the cabinet with all the others and…and besides," feeling both guilty and embarrassed when she saw the smirk on Tom's face, she took a deep breath, straightened her shoulders, and raised her chin saying, "who better than your family to splurge on? I mean…aren't we worth it? Your family…the one's that put up with you and your…your oddities?"

Looking at the defiant chin of the five foot two, hundred and ten pound blonde haired blue eyed menace that was his baby sister, Max smiled and raised his hand in surrender causing everyone else in the room to laugh.

Just learning that Max was a pushover for his sister, Astrid was hoping to learn a little more about him and came back to their earlier subject. "It surprises me that your height would be that important to you," Astrid said to him.

"It wasn't," Sara said softly. "He didn't have a choice." Max was slowly shaking his head, but she wasn't looking at him and didn't notice.

"What?" Jackson asked looking from one sibling to the other. "You did it for Mother, didn't you," he said quietly, then stood up and said louder, "Everything you did was for her and what did it get you?" Max didn't answer and didn't look up, so Jackson walked closer and got louder, "She didn't give any more of a damn about any of us than Father did. She didn't even..,"

"Stop! He did it for you!"

Max slowly closed his eyes and sighed at Sara's shout, this was not the way he wanted Jackson to find out the truth.

CHAPTER 14

Jackson's face turned hard as granite as he stood in front of Max. "What is she talking about? Why do I feel like there is some secret that everyone knows but me?"

Max looked up at him and saw the confusion and anger on his face. He'd tried so hard to spare Sara and Jackson as much as he could, but it was impossible for a ten year old boy to replace the love of a mother and father. Taking a deep breath, Max nodded and poured himself more coffee. "Okay, Jackson." Hearing the tinkling of a saucer being set down, Max looked toward Astrid as she and Tom started to leave the room. "Wait you two."

"This is a family matter," Tom said, "We understand."

"You are as good as family, maybe better," Max said with a chuckle looking at Tom.

"Well, I'm not and…"

"Astrid," Max said softly, "I'd like you to stay."

As they sat back down, Max stirred his coffee then set it down untouched. "Jackson was always a mischievous and busy little guy," Max's soft, calm voice had everyone's attention as he slowly walked to stand at the window. "He was forever getting into one scrape or another. Twins were trouble enough, but Jackson…he was always running around at full speed and as loud as he could be." A smile spread across his face as he gazed into his mind's eye at the precocious little boy his brother had been. "I was forever trying to keep a step ahead of him. One day

Father had guests in the study and a maid was bringing them fika. Jackson came running down the hallway with one of those superballs, do you remember those?" he asked looking at Astrid. "Those damn things would bounce all over the place, helter-skelter. Anyway, one thing led to another and Jackson came running, the maid went crashing along with the coffee and pastries making a hell of a racket." Astrid and Sara chuckled along with Max, but Jackson stood transfixed, waiting for what Max would say next. "Father was furious, as you can imagine, and worse...he was embarrassed that his friends witnessed his son's misbehavior. This was a man who prided himself on an orderly and controlled household. He told the maid, in front of the gentlemen, not to give Jackson any afternoon snack. After they left, he told her that Jackson wasn't to be given any afternoon snack, dinner or dessert and that he should be put to bed immediately. Mother was already getting weak by then, but she tried," he said looking directly at Jackson. "She tried to protest, but her begging and pleading for him to understand landed on deaf ears. He slapped her across the face so hard it knocked her to the floor." The muscle in his jaw tightened and he said through clenched teeth, "She'd interfered in *his* right to punish *his* child." Max walked to the sofa and sat down next to Astrid and she placed her hand in his, but he didn't look at her. He kept his eyes on the carpet as if the words he needed were written there. Jackson slowly sat down on the arm of the chair closest to him, stunned that the mother he thought barely knew of his existence had tried standing up to their father for him. "At dinner that night I sat across from Jackson's empty chair unable to eat; knowing he was up in his bed hungry." Max slowly twisted his ring around and around on his finger and looked up briefly with a sad sort of smile on his face. "Jackson was always hungry, still is. I don't know where it goes! Must be the legs. Anyway, I don't think the old man even noticed until Sara asked me in her sweet, four year old voice, 'you not hung'y Mack?'"

"Well, I'm glad my speech has improved," Sara said giving Max a tearful smile.

He smiled back, then continued, "Father looked over at me and smiled. I will never forget that ugly, creepy smile. He had me and he knew it." Max shook his head, patted Astrid's hand and walked back over to the window. "I had refused to have anything to do with the damn rack from the first day he'd brought it into the house. Some doctor had convinced him that pulling my body apart every day would stimulate growth."

Astrid frowned and said, "But, Max you couldn't have been but…eleven or twelve. Were you really that small that it was…a concern?"

Max smiled, "I was eleven, but I was the smallest in my class. Hell, Jackson was already nearly as tall as me by then!" He smiled at Jackson, but his brother didn't look up at him. "I wasn't just short, I was thin and had no aptitude for sports of any kind. Reading was my pastime and," Max shook his head, "he didn't like it. I had steadfastly refused to cooperate with the doctor and any of his so called treatments…until that night. Father grinned at me and told me that if I got on the rack he'd let me take Jackson a sandwich. From then on every time I refused, Jackson would lose a meal. So, I got strapped in at the ankles and wrists and he turned the crank as far I could stand without screaming and left me there in the basement for three hours." Astrid quickly got a tissue off the coffee table to blot her eyes. Hearing Sara sniffle, Max turned around and saw both of them in tears. "Oh, it wasn't that bad. It was kind of cold down there, but it was quiet. I couldn't hear the old man yelling!" He chuckled and both ladies gave him a watery smile. "Sure enough a couple of hours later I climbed the stairs, feeling a little like jelly, and there was Jackson sitting in the middle of his bed with tears all over his face. I gave him his favorite sandwich, bologna and sliced hard-boiled egg. He looked at me as if I were a god." An easy smile crept across his face and he turned to his brother, but Jackson turned away from him. "He ate that thing in seconds. Luckily I'd brought two." Turning to gaze out of the window again, his voice lost its levity. "The next morning I didn't feel anything like a god. I think it even hurt to blink. I was careful at breakfast to hide how I felt from Father, but as soon as he left for work, I grabbed a blanket and a couple of books and headed down toward the harbor. I knew I'd never have made it at school all day, so I found a quiet spot and spent the day reading and napping. Eventually after six or eight months of racking and measuring the old bastard gave up." Max turned around and smiled. "A couple years later I finally did start to grow, in nature's own good time. Distancing myself more from father, I was able to eat better and fill out. Funny how things happen like that."

"Well, I don't think it's funny," Jackson blurted out, turning to face everyone. "Why didn't you ever tell me it was my fault he did that to you?"

"He was the one that did it, Jackson. Not you. You were not to blame for that," Max said coming toward him, but Jackson moved away.

"God, what a spoiled rotten little shit!"

"Come on, Jackson. You were four years old."

"That doesn't matter. Max that was then. What about now?" He ran his hand through his hair angrily. "What about all the times I've…I've teased you and…and harassed you about it?"

"We are brothers! Teasing and harassing each other is what we are meant to do." Walking up to his tall brother, Max put a hand on his shoulder to stop his pacing. "There was never any malice in it. There's not a drop of malice in you."

As his eyes grew moist, Jackson softly asked, "Why didn't you tell me. Or you," he said looking at Sara, "obviously you knew."

"It didn't matter," Max said putting his hand down and briefly looking away. "That horrible excuse for a human being is never going to be able to hurt any of us ever again. That is all that matters now."

"No, it isn't," Jackson said grabbing his keys and heading for the door. "It isn't," he said again, looking at his brother and walking out.

"Jackson, wait!" Sara called quickly going to the door, but he'd already made it to his car and was driving away.

Seeing Sara's distress, Tom made his way to the door saying, "I'll keep an eye on him." He ran to his car and followed Jackson.

Max went into the kitchen and put away the bag of Hacienda La Esmeralda Coffee, his mind still playing the memories over and over.

Astrid came to him and wrapped her arms around him resting her head against his shoulder blade. As she held him, the memories of that sad little boy sitting on his bed with tears on his face slowly faded away. Max gently patted her hand that was laying over his heart, "It's been a hell of a day," he said quietly.

♣

The next morning Max was surprised to find Astrid up and brewing coffee before him. As he came into the kitchen she practically pounced on him with questions. "So, some of these things I've been writing about in the book…are real?" Astrid asked completely flabbergasted. "How is that possible?" She began to pace the kitchen. "I've been up all night trying to work all of this out in my head and I simply can't! How is it possible to write about something you don't fully understand yourself?" Max looked up at her and before he had the chance to answer, she said, "You're going to tell me it's that witch thing aren't you?"

"Astrid, I don't want to frighten you again."

"Oh, Max, you didn't. I frightened myself. I know you weren't going to hurt me. I'm sorry if…if I made you feel bad or…or guilty just for telling me the truth."

Still harboring the dread of her discovering he was behind the kidnapping, Max was more than ready to forgive and forget. "Don't waste a thought on it."

"It seems I was hiding more from myself than from you."

Max reached out and gently took her hands in his, "Can you tell me what it is that frightens you?"

"I think I could tell you anything," she said with a giggle, "How can you have so much patience with me? You've the patience of a saint."

Max laughed heartily, "Actually, Cashmere I am not very patient at all, but something about you makes me want to be."

"I guess what frightens me is the unknown," Astrid shook her head and frowned, "I guess that makes me sound just like everyone else in the world. How boring!"

"I can assure you, nothing about you is boring!"

155

"So what do I do? Blink, twitch my nose, say abracadabra?"

"You do twitch your nose most charmingly, but that's a different kind of witchcraft! That's more along the lines of you're a girl…I'm a boy!" He wiggled his eyebrows the way he knew made her giggle and reached out to wrap his arm around her and haul her into his embrace.

"So what do I do?" She tightened her arms around him and let out a deep sigh.

"You're doing it right now," he said answering her, but making her frown which he couldn't help thinking was adorable and chuckled. "Aside from that sweet little frown, right now you're holding me in your arms making me feel cared for and comforted."

"You've done that for me many times," she said, "That's not magic."

Max shook his head, "Unfortunately the way I'm holding you and making you feel…any man could do," Astrid shook her head, but he continued, "The compassion you feel for others comes out in your touch. When I was talking to Jackson about my past and you placed your hand on me…some of the pain those memories evoked simply melted away. I didn't feel it as strongly. It's kind of like the feeling you get when you have a headache and put a cool towel on your head; it numbs it, eases it. When Jackson felt bad about putting you in the closet, you touched his arm and his embarrassment was eased."

"So, it's not really something I have control over?"

"The more you practice your gift the more control you'll have. You just have to become aware that your feelings and energies manifested into a genuine physical response." Max leaned forward to just a breath away from her lips and whispered, "You see, if you didn't want my kiss all you have to do is think negative thoughts of anger or fear and it will manifest into a physical attack on me; headache, nausea, confusion. Or," he paused and grinned, "if you wanted my kiss all you have to do is think positive thoughts; desire, pleasure, or comfort and it will manifest into a delightful physical yearning on my part to touch you." Astrid smiled just as his lips touched hers for a warm and tender kiss. "I'd say you," another quick kiss, "Mmm, yes you definitely understand that part."

156

She giggled and placed her hand against his cheek, "So I won't be turning anyone into a toad or anything?"

"Nope, sorry," he said unapologetically. "Your powers are more feelings and emotions. Of course you could scare someone into wishing they were a toad! Seriously speaking though, it is a very powerful ability. You can control how those around you feel at least once you've learned to control your own energies."

"I don't know that I'm all that interested, but…I'm glad if I make you feel comforted. After all these years of making others feel bad, it's nice to make someone feel good."

"It was their own fault they felt bad. They caused you to feel afraid and uncertain and it backfired back to them. Not your fault."

She smile and rested against him enjoying the comfort he gave her and refusing to believe that just any man could make her feel so accepted and safe.

"By the way, just out of curiosity did your family ever take vacations when you were young? I mean, has your family traveled much of the United States or even gone overseas?"

"Yes, once or twice a year."

Max tried to hide his disappointed frown and asked, "Oh, I…I had thought I remembered you saying before that you hadn't been out of Minnesota."

"Oh, I didn't go," she said casually, "they always took Brenda."

"Brenda?"

"Yes, she…well, I'm not really sure how or when it happened," she shrugged her shoulders, "she just seemed to become part of the family practically overnight. That time…" she paused and tentatively looked up at him. Something she'd remembered had suddenly caused her to become nervous or frightened, Max couldn't tell which. "Could you…maybe sit on the sofa with me?"

"Of course," he said grinning, "Mind if we cuddle?"

"I confess, I …was rather hoping…," she ducked her head shyly and he chuckled.

"Cashmere, anytime you want a cuddle from me grab-ahold." She smiled and did as he suggested the moment he sat down.

Giving her a smile and a kiss on her nose, he said, "Now, what were you going to tell me about Brenda?"

She turned so that he couldn't see her face, but he noticed she gently held his hand with both of hers. "That time my brother Jimmy got so angry with me and…and hurt me," Max leaned over and softly kissed her head, "Well, that's when I met her for the first time. Mama was in the kitchen and when she came around the corner I was lying on the couch. She told me to get up and fix dinner. I told her I couldn't breathe very well. She said, 'Great, that's all I need. I guess you want me to take you to the clinic.' The girl, about my age, standing next to her said, 'Oh, she doesn't need all that. It's just sibling being siblings. She looks like she's just trying to get poor little Jimmy in trouble. Girls like her, you know what I mean, do that sort of thing.' She winked at Mama and they nodded their heads. I think…I think she knew that I was…what they all said I was…you know…evil." Max gave her a comforting squeeze. "She told Mama not to worry that by the time they got back I'd be fine. I asked where they were going and she said they were going to Luleå and that I wasn't to leave the house. I didn't know where Luleå was and to tell you the truth I didn't at that moment care. I fell asleep on the couch and woke up in the middle of the day the next day. From then on, Brenda seemed to always be around."

"Luleå is a city in the north part of Sweden called the Lapland. I didn't know how to tell you or what you already knew, but your family has actually made several trips to Sweden."

Astrid sat up a little straighter and turned to look at him. "So, you remembered me saying I hadn't been out of Minnesota yet you knew my family had travelled. Are you thinking…that I've been lying to you?"

Max reached out and caressed her cheek, "No, but…"

"But?"

"I told you I work for Ivan guarding witches. Your family has been being watched by the FBI and the CIA in connection with some crimes in Sweden. I knew you wouldn't be involved with anything like that, but the documents state that your mother was there with two young men and two young girls. Apparently the venal witch, Brenda was there in your place."

"Venal witch?"

"Witches who are open to bribery or corruption. They use their abilities for criminal activities. The question I have is whether or not your mother knew the girl was a witch considering your mother…well, let's just say isn't exactly understanding of your gifts."

"So…you didn't believe that I…"

"No. I know my Astrid," he said and was relieved when she cuddled against him.

"So, all this time…as they called me evil…they were possibly involved in something themselves?"

"Apparently," Max said. Astrid laid back against him, but he could tell her mind was racing trying to make the pieces of her life fit together. Things were about to get a lot more complicated now that there was a venal witch in the picture. Ivan was not going to be very happy. He had a personal vendetta against venal witches and if he were honest with himself, Max didn't blame him a bit. As he held her, her body began to relax, "Here, take a nap," he said moving off the couch and gently laying her head on a pillow, "I have to go out for a while." She was asleep before he even made it out the door.

CHAPTER 15

"I have some information on the Astrid Martin case, but I'm not sure if it's going to straighten things out or make them messier," Max said as he entered Ivan's office.

Ivan didn't look up, didn't acknowledge his presence in any way. Going to his credenza, which stood on the left wall of his office underneath a huge world map, he poured himself a glass of whiskey, lit his cigar, then went back to his desk and growled, "Well, do I have to age another year to hear it?"

Max cleared his throat watching him aware that Ivan the Terrible was even more terrible than usual today. "Apparently there is a venal witch involved in this matter." Ivan stared at him without commenting, so Max continued, "The woman who accompanied Astrid's mother to Sweden was going by the name of Brenda Warren and posing as Astrid."

Ivan tossed a photograph on his desk in Max's direction. It was of a woman and two young men and two young women at an airport in Växjö, Sweden. Max picked up the photo and studied it carefully then set it back down on the desk. Ivan watched him saying, "Are you trying to make me believe that isn't Ms. Martin in that photograph? That she's got a doppelganger out there that just happens to be another witch?"

"Yes," Max answered blandly.

"That photo was taken four years ago just before the death of a Swedish Agent who was a very dear friend of mine."

"I'm sorry for the loss of your friend, but that is not Astrid. It's a photo of Astrid's family and a small woman about Astrid's size with black hair or a black wig, but it's not Astrid."

"Know her that intimately?" Max didn't respond and Ivan grunted. "What else do you have to tell me?"

"That she apparently befriended the family, was instrumental in the family abusing Astrid, and traveled with the family; essentially replacing her. It is unclear, but highly unlikely that the mother even knows the woman is a witch given her intolerance of witchcraft. She encouraged abuse toward Astrid based on the fact that she is a witch and should be punished to 'get the evil out of her'."

"So your theory is this woman is a venal witch and has imposed herself on this family to aid her in destroying other witches?" Max nodded then shrugged his shoulder when Ivan asked him why a witch would do that.

"That much I cannot understand. What would make a witch turn on her own kind? We do know it's happened before for monetary gain, social standing, and political reasons. This particular reason I do not know, but I also think some of the material for Astrid's book came from this Ms. Warren; dreams or I should say nightmares, which the witch had imposed on her. Some of the scenes in her book are completely out of character for the woman I know."

"Maybe you don't know her as well as you think you do," he raised an eyebrow, "it's happened to a few of us before." Max didn't comment. "Astrid could be covering for these people."

"She would never do that. They've spent her whole life trying to beat her down and make her ashamed of who and what she is."

Ivan downed his drink in one swallow and set his glass down hard on the desk. "If a venal witch..." Without knocking, Ivan's brother, Erik walked through the door. "No more of this discussion," Ivan said quickly, looking pointedly at Max. "You're dismissed."

Understanding completely, Max stopped talking and held out his hand in greeting to Erik. When Erik simply looked at him, Max realized his error and tried to recover with a slight bow saying, "It's good to see you."

Erik didn't speak, but gave Max a short nod and walked over to Ivan's desk to set down some papers that were in his left hand. The man's right hand didn't come out of his trouser pocket. Knowing it was none of his business, Max walked out of the room to leave the brothers in peace. He'd really said all he needed to say to Ivan anyway. The ball was in his court now to find out more about the venal witch.

♣

"Your turn, why are you looking at me that way?" Astrid asked Max later that evening remembering when he'd asked her the same question recently. She had been sitting on the sofa, but noticing Max staring at her, she'd started walking toward his desk.

Max sat with his elbows resting on his desk and his chin in his hands. He smiled at the lovely woman standing in the middle of his sitting room and answered softly, "I was thinking what sweet torture it would be to unbutton that blouse one tiny button at a time. I was thinking that with one quick unzipping that skirt would fall right to the floor. I was thinking that you're probably wearing a beige bra underneath that white blouse, so what color panties are you wearing," his voice grew even softer, "Then I was thinking if I glided my tongue slowly and gently along your abdomen would I hear the same sweet intake of breath that I heard the last time I did that to you." Max revelled in the fact that it was exactly what he was thinking. They'd had sex, or to him it seemed more accurate to say they'd been intimate, and here he was wanting her again. *Odd*, he thought to himself.

"I thought you were working," she said, suddenly out of breath. Max slowly and silently shook his head, his eyes never leaving hers. "Well, if we went upstairs you could find out what color panties I'm wearing." With the intense stare he was giving her, she'd expected him to practically pounce on her. Instead, he gradually rose from his seat, took his time meandering across the floor to her then put his arms lightly around her waist. Without warning, her skirt fell to the floor to reveal her pink and beige lace panties. He didn't smile at the surprise on her face, but said huskily, "Some things just can't wait." Max looked down then back up to her face and with his lips just a whisper away from hers he said deep and warm, "very nice." Her body leaned forward aching for him to touch her, but he kept just out of reach. "You're trembling. Are you cold?"

"No," she whispered, "Just…wanting you."

Max bent down to put an arm under her knees lifting her to carry her to his room. She wrapped her arms snuggly around his neck and laid her head on his shoulder. He recognized the soft floral scent of her perfume, the touch of her hand on the back of his neck, fingers weaving into the back of his hair, and felt comforted knowing the way she would hold him and the little sounds she would make as he caressed her. The desire to be with the same woman again…and again…was a new experience; one that made him smile down at her as he laid her on his bed.

"Astrid," he said, gently caressing the head resting on his shoulder.

"Yes," she answered already half asleep after their lovemaking.

"I hope you won't be angry, but…I read the storyline idea you had on your desk the other day. The one you were sending to your editor."

"Why write it if you don't want anyone to read it?"

Max smiled, "Well, I have to say it…it didn't seem like the same kind of scenes you've written before." The warm body that had been snuggled against him stiffened; the hand that had been draped across his chest slowly moved off of him. "I'm not saying it wasn't good. I just meant that it was a bit different," he said feeling he'd touched on a sensitive subject.

"It's alright, Max. I…I don't like it either."

"I know I'm no writer, but…if you don't like it, why…"

"Because I have to," she said sadly.

Now she had Max's full attention, "Why?"

She reached up and kissed him tenderly. "It doesn't matter, really. Would you rather I slept in my own room?"

"Of course not," he said frowning and gently taking her arm as she started to get up. "I like having you here beside me." Realizing he meant it, he reached his hand up to stroke through her soft, black hair and kissed her. "Stay," he said against her lips.

♣

As had become their habit, after dinner they each worked a couple of hours at their desks then settled down in front of the fire to sip coffee and discuss the day's events. Since worrying about how cozy it had gotten got him nowhere, Max simply went along with what felt right. Tonight he was reading the latest bit of story Astrid asked him to read and give his opinion on.

She tried not to keep glancing at him reading, but she couldn't help herself. She was anxious to see if he liked the story. She'd just written it that morning and loved it and was hoping he did, too. It was only a rough draft, but she just couldn't wait to get his opinion. Watching the slight grin appear on his face made her smile. She couldn't help but wonder when it had become so important what he thought of her stories. Once upon a time she didn't care who liked them. She wrote simply because she liked making up her own little world. Now, it mattered what he thought and she wanted this man to share her world.

As if sensing her thoughts, Max looked over at her and smiled. He set down the pages he'd been reading and gazed momentarily into the fire. In her innocent little scene she'd exposed one of their most guarded secrets, the secret to the labyrinth on the Isle of Jungfrun. If a person were to read it and as a lark, try it, they would enter into the realm of the guardian's alliance. Yet she sat there looking at him without a single clue of what she'd be doing to her people. It was clear at the kidnapping that she was innocent, but the problem was how to make her see without hurting her. She was so sweet, delicate, and fragile and he didn't want to do anything to change that. The little girl in her story that danced merrily through the maze, three times windershins, one time doesil and entering the magical realm, made him think of Ermina and the innocence lost.

Astrid said nothing at first knowing that sometimes a person had to digest what they'd just read before they can discuss it. Sometimes you needed to think about how you felt about the scene or the characters behaviors. Finally she could take it no longer, "Well?" she said as he bowed his head. His wrist was resting on his raised knee and he began absentmindedly twisting the lynx head ring on his right hand. She watched him knowing that he always did that when he was thinking. When he looked up at her and still said nothing, she queried impatiently, "Well, Max? Did you like it?"

"I love you."

She blinked, *what did he just say,* she thought to herself. *Surely he meant, I loved...it...right?* She frowned slightly and glanced away and then back at him. "Wh...what?"

He smiled tenderly at her as his soft, warm voice repeated his words, "I love you. I love the way your mind works. I love the way you make me think about things in ways I've never thought about them before. I love the way you make me feel. I love you, Astrid." As her eyes welled with tears he cupped her cheek and kissed her, softly and sweetly as if she were the most precious thing in the world. The kiss changed from tender to demanding as he realized how good it felt to say the words to her. The way she clung to him, the way her body melted against his pressing her heart to his, he knew she felt something; something good, something strong. Right now all he cared about was that he finally loved. He had feared he wasn't capable and that he was more like his father than he'd ever want to admit, but he was wrong; he was wonderfully wrong. His heart, mind, and soul had just been waiting for the right one. The one who's body at this moment was quivering with need the same as his own. By mutual consent they stood up and made their way to the staircase and his bed. Tonight he would make sure she felt how much he loved her.

Astrid did feel it. She woke in the night still in his arms. For the first time in her life she felt truly safe and loved. His face relaxed in sleep, was so perfectly formed; the strong jaw, straight nose, and full lips. Remembering those lips against her skin, making their way across her breasts made Astrid's body begin to hum. Slowly and softly she drifted her fingers lightly up his beautifully sculpted arm to his broad shoulder. He was lying on his stomach, his arm casually draped across her and his face turned toward her. She gave his shoulder an appreciative kiss and breathed deeply of his unique scent of coffee, aftershave, and the woodsy soap he used. Glancing up, she noticed he was watching her and reached up to cradle the back of his head enjoying the feel of his soft blonde hair between her fingers. Her hand slowly drifted to the burn mark on his upper right arm. "Max," she called softly.

"Yes," he replied placing a soft kiss on her shoulder.

"This burn mark, did it happen the night of the fire in your room?"

Max's lips that had been softly kissing here and there froze. "How do you know about that?"

"I was just talking with Jackson the day of the funeral." Max rolled over and sat on the edge of the bed, "I'm sorry. I don't have to know," she said hurriedly.

He put on his pajama pants and stood up, "*Lagom,*" he whispered, walking toward the window, "I just haven't thought of that night in a long time. Yes, that's when I got burned. I ran back into my room to retrieve something and I got licked by some flames." He turned to her smiling suddenly to say, "I got what I went in for though!"

She couldn't help but smile in return then got out of bed, grabbed a robe and walked up to him wrapping her arms around him. "Your book?"

As she wrapped around him, her powers of comfort enveloped him and he was surprised that the memories weren't nearly as difficult as he'd expected them to be. "Told you about that book, did he?"

She only smiled and asked, "So was the fire only in your room then?"

"Yes," he said softly turning to gaze out of the window.

Remembering that Jackson said he was still afraid of fire, she decided to let that part go and get back to the part that had made him smile. "What happened to the book? He said you took it with you to America, but he hasn't been able to find it on your bookshelves."

Max raised her chin with his forefinger and thumb and smiled before kissing her. Stepping away he continued to smile as he reached under his mattress and retrieved the book. "Old habits die hard I guess."

Astrid nearly laughed at the expression on his face. He looked just like a little boy getting caught having a cookie before dinner. "Read it to me?"

"What," he asked with a little laugh.

"Please," she said with a smile, "Open a window into the heart of the little boy Maxim. Let me experience what meant so much to him."

He reached out and played with a tendril of her hair and then placing it behind her ear, leaned down and kissed her so sweetly it brought tears to Astrid's eyes. "Alright," he said warmly. They sat on the bed and she noticed the book was in Swedish and then shook her head. "What?" he asked noticing.

"I'm just laughing at myself for forgetting that of course it would be in Swedish."

He put his arm around her and squeezed, "It's okay. I'll translate. Pancake Pie by Sven Norqvist. In your country they've changed the name to The Birthday Cake."

"Why?"

"Contrary to popular belief...I don't know everything," he said with a chuckle. Clearing his throat, he began to read the story of the farmer Festus who wanted to celebrate his talking cat's birthday by making him a pancake pie. Astrid smiled and giggled in all the places that had made him smile and giggle as a boy. When he was done, he placed the book on his nightstand and turned back to her. As if sensing his need, she tenderly kissed the burn on his arm, another kiss was placed on the jagged five inch scar on his left shoulder, and another kiss on the scar next to his adam's apple, and then eventually his lips. She kissed him with an intensity that reignited his flame and left him no choice, but to make love to her again. When his passion was spent he stayed there, supporting himself over her, reluctant to let her go and move away. Astrid held onto him somehow understanding he needed it and stroked his back until eventually he rolled over onto his own side of the bed and she snuggled against him. She hadn't said she loved him, but the way she held him he believed that whatever she did feel, it was real and it was strong and perhaps maybe one day it would be more. Maybe she could love him.

Max awoke with Astrid's arm across his chest and his phone alerting him to a new text message. Reaching over and trying not to dislodge the warm, soft arm, he retrieved his phone from the side table. It was from Ivan, "A company in Hollywood is interested in making her book into a movie. I'm handling it. It's my job. Do yours."

Max responded, "She doesn't understand."

"Make her understand or I will."

Max didn't respond, but in the morning while he was in the shower his phone alerted him to a new message. Astrid picked up the phone and read. The message was from Ivan, "Get the information we need then dispatch A.R.M..." Astrid set the phone down and walked into her room to get dressed, deep in thought; her own initials were A.R.M. and what could be meant by *dispatch?*

CHAPTER 16

"Everything alright?" Max asked Astrid a few days later as Astrid grabbed her keys looking irritated.

"It's fine. I guess." When Max's only response was a raised eyebrow she let out a breath and opened up. "My editor is being excessively picky. First she wanted me to change the names of all the bad guys, the same guys by the way that those thugs who kidnapped me were asking questions about. Penny seems like a sweet person, at least through her notes, but I feel like she's looking for things to pick at me for." Max didn't respond, knowing that Ivan was actually her editor Penelope. "Now, you remember the little scene I asked you to read?" She waited for his nod. "Well, she thinks I should change the windershins and doesil to clockwise and counterclockwise, no big deal really, she's just afraid some readers won't understand." Max thought it more likely that Ivan was afraid they'd get the idea the story was coming from an actual witch and follow the directions. "She thinks I should change it from three times and one time to twelve times and fifteen times. That would have someone walking the labyrinth all night long! They'd be dizzy before they ever got into the magical realm!" Max chuckled at Astrid's bewilderment. "She even wants me to change the title. I thought…"

Max quickly put a hand over her mouth to prevent her from saying the title out loud. "It's not a good idea for you to say that."

"I don't understand," she said innocently when he removed his hand.

Not really wanting to explain and seeing her grabbing her coat he asked, "Well, where are you going?"

"My apartment," she said as he helped her put her coat on. "Apparently the fire department wants to check the smoke detectors in all the apartments."

"At night?"

"Apparently. Anyway the janitor asked me to come open the door for them."

Jackson walked into the foyer. "Honey, if he's the janitor...doesn't he have a key to your apartment? Couldn't he just let them in himself?"

"Well, yes, I guess he could have," she said slowly.

"This just doesn't add up," Jackson said looking at his brother's scowl.

"Jackson, call Tom and see how fast he can get over here. Astrid, we'll go let the janitor in," Max said taking her coat back off. Under his breath he said, *"Ana ugglor i mossen."* As he went back to his desk for something.

"What?" she asked looking from Max to Jackson.

"He senses owls in the bog," Jackson said putting his coat on. Looking up he realized he hadn't cleared things up for her and smiled, "Sorry, honey. It's just...he got a feeling there's something strange going on."

"I'm sure it's nothing sinister," she said laughing as Max walked back toward them, but the two men didn't laugh.

As soon as Tom arrived the three men headed out the door.

"Max, I know you're hiding something," Astrid said worriedly. "You're thinking there's something dangerous going on...aren't you?"

"Look, I've had a lot of practice taking care of myself. Don't worry."

Maybe it was the witch thing...she couldn't be sure...but Astrid couldn't help a nagging feeling that something was going to go wrong for them. She couldn't put her finger on what, but something wasn't right. They'd reassured her and Sara that everything was going to be fine. All they were going to do was let the janitor in to check the smoke detectors and be right back. Max gave her a little kiss saying, "We'll be back soon," and turned to walk away.

"Be careful," she whispered, "I love you." Max stopped mid-step in the doorway with his back to her.

"One moment, please," he said quietly not looking at Tom or Jackson as he turned around. Looking only at the ground, he came to her and gently took her elbow guiding her into the sitting room where he closed the doors behind them.

Jackson looked at Sara, "I find myself recalling a yuletide song, Do You Hear What I Hear?" The three of them enjoyed a chuckle as they waited for Max to return.

Safely inside, Max stood with his back against the doors and closed his eyes scared to believe what he'd just heard. His breathing became rapid and he clenched and unclenched his fists three times before he had the courage to look into her face. He'd told her days ago that he loved her, but she hadn't responded. He'd waited, hoped, and laughed at himself for needing so desperately to know if she could ever love him. Now, he couldn't bring himself to ask her to repeat it. His heart was near to beating out of his chest as his eyes begged for the confirmation his voice could not.

"I didn't tell you the other night because I didn't want you to think I was simply saying it because you said it first," she said in the soft, cashmere voice that he loved. "I wanted you to know that I really meant it. So I've been waiting for the right time." She came to him and placed her open palm over his heart. "I had hoped you'd feel it, in here." Looking at him with her blue-green sea goddess eyes she said what he'd waited his whole life for, "I love you, Maxim. I love you so much."

The warm sensation that flooded through him was like diving into a hot tub, his eyes involuntary closed to absorb the moment. This time when her use of his full name made him quiver, he smiled, feeling it was like coming home after a long day; only in his case it felt like a lifetime of waiting. As his eyes drifted back open they looked into the face he adored. He placed his hand over hers on his chest and said quietly, "I did feel it, but the words are nice to have."

The kiss that started soft and comforting grew in its intensity as his arm went around her to pull her closer. His passion took her breath away and it took her a moment to recover enough to say fervently, "Please, Max, come back to me."

The worry was evident both on her face and in the slight shake in her voice. His hand came up to hold her face. Looking deeply into her eyes he said firmly, "My darling girl, I have waited all my life to hear those words from someone. Now, to hear them from the woman I love with all my heart...," Max paused and swallowed the lump that had suddenly appeared in his throat, "Nothing," he took a deep breath, smiling at her, "absolutely nothing, will keep me from coming back to you. I promise." His lips met hers, warm and tender; strong arms wrapped snuggly around her. "Thank you for telling me," he whispered into her ear. Astrid melted into his warmth listening to the steady rhythm of his heartbeat. With a quick peck on her nose he turned and walked out.

Astrid watched the men get in the car unable to stop the feeling that something dreadful was about to happen.

When they got to the apartment everything was dark. Even the street lamps that usually lit up the walkway were out. There was no janitor or firemen lurking around. The dead silence was unnerving and all three men were on high alert convinced something just wasn't right. Max unlocked Astrid's door and pulled out his gun. Just as he got one foot inside, someone threw a large sack over his head and down his arms then knocked him to the ground. As they tried to pick him up, someone shouted, "It ain't her!"

Unable to see much in the dark, Tom and Jackson started throwing punches at everything that came their way. Just as Max got the bag off of his head someone kicked his hand knocking the gun away. Max punched the back of the assailant's knee, got up and stomped down hard on the ankle of the man now kneeling on the ground. Hearing the crunch of a broken ankle, Max looked up in time to see Tom get knocked hard against a wall and then beaten in the face with brass knuckles. Max grabbed the brute from behind and punched his face as Tom slowly melted to the floor. Enraged, Max continued to pound into the man's face with a solid right to the jaw and an elbow to the nose spirting crimson onto the carpet. Seeing Tom on the floor, Jackson punched his opponent a few more times in the ribs then tossed him aside to rush to Tom. "I'm…I'm alright," Tom said trying to sit up and take a breath. Then he suddenly shouted, "Max, look out!"

One of the attackers swung a baseball bat at Max's head. He ducked, but it still managed to make enough contact to be heard as a sickly thud. Jackson rushed forward narrowly missing another swing of the bat. The brute Max had been beating earlier came to kick Max in the ribs as he lay on the ground. Someone was helping the one with the broken ankle out of the apartment and the men heard them yell, "Burn the witch, she's inside, burn her!"

Two more men came running in throwing gasoline all around the room. "No!" Max yelled, using the furniture to help him stand, "No!" Panic over took him and he grabbed one of the men with a gas can and shoved both out of the apartment's front window. He looked over and saw Jackson on the ground with a large man kneeling over him punching him over and over again and his brother was no longer fighting back. In full fury Max grabbed the back of the guy and slung him toward the door then turned to discover fire had broken out in the kitchen. Tom rushed over to help stand up Jackson. "Get out of here," Max told them and raced into the little kitchen as the fire started spreading. With a glance at the wall he saw little pictures of fairies and other mystical creatures, the counter held a charming collection of spice jars shaped like little houses; pieces of Astrid. They'd already taken so much from her over and over again and these things were all that were left. He started grabbing the pictures from the wall as the kitchen was engulfed and the fire began to spread to the dinette. The smoke was getting thicker, but he felt around blindly for the fire extinguisher. The heat was already beginning to make his skin hot, but he grabbed anything he saw that belonged to the woman he loved; afraid he'd miss something that meant something to her. Piling up the belongings in one spot, he picked up the extinguisher and attacked the flames here and there. Unaware Tom was behind him, Max stumbled forward when a man punched Tom and knocked one man into the other. Max turned around and knocked the man out with the extinguisher. "Tom! Get out of here," he yelled continuing to battle the flames.

"Come on, Max," Tom yelled back as the fire spread through the living room.

"I can get it put out," He glanced at Tom, "Where's Jackson?"

"He's safe, but this fire is too big and you're injured," he said seeing the blood ooze down Max's head. "Come on!"

"I've got to try. Just go!" Max continued fighting the flames and picking up mementoes as he went toward the spare room.

Both men were coughing and nearly blinded from smoke. Tom felt dizzy and reached for Max, "It's no use, come on. I'm not going without you."

"Take these out of here," he said handing some items to his friend. I'm coming, you go on."

Max walked back through the smoke trying to put out the fire and Tom lost sight of him. Losing his way in the smoke, Tom ended up in Astrid's bedroom. He tripped over something on the ground and as he fell onto it, realized it was Jackson. The attackers had apparently hauled him back into the apartment and dumped him in the bedroom. "Jackson! Jackson," he yelled, shaking him. Seeing the apartment was now engulfed in flames the arsonists started running off leaving their injured comrades to fend for themselves. Jackson rolled over and started coughing.

As Tom helped him up, he asked, "Where's Max?"

"He was trying to put the fire out."

"He's afraid of fire!"

"Then why in the hell is he…"

"Because he's Max!" They fought the smoke fanning it from their faces trying to find him and hold on to the few meager things they could take back to Astrid. Finding a recycling shopping bag, Tom put all the things they had in it and set it outside the door.

The smoke and lack of clean air was making Max feel a bit dizzy and disoriented. For a moment his mind went back in time, to his old

174

bedroom and he could see the flames all over the bookcase and spilling out onto the little rug next to his bed. *The book!* his mind screamed, *gotta get the book!* Max stumbled walking forward and began to crawl toward the bed reaching for it…the thing that meant more to him than anything else, but the flames were coming closer. Finally…finally he reached the bed, but where was the book? *Where is it? Where is it?* His mind raced to understand as he felt underneath the mattress. That was where he'd always kept it. He'd always remembered to put it away so his father couldn't take it. Why wasn't it there? His throat felt raw as he continually coughed, failing to clear his lungs. He shook his head a moment trying to clear it and realized this wasn't his bedroom. The book wasn't here. That was a long time ago, but for that brief moment it had seemed so real. Tears formed in his eyes thinking back to that night; the pain from the burns, how close he'd come to losing his most prized possession, and knowing who'd caused it all. He laid his head down on the floor knowing that he hadn't the strength to get out this time. This time…disoriented and weak…the fire won.

"Max! Max!" Tom yelled feeling his way through the apartment since seeing was out of the question. The mere moment he'd left Jackson to place the mementos outside, he'd lost sight of him. The smoke was a deep gray cloud that seemed to wrap itself around him. Holding his hands out in front of him, he felt the long, broad back and knew unmistakably it was Jackson. The heat from the fire scorched their eyes causing tears to build and making it even more difficult to see. Tom's lungs wanted to close against the invasion of the smoke, but he continued to try to yell, "Max, where are you," but his throat was rejecting the exercise. Still dizzy from his earlier encounter, Jackson stumbled, "Jackson, get out of here. He'll never forgive me if…"

"I'm not…leaving with…without him," he stammered.

They finally found him, nearly stepping on him, as he lay on the floor in Astrid's bedroom. Each grabbing an arm they pulled him. Tom grabbed the canister from the floor and used it to clear their way to the door. Max woke up coughing and with their help, staggered to the door. The fire department had arrived and were helping people evacuate the building. Using the back stairway, they staggered down the steps and around the building to get into their car leaving unnoticed. Max laid down in the backseat while Jackson sat in the passenger seat with his lap loaded with all that was left of Astrid's belongings. As Tom drove them to Max's house, Jackson couldn't stop looking over his shoulder at his brother's still form. Aside from a few coughs, Max barely moved and Jackson was all too aware of just how close they'd come to losing him. The thought made an unnerving and confusing pain in his chest. Besides each other, Max was all they'd ever had. He turned away to gaze out of the car window wondering what in the hell they would do if they ever did lose him.

CHAPTER 17

The front door burst open suddenly causing Sara and Astrid both to jump to their feet. Jackson and Tom were dragging a bruised and bleeding Max through the door and into the sitting room. Their clothes were singed and they all reeked of smoke. "Oh, Max!" Astrid exclaimed racing to him as they laid him on the couch.

"What happened?" Sara asked as Tom ran out to his car. Jackson didn't answer her, but sat down in a chair and stared fixedly at Max. Tom rushed back in with his medical bag and Astrid moved out of his way so he could kneel down next to him as Sara wrung her hands looking from one man to the next. "Why didn't you take him to the hospital? You all look like you need it!"

"He wouldn't go," Tom yelled then winced at the pain the act caused his bruised jaw. He was angry that Max had refused then angry with himself when he saw Sara's worried face.

"I had a promise to keep," Max said hoarsely looking up at Astrid. "I told you nothing would keep me from coming back to you."

"Max, you…you maniac," she said with no aggression.

"What happened?" Sara asked again.

"When we got there a couple of fellas were already there," Jackson said, "While we danced with them, someone set the place on fire."

"Oh, Max," Sara said.

Max closed his eyes, unable to look at her knowing where his sister's mind was going. "Jackson, could you get her things out of the car," he asked hoarsely.

"What things?" Astrid asked.

Tom had torn the sleeve of Max's shirt open and was searching in his bag for something when he stopped to say, "Max went through the smoke grabbing anything he could find." Jackson came in with his arms loaded with Astrid's things. She looked down at them then back at Max as Tom continued, "He tried his best, but the flames were just too much. When we found him passed out on the floor..."

"What?" She cried out in alarm, "Max, for this?" Her hand came up to cover her open mouth and her eyes welled with tears looking at the man she loved lying on the couch with several scorch marks on his clothes. "For this?"

"I know what...," Max started to sit up, but was began coughing, "what it's like for...the things that matter to you to be...senselessly destroyed," he said, surprising all of them with the emotion in his voice and the unshed tears in his eyes. He blinked his eyes rapidly and then turned away from everyone, but not before they'd all seen the shadow of fear on his face as he'd been reminded once again of the last time he'd been caught in a fire.

"Here, Jackson," Tom said, handing him a bottle. "That will take some of the sting out of your eyes from the smoke." Jackson tilted his head back and placed the drops in while Tom put some burn cream on a bright red mark on Max's arm.

Max kept his face averted, and Sara pulled Astrid into the corner of the room. Not knowing what she already knew, Sara tried to offer Astrid an explanation for Max's behavior. "When Max was about eight there was a fire in his room. He had been tending Mother earlier in the day and when he came to his room, everything was engulfed in flames. It had started at his bookcase and all his books were ruined. His shelves of school projects and other toys and things important to a boy were ruined, but that bookcase...," she shook her head a moment and then cleared her throat to continue, "Our nanny found him crawling out of his room on his hands and knees and rushed him to the hospital clutching the one thing he'd managed to save, his favorite book. Apparently he was always afraid something would happen to it, so he kept it hidden under his mattress. He was in the hospital for several days with third degree burns on his arm, back, and leg. Jackson and I were only about a year old, but according to our cook, the nanny was fired for taking him to the hospital without Father's permission. It all seemed very strange to me and of course Max has never talked about it." A ghost of a smile passed over her face before she whispered, "I sometimes think he's still haunted by that night."

Sara walked over to Jackson to clean up his bloody arm and lip. "I hope you gave as good as you got," she quipped and he leaned forward and kissed her forehead. She'd expected to see his usual smile when she looked up at him, but all his attention was on Max lying still on the couch.

Having heard the whole story now about the fire and the book, Astrid walked over to Tom finishing up tending to Max's injuries. Tom stood giving her a reassuring smile and she knelt down to take Max's hand in hers. He didn't move even to squeeze her hand and she knew his mind was caught up in the painful memory of his childhood. Attempting to put her new found powers to work, she gazed at him imagining herself wrapping a blanket of love and comfort all around him. It was painful to see another injury; another burn to add to the others. She leaned down and softly kissed the fresh bandage and whispered, "I love you, Maxim. There was nothing in that apartment that means as much to me as you do."

Max heard her quiet sob and turned his face to her. Looking at their joined hands, he brought them up to his lips to place a kiss on the back of her hand. Tom had bandaged a wound on the side of his head and as she stared into his eyes, she reached up and gently caressed his head.

Sara went over and motioned for Tom to have a seat in a chair. She wiped the blood off of the cut above his eye. He looked down at her and his eyes softened, "I'm okay." As one tear landed on her lower lashes he wiped it away with his thumb, "Is that for me?"

She sniffled, "It might be," she said, gently running a finger down the livid bruise that ran from his cheek bone to his jaw. "What...," she sniffled again, "what did they hit you with?"

179

"Brass knuckles."

"I thought those were illegal."

Her innocence made him smile, glad that regardless of what she was exposed to, she was still innocent, sweet little Sara and that thought alone made his wounds hurt a lot less. "These kind of guys don't care about little things like legalities." They smiled at each other as he wiped another tear off her cheek.

"Hey, what's going on over there?" Jackson called out to them from across the room with a frown on his face. Tom stood up and walked away to put his medical supplies back in his back.

Noticing something in the way Jackson was watching his brother, Astrid walked over to him and knelt down in front of his chair. "He's alright, Jackson," she said softly placing a hand on his arm. Jackson placed his hand on hers, but didn't speak. "Jackson," she said trying to get him to look at her. Lowering her voice to barely a whisper she said, "The fire didn't get him." Having his fear spoken out loud, Jackson was unable to hold in his emotions. He bent his head down and his shoulders shook as Astrid wrapped her arms snuggly around him.

When he had himself under control again, she handed him a tissue and he said, "Thank you, Astrid. I'm alright. Please," he glanced over at his brother lying on the sofa with his eyes closed, "don't uh…say anything to Max. It's just…"

Smiling at the tall and completely unaware wonderful man she said, "I won't say a word."

Jackson walked out toward the kitchen while Astrid walked over to the bag full of her things and kneeled down to glance into the bag. Tears formed in her eyes and she didn't try to stop them rolling down her cheeks. "I'm sorry we couldn't get more of your things," Max said coming up behind her.

"I don't care about the things," she said so sadly he came down on his haunches to put his arms around her. "I just don't understand all this; burning my things, attacking you, kidnapping me…Why!"

Her sobs continued as he escorted her to the bottom of the staircase. "Get some rest. You feel better in the morning and we'll see what we can get sorted out," Max said as she nodded. "Astrid, I need to ask you something."

"Yes," she said drying her face with a tissue.

"The other day, we were talking about the other scenes in your book, the ones you don't really like."

"Yes,"

"You said you had to write them. Why?"

"For years I've had these nightmares and someone told me that writing things down, especially things you can't say, helps to make you feel better. So, one day I wrote down one of the nightmares and it went away. Since then, when I have one that just keeps happening, I find that if I write about it, it goes away."

"Okay, that makes sense, but...why put them in the book?"

She frowned and rubbed her temple as if she had a headache, "I don't know. It seems like someone suggested it, but..." she chuckled, "I must be tired. I can't remember who it was, but it works. Not only do the nightmares go away, but I just don't even think about them anymore; almost...as if they didn't happen. Besides, destroying witches in the book made me feel like I was destroying that part of myself."

"No part of you needs to be destroyed," he said trying to keep his anger in check.

Astrid kissed him gently, "I want to believe you, Maxim. I really do, but right now I'm looking at the man I love who is burned, bruised, and reliving memories he shouldn't have to relive...because of me." She turned and slowly went up the stairs to her room.

"*God natt och dröm sött,*" he said softly watching her then went to his desk.

Sara sniffled and held a tissue to her nose having heard the Swedish roll off of her brother's tongue. He'd said those exact words to her every night when she was young. "How can you tell her to have a good night and sweet dreams with all this hanging over her head?" she asked him. "You've got to explain to her about the book." Sara pleaded.

"You want me to endanger her even more?" Max said without looking up at her.

"You don't know it will."

"I'm not willing to take the chance," he said trying to text Ivan to set up another meeting now that he finally had some sense of what was going on.

"Are you going to tell her it was her own brothers that burned down her apartment?" Jackson asked.

"What?" Sara turned to him.

Tom came towards her, "The guys before were working for Ivan and just wanted him out of the way to grab her, frighten her, or get information. This time…these guys were out to kill her and her two brothers were with them. The brothers were worked up into some crazy frenzy. They were chanting, 'kill the witch' when they torched the place." He turned to Max, "Tell her about her brothers' involvement at least."

"You don't understand. She's already been through so much with her family. To find out they're behind the fire…," Max took a deep breath and hung his head, "I simply don't know how to make you understand how much that's going to hurt her."

Softening his tone a bit, Tom said, "This whole thing has gotten out of hand, Max. Protecting our people is one thing, but Astrid has a right to know what's going on around her. She's got it coming from more than one side now. Tell her who she is, tell her what's going on. It's her life…you've got to let her run it."

"Tom, you are the epitome of fair and reasonable and respecting boundaries…," he smiled at his longtime friend, "but I am not. I can't let her walk blindly into a bad situation."

"It wouldn't be blindly."

"She knows things that most witches, who know they're witches, don't know and I think I finally know how, but I've got to handle this carefully." He looked Tom square in the eyes, "Have you heard of what she wants to call the book?" Max wrote it on a piece of paper.

After reading it, Tom quickly grabbed it and tossed it into the fire. "Well, hell! He wants her dead anyway," he shouted raking a hand through his hair.

"I'm still trying to make him see reason," Max said throwing himself into the chair behind his desk. "I'm still working on a way to…"

"What? Make everyone happy?" Tom looked over at Sara dabbing at her face with a tissue and his gut clenched. "Maybe this alliance is getting a bit out dated," he said softly, "we're now hounding one of our own because she has knowledge. Isn't that what the witch hunting was all about in the first place?"

Feeling as if she was being left out of something important, Sara asked, "What does she want the title to be?"

Tom clenched his jaw and turned a steely gaze to Max, "Not even on paper," he said in a low, strong voice Max had never heard him use before. Max didn't argue both because he agreed it was safer for Sara not to know and because it was the first time Tom really stood up to someone on Sara's behalf and he was hoping she'd notice.

Scowling and getting up from his desk, he handed his phone to Tom. "It would seem now is not the time to disband the alliance." The text he showed Tom was about a witch nearby whose landlord just discovered she was a witch, threw her out of her apartment and told others in the neighborhood that she was worshipping the devil. They beat her so badly her guardian barely recognized her. Ivan wanted Max to *take care of things*. He looked over at Sara, "Could you stay a while? I have to go out and I wouldn't want her to come down stairs and be all alone."

"Of course," she said, "but are you sure you're well enough to go out? It is two o'clock in the morning."

"I'm needed," he said dismissively, heading for the door.

"With everything that went on tonight…maybe you shouldn't be here alone," Tom said uneasily.

Sara smiled, "Well, you could stay and keep me company."

"I can stay," Jackson said, coming from the kitchen with a sandwich in his hand. "I can take care of my sister." Just then Tom's phone alerted him to a text. Guessing what it was Jackson said, "The alliance would probably want you to go with him anyway."

"Yes...uh...of course," he stuttered after reading his text, "I'll...uh, I'll say goodnight then." He and Max walked out the door together and Sara elbowed her brother in the ribs.

"Hey, what was that for?"

"I really don't think you need it explained," she said walking toward the kitchen to brew a pot of coffee.

♣

"Good morning," Max said the next morning as Astrid entered the kitchen.

Astrid looked at him and noticed the shadows under his eyes. It was obvious he'd not rested well. She reached up and gently stroked his cheek. "Good morning, Maxim," she said sadly as she got up on her tiptoes to kiss him.

"Everything alright?"

She nodded, but he wasn't the least bit convinced. "Do you have plans today?"

"Not really," she said backing up a few steps.

"Good. Spend the day with me."

Unable to resist his boyish grin, she smiled back saying, "What will we be doing?"

"Anything, everything, but mostly...nothing."

He pulled her into his embrace just as she said on a heavy sigh, "That sounds wonderful."

Max chose to drive down the most scenic route he knew of enjoying the winding of the road and the comfortable silence they both found comforting. With no particular agenda and just enjoying being together, Max couldn't remember the last time he'd been so at peace. Eventually making their way to the Riverfront District, Max said, "Care for a walk through Mills Ruins Park?"

"That would be nice. I've heard of it and driven past it plenty of times, but I've never taken the time to explore it."

Max looked genuinely surprised. "Lived here all your life and you've not experienced the landmark that got the city up and running! Shame on you," he said smiling. Assisting her out of the car he began his history lesson. "In the nineteenth century, this area of mills formed the largest direct-drive water-powered factory in the world. This, my darling girl, was the international leader of flour production. Flour was sent nationally and internationally right from this spot and consequently, Minneapolis was born and became a major player in the world of industry and commerce."

They walked along the trails leading to the ruins of the flour mill and then beneath the historic Stone Arch Bridge. Astrid reached out and touched the stone reverently, "It's so beautiful. Imagine the men building this structure," she said with a smile, "I wonder if they had any idea how important and how…appreciated their craftsmanship would be."

Max smiled, "I should think any craftsman or artist wonders about that at some point; will all the time and energy put forth in something be considered and appreciated." She turned to him then and kissed him. He lingered there at her lips for a few moments taking in her warmth and the floral smell of her perfume. If he wasn't mistaken, she was wearing Lily of the Valley and the thought made him smile. They continued meandering along the trail with no particular destination in mind and then Max stopped. "For me, this is one of the most beautiful spots in Minnesota," he said as they stood admiring St. Anthony's Falls. "You know, this is the only waterfall on the entire Mississippi River?"

Astrid laughed causing him to pause in his lesson and frown at her. "I always thought it sad that you lived here missing Sweden so much, but you seem to have just as deep an affection for Minnesota!"

Max smiled, "I guess I do get carried away," they strolled hand in hand enjoying the brisk breeze from the Mississippi River. "The truth is, this area reminds me of Oskarshamn; the water, watching the boats in the harbor, and the history."

"Max, why is it you don't go back to Sweden?" He stopped walking and she turned to face him, feeling the longing in his energy. "At least a small vacation, just to see the sights you miss?"

"I guess because…," he reached out and played with a tendril of hair next to her cheek saying softly, "because…I'm a coward." She would have made a retort, but before she could, he leaned down and kissed her so tenderly any thought of admonishing him flew from her mind. "Come, I must feed you," he said with a little grin, trying for a bit of levity after the moment that to Astrid seemed riddled with sadness. "There is a little café here, but…,"

"One-night!" a buxom blonde woman practically screamed. She was jogging as fast as she was able in her four inch heels right to Max. Reaching him, she wrapped herself around him and kissed him. "Just the man I need tonight."

CHAPTER 18

The woman was out of breath from her run and her lip-lock, but still managed to say with a pout, "Oh, please, Max. Break your rule just this once," she said before Max was able to pull her off.

Stepping back from her, he glanced at Astrid, noticing the look of complete shock, then back to the excited woman, "I'm sorry, uh..." he cleared his throat.

"Come now, Max you remember my name." She pressed herself against him again putting her hand around his neck and up into his hair, "Hired Gun Gunther never forgets anything," she purred.

"Of course I remember, Louise, but..."

She put her hand on his package and gave it a little squeeze, "It's Friday night and I have no plans," she whispered in his ear, "One night with you was just not enough."

Max grabbed her by both arms and pulled her off of him. "I'm sorry, Louise," he said firmly and reached back to take Astrid's hand, "I have plans tonight and if I have my way," he looked up at Astrid, "a lot more nights." They walked away leaving the woman with her mouth open and darts shooting out of her eyes at Astrid.

"I didn't warrant an introduction?" Astrid was practically running to keep up with Max's long strides.

"No, *she* didn't deserve an introduction," he said testily opening the passenger side door.

As she stepped in the car she inquired, "One-night?" Max groaned and shut the door. "We've had more than one night so...what does that mean?" she asked quietly when he'd gotten behind the wheel.

"It means nothing," he nearly shouted, then clenched his jaw and gripped the steering wheel with both hands, "I meant, she means nothing." His embarrassment was making his palms sweat and he roughly rubbed them on his jeans. "Astrid..." he felt at a complete loss for words. *What do you say when your carefully crafted reputation rears up and bites you in the ass,* Max asked himself. Never had he prepared for his rule of only spending one night with a woman to become a nickname and for some women, a challenge. He ran an agitated hand through his hair and twisted his lynx ring around his finger several times waiting for the right words to come to him.

Mistaking his silence and his anger, Astrid gripped her hands in her lap and said, "Max, please don't be angry. I...I never knew I was the jealous type," she said with a nervous chuckle, "I've never been in the situation before to find out, but...it's just the thought of you being with someone else the way we have and her holding you and touching you the way I do...it just makes me sad. I..."

As she spoke, the words he needed quickly fell into place and he turned to look into her beautiful blue-green eyes to say quietly, "You said, the thought of me being with someone else the way we have." She nodded sadly and he reached out and caressed her cheek. "Cashmere, I have never been with any woman the way I've been with you. Before you, I had never made love to a woman. Sex? Yes, a...a few times," he said with a grin, "but not love and you have shown me that there is a very big difference. As for someone holding me or touching me the way you do," he shook his head, "no one has ever touched me with so much care, kindness, and tenderness. I guess most women think guys don't need that and there are plenty men out there that try to act like they don't. You've offered it to me and...it fills a void. I am sorry that my past hurt you, but please don't dwell on it. You've cast a spell over me and I want no woman but you." When he leaned in his lips caressed hers leaving no doubt in her mind that she was the one he wanted. As he ended the kiss, he kept his cheek against hers to whisper in her ear, "You do things to me. I meant what I said to her. I want a whole lot more nights with you...just you." Astrid closed her eyes enjoying his words, his aftershave, and his warmth. She smiled at him when he leaned back to look into her eyes and couldn't help thinking that she wanted a lot more nights, too. Turning back to the steering wheel he said with a grin, "Now, lunch for my lady."

At lunch, she reminded him of his history lesson and his belief that she'd been remiss in her appreciation of her own city. "You know you fuss at me for not knowing my city's history and here you are, a Swede who hasn't been to the American Swedish Institute! Shame on you, Mr. Gunther." She was rewarded for use of his sir name with a glare over his fork. Giggling she said softly, "I mean, Maxim."

He reached out and took her hand to place a kiss on it before saying, "I make you a promise that I will go to the institute and wallow in my own heritage."

"Thank you."

"But not today," the little frown she gave him made him smile, "after this most delicious lunch, I am taking you to another of my favorite spots."

"Where is that," she asked, but he shook his head and offered no other information. "You know you really have an issue with old fashioned signs of respect like, Mr., Sir, and things like that."

Max silently set down his fork and took her hand in his. "I understand that it's supposed to be a sign of respect, but for me...it feels more like subservience and domination." His thumb softly stroked the back of her hand and she leaned closer to him. "You see, Father demanded that so-called respect from my mother and...it was just one of many things that...broke her." The emotion in his voice made her wish she hadn't mentioned it, but at the same time glad that he was opening up about a subject so difficult him. "He cheated on her, a lot," he said shaking his head, "Practically flaunted it in front of her. He belittled her; shouting and pointing out what he considered her failings as a wife, a mother, and a human being. She cried and cried until she had no tears left and it was as if she just sort of faded away."

"Makes you wonder why she stayed with him," Astrid said softly.

Max shook his head, "Would you believe she loved him? Sometimes when I would be reading to her she would try to make me understand and say that he hadn't always been the man he was now. There had been a change in him and she blamed herself so she couldn't just walk away. It always seems odd to me that the people demanding the most respect are the ones giving the least amount to others. I just...don't want to lose sight of the fact that we all deserve respect in equal measure. I'm sorry if I seem...obsessive about it."

"Don't apologize," she said smiling at him, "I think you're wonderful," she leaned in and kissed him lightly, then put his fork back in his hand and said, "Eat, I want to see where you're taking me next!"

Snuggled close together, they returned to eating the delicious lunch of Walleye and Astrid didn't know what she enjoyed more, the fish, or Max's description of his own attempts at fishing for it.

After lunch they headed out to a much less populated area where the road got smaller and the land got wider. Eventually he turned onto a dirt road that turned and twisted with large tress hanging over the road making interesting patterns of shade on the ground. Astrid could easily imagine a picnic under one of the huge oak trees. Max pulled off the side of the road and smiled. "I'm afraid we'll have to walk from here, but it's not far." Hand in hand, they walked through a field of wild flowers and various foliage hearing a scurrying sound now and then of some small creature. Astrid thought they were probably wondering what they were up to. She'd been looking down at the ground when he stopped and said, "Well, this is it."

Astrid looked up and past his grinning face to see a small yet busy gurgling stream with a small wooden structure perched atop a little hill next to it. The pretty gazebo was unlike any she'd ever seen before. It was octagon shaped and the wood was intricately carved in some designs similar to ones she'd seen at the institute that were said to be authentic Swedish traditional carvings. It was left unpainted, but the wood was sealed to keep the natural look. Various flowers were planted here and there around the sides. "This is...the most beautiful thing I've ever seen," she said slowly walking up the three wooden steps. "How ever did you find it?"

"I bought the land when I first arrived here," he said coming up behind her. "I wanted to be away from everyone else for a while. This was the most remote place I could find...at least that was for sale. Not exactly being a carpenter," he said with a chuckle, "it took me a year to build it."

Astrid gasped, "You," the shock was impossible to hide, "you built this?" He just looked down at the ground shyly and ran his hand down one of the pillars. "You are an amazing man, Max," she said quietly.

He shook his head, "No. Many better men wouldn't have taken so long."

There was a hint of insecurity in his voice and Astrid's heart swelled with love that he was willing to share with her something that meant so much to him. "It was a labor of love and you took your time to tend it," she said taking his hands in hers. "Did you even do the carvings yourself?" Astrid turned his hands over and lightly ran a finger over the small calluses.

Max watched her fingers and enjoyed the comforting sensation it brought, "Yeah, not exactly Turnblad Mansion quality, but...," he looked around at his accomplishment, "I enjoyed the process."

"Well, that's what matters the most; enjoying the process not the end result. If my opinion matter though...I think it's beautiful."

"It just so happens that your opinion matters quite a lot," he said warmly.

"The benches were a wonderful idea. What an amazing place to sit and watch the water. I think I could sit out here for hours," she laughed, "maybe days."

"I thought about building another *Långa Soffan,* but I'm a man not a machine," he said with a chuckle.

"What is *Långa Soffan?* And don't laugh at my pronunciation!"

"Sorry," he said failing to hide his grin, "It's a bench in Oskarshamn that is seventy two meters long. The name actually means long sofa. It was originally built for the wives of the sailors to sit and wait for their men to come in."

"Sounds very romantic. This," she said spreading her arms out to the gazebo, "is very romantic. Who else knows about this place," she asked thinking that she already knew the answer.

"No one," he said softly, fingering one of the carvings. "I haven't even told Sara and Jackson because…well, it seems a little…I don't know really," he laughed at himself.

Looking around she suddenly thought of something. "Oh…oh, Max. The flowers…"

"Yeah, their dying back a bit with the cold settling in."

"No…did you do this gardening yourself?"

Max looked at the almost alarmed look on her face then back down at his gardening effort and chuckled, "Yeah, is it that bad?"

"No, of course not," she said.

The alarmed looked changed to one of joy and she began to laugh. Feeling left out of the joke, Max said, "I come out here once a week to mow the grass and keep the weeds back and just kind of piddle around a bit."

"In jeans and a t-shirt?"

"Well, certainly not in a suit!"

"With…a shovel?"

"Of course. Do you think I'd use my hands to dig?"

"No, but I thought…" Astrid looked at him and shook her head, "I saw you with the shovel and wearing those dirty clothes and I thought…"

"What, that I'd just buried somebody," he said with a chuckle, but with one look at her face, he stopped and got serious. "Astrid, you thought…"

"Sorry," she said grinning. Max shook his head raising an eyebrow at her. She laughed pulling him into the center saying, "Kiss me in the middle of this beautiful structure."

More than willing, he did as requested then grew serious and asked her, "Why were you sad this morning?"

Wrapped in his arms, she tucked her head down to rest on his chest. "You didn't rest well last night. I know. I could see the shadows under your eyes. You were in too much pain…and perhaps…haunted by too many memories to sleep and it's my fault."

"It's not your fault when other people behave foolishly."

"I'm not so sure about that," she said moving away from him to look out at the little stream.

"What?"

"Really, what kind of person am I?"

"A good one," he said as she rested her head gently against a pillar.

"No," she said. Max came up behind her and turned her around. "Max, you've been very kind to me and…you make me feel like…I don't know…like I'm just like everyone else, but it's simply not true and I can't ignore the nagging feeling in my heart."

"What feeling?"

"That I'm just a mistake that happened," Max shook his head, "I wasn't planned or expected or even…," tears welled in her eyes and she took a breath to turn away from him saying, "I wasn't even wanted." She tried to go down the steps, but Max held her arms from behind her and pulled her back against his chest. "What kind of person can I be if my own mother didn't want me…," she said brokenly, "didn't love me? Even regretted created me."

Her sobs grew and Max turned her around to hold her tightly. "Astrid, we are not defined by how our parents feel about us."

"Mothers love their babies…it's…in their make-up…they can't help it."

"You can't paint all parents with the same brush. Not all mothers love their children any more than all fathers. My father hated my existence to the degree that he punished my mother for giving birth to me for the rest of her life."

She shook her head stepping away from him. "I know you didn't have a good relationship with him. You told me about the rack and…"

"No, Astrid. It was a hell of a lot more than that rack," Max walked over to one of the benches along the wall of the gazebo and sat down with his hands in his lap. Although he didn't look up and she couldn't see his face, it was obvious what he was going to say next was difficult for him by the way he gripped his hands until his knuckles were white and the muscle in his jaw tightened. "I know how it feels to be brought into the world unwanted." She looked into his eyes questioningly and he smiled faintly. "My mother wanted me, but my father did not and when you're born into that...hell, you somehow feel the need to spend your life apologizing for your existence." Astrid nodded and sat down beside him on the bench. "My father hated me so much that he threw me into the ocean one night in the hopes of getting rid of me." Astrid lovingly placed her hand on his. "You once asked what happened to the little witch that made her attacker vomit uncontrollably." He saw her nod through the corner of his eye and continued, "Ermina was a dear little friend of mine. Her mother was our housemaid and her father was our gardener," he smiled briefly, "He was amazing and would probably laugh his head off at my attempts," he gazed out at the water.

"Maxim," she said softly, "There is no more beautiful garden than a garden tended with love."

He smiled and kissed her hand that held his. "Ermina was younger than me but had the most wonderful...I guess outlook is the word." Max brought her hand to his lips again then to his cheek before releasing it to stand up and walk down the steps toward the stream. "I tended to be a serious chap and she was forever making fun of me for it and trying to make me laugh," he said smiling as Astrid walked along with him. "Anyway, one day she was attacked by an influential man of the town and her powers emerged. Afraid she'd tell someone the truth of his behavior, he rallied the town against her saying that the evil witch had put a spell on him. Her parents came to my father for help, but he refused to side with his servants against this important man. They stoned her to death and she died in my arms."

"Oh, Max," Astrid cried taking ahold of his arm and burying her face in his shoulder, "I'm so sorry."

"That night when he came home..." he tipped his head down and shook his head, "he'd apparently heard about his son siding with the

194

witch. He snatched me out of my bed and hauled me down the stairs. Mother was in the foyer, crying and pleading with him to tell her what was wrong. I was still undersized then and I must have looked a bit like a rag doll being slung around." He chuckled, but instead of sounding jovial it sounded hollow and sad. Astrid reached up and gently kissed his cheek. Max nestled his head against hers a moment then continued, "Anyway, when she blocked the front door he pushed her aside and for a moment I thought he'd...I quickly tried to straighten my spine a bit and not look so pathetic. I told her everything was alright not wanting her to get hurt trying to intervene. She looked so frightened for me," he said with a little smile, "I forced back my own fears and gave her a little nod as if everything was under control. It was a relief when she backed out of his way. The hand around my arm nearly cut off the circulation as he pulled me down the steps and shoved me into his car. We drove to a deserted piece of land that stretched out over the ocean. I remember...it was pitch black out and...I don't know," his voice softened to a near whisper, "it was so...quiet...so still. The only sound was of the waves crashing against the land and rocks below." His brow furrowed as he looked off into the distance, "It's so strange because...I can still feel how cool the breeze was up on the cliff. I can still remember my heart nearly beating out of my chest with fear and even now...all this time later...I can...remember the fear," he voice had grown cold and distant and frightened for him, Astrid put her arms around him and held him trying to bring him any comfort she could. Although he'd pushed the memories aside to get on with his life, she knew that the terrified little boy was still there and always would be. As the birds flew overhead and the stream gurgled, they sat in silence a few moments before a squirrel running up an oak tree brought Max back into the present. Blinking a few times and taking a steadying breath, he dipped his head down and with a slightly stronger voice, he continued, "He grabbed me by my shirt front and flung me toward the edge. The same cold eyes as mine looked down at me and he said, 'You defied me and embarrassed me in front of this entire village. If you survive I'll forgive you. It will show that my soft, undersized son may have value after all. If you don't...well, I guess we know what that means.' Then he gave me a shove and down I went." Max walked closer to the edge of the stream and bent down to pick up a small pebble. "It was odd really," his voice took on a lighter tone, "I'd missed the rocks and for a few moments I felt nothing; just a quiet and calm floating sensation, but then…then the cold penetrated and the water was so frigid it was difficult to draw breath." He threw the pebble into the water then looked down to select another. "I struggled against the waves trying to keep my head above water, but when a wave got me and my head was underwater I realized how much more peaceful it was under there. It was quieter and I couldn't see the figure of my father any more. I wasn't struggling and the water just toyed with me back and forth and I relaxed." Astrid reached into her pocket for a handkerchief and wiped her face. The thought of the little boy letting go of life was too heart wrenching to imagine. "I could picture my mother's face as I was hauled away and tried to remember it in my mind. I thought I would never see her again you see and…and I didn't want to forget the way her eyes looked into mine," his voice was so soft and quiet it seemed to float on the breeze as the memories flooded his mind. The breeze was cool and he lifted his face up to the sky, closing his eyes a moment remembering the mother he loved. Eventually remembering himself and the story he was attempting to relate, he cleared his throat and began again. "It seems so strange now, but…somehow, under that water…," he ducked his head down and said quietly, "I heard her."

"Who, Maxim. Your mother?"

"No," he said turning to look at the owner of the cashmere voice that touched his soul, "It was Ermina."

196

CHAPTER 19

"She called to me," Max said as the cool breeze blew across the river and into his hair making it flutter. It gave him an odd sense of relief to be getting the memories out of his head and told to the one person he thought could really understand. On a sigh, he continued, "Remembering her...thinking of her, I remembered the twins. They'd only just been born into a very scary world. They'd need looking after, protecting. I realized I couldn't just leave them with him. Ermina continued to call to me. I know it must sound crazy."

"No, not to me," she said with a soft chuckle.

"I followed that sweet, giggly voice through the water. Every time I got tired and stopped swimming she'd fuss at me the way she used to and I'd get going again," it was good to see him smile and Astrid hugged him. "She led me to a little island in the Baltic Sea situated in the Kalmar Strait between the mainland province of Småland and the island province of Öland, part of the municipality of my home...Oskarshamn. There, on the Isle of Jungfrun she stood waiting for me." He smiled at her as her mouth fell open and a hand came up to cover it.

"You mean it really...it exists," she whispered.

"There she stood, laughing at me as usual. I knew it was just her spirit and not her, but...," he looked down at the lovely girl in his arms, "seeing her smiling, happy face after how things had been the last time I'd seen her...I don't know it just...made things okay somehow. That night she showed me to walk the labyrinth, three times doesil and one time windershins, to open the portal. I was taken into the very caves you've been writing about. There, deep in the mouth of the cave standing around an altar was a group of people willing to pledge their lives to prevent something like that from ever happening again or at the very least to prevent it from going unpunished."

"The Witches Guardian's Alliance."

"Correct. They explained to me about the Torsaker Witch Trials and how many lives were extinguished for no real purpose or reason…just a few silly men giving a harsh example of how cruel humans could be to each other. They explained to me about the old magic and how beautiful the world could be if we just accept it. For the first time in my life I felt there was a reason for my existence. Mother loved me, Jackson and Sara needed me, but this group…wanted me. Maybe in a way I should thank that old bastard."

"No," Astrid said clinging to him and hating a man she's never known. "Never that, but…"

"Yes?"

"Nothing, I…I just can't believe it's all real and I thought…" she shook her head unable to finish her thought and hugged him closer. "I'm sorry for how you were treated, Maxim."

Instantly feeling the comforting energies she was sending him, Max's tone softened and he gently stroked her hair as he held her. "They consider us unworthy of their love, but actually they are unworthy of ours. They are the ones who are black-hearted, twisted, and immoral; not us. Do you feel I am unworthy of my father's love?"

"Of course not."

"No more than you, my beautiful, compassionate, darling friend are unworthy of a mother's love. By the way…Jackson and Sara don't know about the ocean. They think…Father told them a story one time about me falling in. The sick grin that bastard gave me when he told them would curdle milk," taking her hand in his, he looked down at their joined hands, "I don't want them to know."

"Why," she said in the soft voice he loved, "afraid they'll think you're a superhero?"

He shook his head, "Certainly not…it's just, well…kind of a private thing." She nodded and offered a kiss. He responded with a kiss in return then stepped away to turn back to the river and said quietly, "My siblings would certainly not think I was any kind of hero," he frowned suddenly and she walked up behind him to put her arms around him. "Sara especially, she thinks…"

"What?"

"Well, one day she told me that she knew what I do for Ivan. Seeing her face when she said it, the disappointment," he shook his head, "I felt as if my legs had been cut off at the knees and I was sinking to the ground. I know when we were young, she loved me…but what does she see when she looks at me now? A thug? A hired gun with no thought to his actions? Does she truly understand why I've made the choices I've made? Does she…does she see my father?"

"Ask her."

"I can't. I…," he chuckled, "I'm afraid of her answer."

"Max *Günther* whose name means, warrior…isn't afraid of anything."

"And here I thought you knew me."

"I do."

He smiled at her and asked quietly, "How did you know *Günther* meant warrior?"

"Jackson. He was teasing Sara a few Sundays ago saying he was going to get her some tactical gear! She told him that since it meant warrior in German Mythology and you guys are Swedes it doesn't count."

"Where was I during this interesting conversation?"

"Finishing the Pyttipanna, which was delicious, but that's probably because of the meaning of Maxim."

"I shudder to think."

"It means, The Greatest."

Max started laughing and choking at the same time. Taking a deep breath he said, "So you're telling me that with my two names together it means, "The Greatest Warrior?""

Astrid nodded her head, "Yep, and it really annoys Jackson whose name only means, Son of Jack."

"Come on…that's ridiculous," he put his hands on his hips, "There's nothing in that stuff. First of all, in this country it's Gunther not *Günther*. Second, I am *not* a great warrior…I'm not a great anything! Third, he is not the son of Jack, he is the son of Karl; nothing to rave about I grant you, considering what kind of a man he was, but there it is." Max shook his head at the absurdity of it all. "That's all I need is one more reason for Jackson to…," he put his head down not able or not wanting to finish his thought.

"I think you're great," she said making him shake his head, "Maybe too great. I feel rather foolish being such a coward about the trivial things that have happened to me knowing what torments and abuses you've endured."

"Don't be ridiculous. It isn't a contest. Of course it does give us a bit of a connection," he said grinning.

"Connecting is good. Maxim," she said and her soft voice reached out warming his soul, "I love you."

All thoughts of fathers, brothers, or family members of any kind left his mind and he pulled her into his embrace to kiss her slowly and passionately. After a moment to settle his heart, he pulled his pocket knife out, walked back over to the gazebo and started to carve into one of the pillars. "What are you doing?" Astrid asked running up to him in alarm. She watched as he carved, M.G. plus sign A.M. and made a heart. "Max, really. How old are you?"

"A man is never too old to carve his love into a tree…or in this case a gazebo."

They laughed and she wrapped her arms around him, "Thank you for bringing me here. Thank you for sharing a piece of yourself." They sat on the bench in the gazebo together listening to the gurgling of the stream and the whistling of the birds. "You know," she said, just a little bit drowsily lying in his arms, "it's Sunday. What's for dinner?"

"I thought about shocking them with something very American like pizza or hamburgers, but…"

Sitting up to face him she asked smiling, "But, what?"

"I just don't think I have it in me to make them that happy!" Astrid giggled and the two held hands making their way back to his car.

♣

"It was a great dinner last night Max," Jackson said sitting in front of the fire the next afternoon.

Max was sitting at his desk shuffling through e-mails so he was unable to see his brother's face, but the surprise of the comment was enough to stop his activities. "Thank you, Jackson," he answered quietly.

"No, I mean…," Jackson bent his head down and Max could see he was gripping his hands in his lap.

"Something bothering you," Max asked as he stood up from his desk.

Jackson was still a moment, then ran a hand through his hair and said, "It's just that…last night everything felt," he let out a sigh, "like it's supposed to with family."

"Isn't that a good thing?"

"Max, I love Astrid."

Max nearly fell over where he stood. All these years they'd never had a woman come between them. He'd always figured it was because there was such an age difference between them, but…they've just never before been interested in the same kind of woman. Why now! With the woman he loved? "Jackson," he started to try to find the words to respond, but luckily Jackson turned around in his seat and spoke first.

"She's become like another sister to me and…Max what's wrong," he asked noticing how his brother looked as though he was going to pass out at any moment. Jackson got up and went to him, "Damn, you look like you're about to toss your chips!"

"I'm…I'm fine, Jackson," he said taking a breath and starting to smile at himself for being a fool. "I've got to stop jumping to conclusions." Jackson just frowned, "I'm glad she's important to you," Max said with a smile.

"Well, yeah, but…the kidnapping…have you told her the truth?"

201

"No, I haven't told her I was the one behind the kidnapping. There is no reason to dump that on her just to ease my own guilt," Max said straining to keep his voice low.

"Don't you think it's a deception though?" Jackson asked knowing how Max himself felt about not being told things. Good, bad or ugly Max always wanted to know everything. Astrid loved Max, they all knew it. Surely she'd understand, so why was Max being so insistent on keeping her in the dark? As soon as the thought entered his head another thought entered as well, maybe she wouldn't understand. She'd been kidnapped and injured all on Max's direction. He remembered how she'd looked when Max brought her back. With a huge blue and purple bruise on her cheek, she'd cried tears of joy at seeing all of them. She'd actually worried about not being able to thank all of them for their kindness toward her. She'd been heartbroken at the thought of never seeing any of them again. Jackson hung his head down. They'd all known the truth and none of them had told her. The thought of Astrid, whom he'd come to regard as another sister, hating him for his deception convinced him to agree with Max. "Alright, we won't tell her they kidnapped her on your orders."

"I'm afraid it's too late." Astrid said walking slowly into the room stopping just inside the doorway. "I guess you should have shut the door if you were going to have this kind of conversation. I feel like I'm watching a soap opera telling the bad guy, 'look behind you.'" She stood with her back straight as a board, her face expressing no emotion. She addressed Jackson, but only had eyes for Max. "Jackson, would you excuse us, please." Jackson looked at Max and then back to Astrid. Not knowing what he could possibly say to help he decided leaving was probably his best course of action. Without saying a word he left and closed the doors behind him. Astrid and Max stood staring at each other with no sound except that of the clock ticking. Finally she spoke, but the tone was not the soft and comforting one Max was accustomed to hearing from her. This tone was rigid and controlled. "You paid men to kidnap me?"

"Yes."

"To get information about my book?"

"Yes."

"You paid men to grab me, throw me in the back of a car, and tie me to a chair? You paid men to threaten that I would never see anyone I cared about ever again? You paid men to take away all my control, to put their hands all over me and do whatever they had to do to get me to answer your questions?"

Max didn't blink and didn't flinch to her accusations, but he did add, "They were given instructions not to touch you or to hurt you."

A slight grin appeared on Astrid's face, but it wasn't warm and friendly. She slowly walked over to his desk and her hand caressed the bud of the fresh lily that had been placed there just this morning. She looked up and saw Max's eyes watching her hand. "Is that why you suddenly sprang from the shadows? Because your orders were not being carried out properly?"

Max's face hardened, "I killed the one that struck you. I killed the one that put his hand on your thigh. I killed the one that held a knife to your throat. They weren't supposed to touch you." She was already angry and disappointed in him, he saw no reason to cover things up or sugar coat them.

Astrid stared at the lily in her hand acknowledging the tender stem that could so easily snap in her hand. Like love, flowers were delicate and easily destroyed. With her hand still holding the lily, she looked at Max watching her stroke the flower's petal. His eyes were hard, his jaw clenched, and there had been no emotion in his voice as he'd described what he'd done. It broke her heard to think that maybe his heart had hardened so much that human life meant nothing to him. "Is that all you have to say about it?"

"What else should I say?" It unnerved him seeing the lily in her hand that she could so easily crush. His heart beat faster wondering if she would. "You want me to apologize for killing those men? No. I did what needed doing." He watched her beautiful face imagining what she must think of him. His cold and calculated talents that had made him the success that he was at his job was the very thing he sometimes couldn't come to grips with himself. The despair in her eyes sliced into him opening up every fear, every self-doubt, and every insecurity he'd ever had. Suddenly he was the lily held in her hand, one wrong move and he'd wither away; unwanted, unloved, and unnecessary in the world. As he took a deep breath trying to slow down his heartbeat, she moved away from his desk leaving the solitary flower precisely as she'd found it. "I could see your powers had begun to manifest. Your fear was turning to an emotion you could use; anger. I knew those men and I've known plenty others like them. It would have just fueled their bully mentality." His jaw twitched and his fists clenched as he tried to reign in his anxieties. "They had already hurt you once. I killed them before they had a chance to do it again."

"I see," she answered simply walking back to the door.

Max tried reaching a hand toward her, "Astrid, I...,"

"You'd been there all along, hadn't you? In the back of the room?" She took a step back away from him. It was only a step, but to Max it seemed like kilometers.

"Yes," he answered.

"You just watched while I sat there with no control, terrified, humiliated, and confused. You just watched...until your orders weren't followed. That's when you decided to act. When what *you* wanted didn't happen."

"I didn't let them hurt you, I...," his voice sounded panicked even to his own ears.

"Didn't let them hurt me?" She shook her head looking down at the carpet and said quietly, "Not all pain is physical. How could you do that?" Max briefly closed his eyes to the bitter accusation in her question and then swallowed the self-loathing that formed in his stomach when she asked, "How could any man do that to someone he says he cares about?"

He wished she'd yell, shout, or show her anger in some way. Instead she just stood there looking so dreadfully disappointed in him. Perhaps she didn't consider him worth expending the energy to be angry. Perhaps he wasn't. He stepped toward her and she backed away. Quickly he stepped forward again and took her arms beginning to feel panicked, "Look, this all happened before I really knew you. My people were in danger and I was told you had answers you weren't sharing and I had a job to do. Lives had already been taken!"

"What?" Astrid said concerned etched all over her face.

"It…it doesn't matter right now," Max said angry with himself for slipping and letting his insecurities cause him to say more than he'd intended.

"Of course it matters! What lives were taken? What have they to do with me?"

Watching her chest rise and fall as her breathing became rapid, Max attempted to calm her down, changing his tone and saying gently, "Astrid, let's sit down and…"

"No! What lives, Max?"

Looking into her face he knew she wasn't going to let it go. She was so sweet, so innocent, he knew she would take the news to heart and blame herself. Clenching his jaw at his own stupidity, he ran a hand through his hair trying to think of the best way to tell her. As softly as his voice would allow he said, "Two witches and a guardian of the alliance were killed after…after things were read in your book." The look of horror on her face made it difficult for him to breath. "They took…things you'd said and…researched a little and…discovered how to recognize a witch and performed a ritual that…that killed her. The guardian tried to put a stop to it and got caught in the middle. The other witch was…tortured in the same way as the one in the end of the book. Three other witches; one here, one in Iowa and one in Mississippi who had been in hiding, were discovered using the methods from your book."

"But…but that was just…made up…it wasn't…"

"The spells are real. The methods of identifying witches are real," he said quietly watching her expression go from bewilderment to horror.

CHAPTER 20

Astrid reached out to grab the door frame as the room began to spin. Her stomach clenched as she thought about what Max had said before about her receiving messages from the spirits.

"It's not your fault, you had no idea it was all real," he said quickly as her face paled and the realization of what he was saying began to sink in.

"That was the reason behind the...the ambush at the hotel, the...kidnapping, my apartment being burned. It was all to shut me up?"

Max ignored the comment about her apartment. There was no reason to tell her who had actually done it; no reason to cause her more pain just to try to save himself, but the other things, "Some things were to shut you up, some to find out where the information came from, and in the case of Brenda...she was trying to keep you talking."

"So, I've been under attack from three sides and didn't have a clue what it was all about." Astrid shook her head trying to make sense of everything. "Why not just refuse to publish my book?"

"You would have just gone to another publisher and...the story is good. You have real talent as a storyteller. Any other company would have recognized that and made you an offer. We'd have had no control."

Instantly seeing the look on her face, Max realized too late that he'd chosen the wrong word. "Yes, control. That's what this has been all about isn't it? I guess the apple didn't fall far from the tree. All those years of your father trying to control and now look at you. You've placed yourself in a position of controlling other's lives."

Max knew she was deliberately hurting him, but couldn't stop it from working perfectly. All the years of worrying he'd turn out like his father and here the woman he loved was pointing out that he was. He ignored the sudden nausea, saying, "Astrid, all that is in the past, let's leave it in the past. We love each other. We can…"

"I don't love you," she stated, knocking the wind out of him and making the nausea rear its ugly head again. He looked into her face finding it difficult to get a breath. There was nothing in her face, no warmth, no kindness, no emotion at all. She just stared at him like some small and insignificant creature. He stood motionless as sweat dripped down his back and beaded on his forehead. "I loved the man you wanted me to believe that you were. I trusted the man you wanted me to trust. I can't love someone I don't know."

"You do know me," he said unable to hide the slight quiver in his voice, "You know me better than anyone ever has." At her silence he slowly started shaking his head from side to side. "Astrid." She started to turn away and he grabbed her. "Listen to me!" he nearly shouted, her coldness scaring him worse than any enemy ever had, "The kidnapping was set up before I knew you. I meant to call it off, but then it seemed the only way to get the information I needed. I wanted to tell you, but I…"

"Couldn't because you knew I would despise who you really are; cold, calculating, and obsessed with control? Let go of me," she hissed. "I thought they were going to kill me! You knew about the times I'd been locked in the closet, stripped of any power or control over my situation."

Max shook his head slightly, "Astrid, this was set up before…before I understood…I…,"

"I thought I'd never see any of you again." Her laugh was hollow and sad, "I guess that wouldn't have mattered to any of you."

"What in the hell does that mean?"

"I saw the text from Ivan on your phone the morning after I'd fallen for your, 'I love you' line."

"That was not a line, Astrid you know that!"

"The text said for you to kill me." She looked at him sadly. "I was too stupid to be afraid. I thought I must have misunderstood or...or he'd sent the wrong message or something. How many times did Sara drop hints about things being or not being a killing offense?" Again she laughed the hollow, sad laugh that spoke volumes of how deeply he'd hurt her. "I simply didn't want to believe that all that time you'd been just waiting...waiting for the right moment."

"You don't understand. Ivan gave me orders, but..."

"He gave you orders, but did you ever just tell him, no? At any point?"

Max hung his head and said softly, "Not...not in exact words."

"Just like how you never asked me where the information for my books was coming from. Tell me the truth Max, after you told me you loved me," he looked up at her, "were you still trying to get information from me?"

He swallowed hard and turned away saying, "Yes."

"After you got the information you were supposed to silence me?"

"Yes."

"You and your alliance think you're so much better than the witch haters, but are you?" Max's head whipped around to look at her, "You can't hide history, pretend it didn't happen or change it to suit your conscience. Maybe the souls that were killed want their story told. Maybe if it came to light what really happened they could rest. I understand that maybe some things that were in the book shouldn't have been, but are secrets ever really a good idea? This one didn't work out so well...at least for me," she said sadly.

Max shook his head, "I agree with what you're saying, but there are still a few people who will always try to stand as judge and jury on the rest of the world. They are the ones we are fighting against and controlling the information out there is just one way we're trying to do that. I realize I should have just talked to you about everything. I didn't think you would just tell me where you got your information from and I was afraid that the more you knew the more danger you'd be in. If Brenda caught on to what we were trying to do...I simply didn't know

208

what she would do. I tried to ask you questions, but the way you hesitated answering sometimes…I thought you weren't telling me intentionally….I didn't realize until later that you didn't have the answers. I thought you were being cagey and secretive and I was concerned for my people. There was no reason for you to tell me the truth so I thought you wouldn't."

Astrid looked at him in disbelief. "There doesn't have to be a reason to tell someone the truth. All you had to do was ask. I have nothing to hide. Besides, I did tell you. I told you how ideas pop into my head when I take baths." An ugly sneer came across her face, "You didn't believe a word I said. You just thought of me as some kind of nutcase." She looked at the floor and then back at him. "I thought we had something; the kind of thing I'd always dreamt about. I guess it doesn't really exist. You know that old saying that it's better to have loved and lost than never to have loved at all? Well, it isn't true. Not for me at least. I have never hurt this badly before. I thought Jackson and Tom and Sara were my friends, but it's all been a lie." She smiled a sad little smile as tears cascaded down her cheeks. "I thought you really loved me. I thought for once, somebody…"

"Astrid, please listen to me," he said gently, "I was trying to…to help you. You'd already been hurt so much by your family. I didn't want you to be hurt more. Let me explain everything that I should have explained before."

"Why? For more lies, half-truths, and everybody else in that family?" She tried taking a deep breath, but her sobs prevented her. "I don't want to listen, I don't want to talk, and I don't even want to take the next breath." Max's heart clenched at the sound of her sad chuckle as she said, "I guess this is what dead inside feels like. Well, half the battle is over now you'll just need to kill the outside." She looked up into him and the despair he saw there nearly brought him to his knees. "I just feel empty," she said as she opened the door to the sitting room and stood in the foyer.

"Astrid, I do love you." Max said softly attempting to come toward her, but she backed away again. "Sara, Jackson and Tom *are* your friends."

She shook her head, not believing him. The soft voice that usually brought him comfort was now piercing through him with its pain and distrust. "All because of some stupid made up story that it turns out…I didn't make up after all. The fates definitely dealt me a nasty blow." Her brow furrowed and her hand gently rubbed her chest. "Strange how…it even hurts to breathe," she said with tears coursing down her cheeks. She walked toward the door just as Sara came through.

"Good bye, Sara," she said passing her.

Sara looked from her to Max, but Max just hung his head down. "Good bye? Astrid, where are you going?" she called as Astrid quickly ran to her car.

"To the river," she called back as Max entered the foyer.

"What's happened?" Sara looked from one to the other, but neither looked at her.

"Astrid, wait. Don't leave like this," Max called to her.

"It's done, Max. We're done, the book is done, and most especially…I'm done," she said sadly, but then a strange smile stole over her face. "Is that why you took me to the gazebo that day? To kill me…throw me into the river?"

"No," he said firmly.

"Is that why you told me that story of what your father did to you? Were you trying to gather the courage to do the same to me? Find out if I'd survive?"

Max balled his fists and shook his head, "How can you even think that?"

She looked at him sadly, "Once upon a time I would have never thought you capable of something like that, but now…," she shook her head and turned away, "Don't worry, Max. I'll finish what you obviously couldn't that day," she said walking away.

Max frowned, "What does that mean? Astrid…,"

"Astrid," Sara called the pain on both their faces being impossible to ignore, "Why are you going to the river?"

Astrid opened her car door. "It was the last place I was truly happy," she said wistfully, "Funny and a bit macabre; don't you think? Considering what it could have been. I need to do a little research."

"What kind of research," Sara asked, thoroughly confused by their conversation.

Looking into Max's face Astrid said quietly, "To find out how deep it is. Tell Ivan the job is done. Goodbye, Max," she whispered looking at him with tears welled in her eyes.

Just as she sat and shut the door Max realized what she'd meant and came running out of the house. "No! Astrid, no!" he shouted trying to grab the side of her car and she turned to go down the driveway. She gunned the engine. "Astrid, no!" he tried to hold on, but she swung a sharp right and knocked him off. Not stopping to find out if he was alright, she raced down the drive. Max ran into the house and grabbed his keys then raced down the driveway after her. Having noticed Jackson's car out front, Sara ran inside to find him.

Max drove as fast as his Jaguar and afternoon traffic would allow. Although he knew she'd only said all that nonsense about him bringing her there to kill her to hurt him, at least he hoped, it still felt like the most logical place she'd go. It was safe, secluded, and somewhere she'd been happy. Unless of course she really did believe, *No, that's ridiculous,* he thought to himself.

When she wasn't there, he wasn't sure whether he was relieved or frustrated. It had been the only clue she'd left of where she might be. He pulled the car over to the side of the road to give himself a moment to both catch his breath and to try to think of where she would have gone instead. Every time his mind tried to imagine her hurting herself because of him, he gritted his teeth and shook his head refusing to let the thought take root. *When exactly did you become the monster you swore to protect her from,* he couldn't refrain from asking himself. Gripping the steering wheel as tight as he could and enjoying the pain it caused his hand, Max took a deep breath. *You fool,* his mind refused to be silenced, *you lied, manipulated, and confused her for your own selfish gain. You've worked to be considered intimidating, forceful, and dangerous and now? Now you're going to try to convince the most beautiful, compassionate, and loving woman you've ever met that you're not a monster? Good luck with that!* Deciding inaction would certainly lead to the disintegration of his sanity, Max pulled his car back onto the road to head toward the West River Parkway. She loved the river and regardless of her comment about harming herself, it was as likely a place as any for her to escape to. Meanwhile, he called Sara, "Are you with Jackson?"

"Yes, we left after you did and are driving over to the Loring Park area. I thought we'd check the Sculpture Garden," she said softly.

"Good idea. She loves that place," he responded just as softly. "Can you give Tom a call and ask him to head over to Lake Street and near the Institute? She uh…she wasn't where I was hoping she'd gone."

"I'll call him. Try not to worry, Max." He hung up without answering her and she quickly called Tom. "Tom there's been a…well, situation." She explained to him what she could and as she knew, he was eager to join the search. Always conscious of his tender heart, she was careful about what exactly she said about how Astrid left.

When she hung up with him, Jackson said, "You sugar-coated that pretty well."

"I couldn't tell him what she'd said. About harming herself. Not after what happened with that other girl that meant so much to him. He cares so much about people and…"

"And you think he needs a mother hen to look after him?"

"I'm not trying to be a mother hen it's just…he's so kind and things like this seem to affect him differently than you two," she said frowning at him.

"You're learning to keep secrets as well as Max does," he said under his breath. He didn't have to look at her to know she'd have been hurt by his words. "I'm sorry, Sara," he said quietly hoping she'd let it go and was relieved when she did.

Max drove in silence with the image of Astrid's heartbroken face right in front of him. Her bright yellow Volkswagen Beetle should be fairly easy to spot, but he didn't see any yellow cars or any Volkswagen Beetles of any color anywhere as if they'd all suddenly vanished. *The first day you met her you introduced yourself as working for her publisher. You wouldn't know a sci-fi book from a historical novel. You're a hired thug working for a bigger thug,* his mind reminded himself as he drove along the water wondering what in the hell he was going to do if he didn't find her and noticing the time ticking away. The more time ticked by the farther away she seemed; so he rolled his watch over so that he couldn't see the face then reached over and reset the dash clock several hours behind. It was the only way he could think of to control time.

CHAPTER 21

When he didn't find Astrid's car near the Institute, Tom returned to Max's house remembering Max had her car lojacked just a few days ago. As soon as Tom thought he had something he called Jackson.

"Yeah? Any news?"

"Yes. According to the computer she's headed south on Zenith Street toward West 38ᵗʰ Street."

"The computer?"

"Max had her lojacked a few days ago."

"Jeez, I wished we'd have thought of that before," Jackson said shaking his head.

"I think we just panicked," Tom said with a chuckle. "Are you anywhere near Zenith Street?"

"That's not too far from us. Let Max know we have a lead, he's still down by the river." Jackson hung up unsure what they'd do or say when they caught up with her, but at least they'd know she was safe.

"Are we close?" Sara asked anxiously.

"Yeah," He looked over at his sister's worried face. "It's okay. We'll get there and talk some sense into her. As much as Max is worried about what she'll do, I don't think she'd really try to hurt herself. She's been through a lot of crap in her life. She's a fighter, she'll keep fighting."

"I hope you're right. Max couldn't take it if..." Sara couldn't bring herself to finish the sentence which was just as well as her phone began to ring. It was Tom again, "Yes?" She turned to Jackson, "She's on East Calhoun Parkway." She turned her attention back to the phone, "Okay,

Tom we're headed there. What? Jackson, he says she's turned right onto West Thirty-Sixth Street." Sara held onto the phone feeling her emotions were running all over the place. She was worried for Max, worried for Astrid and feeling guilty for her part in hurting her, and she was worried about Tom. He'd hated the deception from the very beginning. He'd been afraid something like this would happen. "Okay, Tom," she said softly then turned to Jackson, "She's turned left on Park Avenue. She must be going to Lake Street."

She stayed on the phone with Tom as they kept driving and a few minutes later she heard him shout, "Oh, no. Sara, you guys...hurry."

"What is it, Tom? What's happened?"

"According to the computer...she's crashed right there at that old cemetery."

"What old cemetery?"

"The one on Lake Street and Cedar Avenue."

"I don't remember any cemetery over there," Jackson said.

"It's uh...uh the Pioneers and Soldiers Memorial Cemetery," Tom said. The minutes seemed like hours as he waited for them to get to the sight registering on the lojack website. "It's the oldest cemetery in Minnesota built in 1853."

"I take it you've been there, researched it?" Sara said with a smile knowing how much Tom loved history.

Her smile faded when she heard the sound of his voice as he responded, "It's quite sad really. Half of the twenty thousand residents are children."

"We're almost there now, Tom...we're...Jackson?" Jackson had pulled up next to a police car. "Tom, I'll call you back. She's crashed into a stone pillar and the police are already here. I'll call back." She hung up the phone and rushed to catch up with Jackson already out of the car. They slowly approached the officer already on scene. The little car was totaled. It had plowed head on into one of the decorative stone pillars that connected the rod iron fence that surrounded the cemetery.

"Hold on you two," the officer said putting his hand up to stop them coming any further toward the car.

Jackson held Sara's hand and told the officer. "It's alright, officer. She's a friend of ours. How badly is she hurt?"

"We don't know. No one is in the vehicle. You say you know the owner?"

Sara raced to the car. "What do you mean she's not in the vehicle? Where is she?" Sara looked in the car, "Why didn't the airbags deploy?"

The officer shook his head explaining, "These old cars often don't have airbags or when they've been in accidents they don't get them reset. We see that sort of thing all the time."

"So she could be really hurt!" There was blood smeared in a few places and Astrid's handbag was in the passenger seat. Sara looked up at her twin, "Jackson, where is she?"

Jackson shook his head putting his arm around her and listened as the officer spoke into his radio then turned back to them, "We've got a couple officers scouting the area. The strange thing is that there doesn't seem to be any tire tracks. Looks like she didn't even try to hit the brakes. When I arrived on the scene the door was already open, but it doesn't appear as if she fell out. Most likely she just wandered off, but…if there was any kind of head injury…," Someone called on his radio and he walked away to answer it.

Sara called Tom. "Have you called Max?"

"He called me and I had him come back to the house. He's just pulling up now. What's the latest…," Sara told him everything this time including the officer's comment about her not hitting the brakes. He was silent a moment digesting all the information then softly said, "Okay. I'll let him know. Are you two coming back? He's just walked in…yeah, okay." Tom put his phone away as Max rushed into the study.

"Is she here?"

"No. Max…"

"Well, have Jackson and Sara got her?" He asked frowning.

"No. Max…I…"

"I thought that was why you had me come back. Damn it, man." He started to turn away and Tom stopped him by grabbing his arm.

"Max!" Tom took a deep breath and looked Max in the eyes. "We found her car."

Max stood motionless a moment as Tom held his eye contact. "What do you mean you found her car?" He had seen Tom in this pose before. Keep eye contact, make the person aware of the seriousness of the situation, just like he does when he's got bad news for a patient.

Tom moved over to the desk and sat on the edge. "The car was found totaled. It ran into a stone pillar outside the old cemetery. When the cops got there she wasn't inside."

Max swallowed hard and tried to assess the situation. "Could she have been thrown?"

"The cops say no. They're looking around in case she just walked away."

"What else, Tom? There's something on your mind you're not wanting to say."

Tom half smiled. Max knew him well. Hiding anything was not an option. "There was some blood in the car. Her handbag with her wallet and i.d. are still in the passenger seat."

"You're thinking someone took her?" Max frowned thinking of whether or not it was a plausible answer.

Tom nodded slowly. "If she just left, why didn't she take her bag? Why haven't they found her?" Tom tucked his head down a moment then said, "Sara told me what happened, but I can't believe she'd really just up and walk away? For that matter, could she just walk away with whatever injuries she sustained? There were no airbags in that beat up old thing."

Max turned to leave. "Heiss," he said with disgust, "If he took her, I'll kill him," and he started for the door.

"Max! Wait!" He stopped just at the door. "How would he even know where she was?"

"He's been watching her ever since the day I was not answering calls."

"Okay, but you are in no condition to go anywhere. Stay here in case she calls or something. I'll go see Ivan and find out if he knows anything

217

about any of this. Remember, we've got that venal witch to worry about as well. It may not be Ivan and pissing him off will only complicate things." Tom understood the anger and frustration on Max's face, but he knew that anger sometimes made you make mistakes. Max was in no condition to meet with Ivan Bronius about anything especially not about the woman he loved.

"Tom, you know how Heiss works. If he's been given this assignment he'll have already...," Max bent his head down and sighed, "he'll have already killed her."

"Maybe not," Max was slowly shaking his head, "I'm very good at keeping things calm. Trust me to handle Ivan. Right now that formidable temper of yours could make this a lot worse," he smiled, "Not that you don't have reason. I know what she means to you."

Max stared at his old friend a few moments then admitting he had a point and his friend was only watching his back, Max nodded and turned back toward the study. "Tom."

"Yeah?"

Max sighed heavily, "Nothing just...let me know...when you know."

"You know I will."

Max briefly looked out the window as Tom got into his car. It was already dark outside. He didn't know what worried him the most, someone having taken her or her being out there alone and injured in the dark somewhere. She was hurting emotionally and now physically. She was angry, frustrated and worst of all sad, hurt, and feeling all alone. He knew what it felt like when you thought someone didn't give a damn about you; his father had made sure he knew that feeling. That was how Astrid felt when she'd left. Right now she felt as if she had no one to turn to and he'd done it; he'd made her feel that way. Knowing how that felt; the emptiness, the loneliness, *how could you have done that to her,* he asked himself shaking his head back and forth. He rubbed absentmindedly at the ache in his chest. Suddenly he swept his arm across his desk. Most things went immediately to the floor, but the bud vase flew and slammed into the wall before falling to the floor as broken glass and mangled flower. Seeing it hit the wall, Max saw his father slapping his mother to the ground and white hot pain ripped through his chest. The flowers that before had been a comfort now seared him with pain at the thought of being comforted knowing he didn't deserve it. Then a thought suddenly occurred to him, would comfort even be offered? The not knowing, the possibility that she would rebuke him was nearly paralyzing. With a loud, guttural yell he flipped the credenza overtop itself; papers, maps, the printer, and a camera all hit the floor. Adrenalin pumping, the coffee table was flipped upside down sending the candy dish crashing with little chocolate candies going everywhere. The little gnome figures that had so enchanted Astrid when she'd first arrived were tossed in all directions. Stomping to the fireplace to sweep off the mantle, he spotted the music box. The room quieted as papers drifted down to the floor and things that were rolling found stopping spots. He slowly picked up the box and opened it. As the music began to play, his mind drifted to his Mother, Ermina, Jackson, Manette, Sara and Tom; all the people who would be so disappointed by his actions and gently he closed it and put it back on the mantle next to Astrid's little spun glass piano. With his energy drained away and with his shoulder braced against the mantle, he gazed into the fire thinking about the day she'd looked into his eyes and told him about what the little piano meant to her.

♣

Astrid came into the study unnoticed. Max was standing by the mantle staring into the fire holding her grandmother's piano. Sensing a presence he glanced her direction and blinked several times trying to make sense of what he was seeing. Seeing the mess all around the room, she pointed at the fragile piece he held in his hand and said, "Thank you for not breaking it."

Relief overwhelmed him as he rushed to her and put his arms around her. "I would never break something that means so much to you," he whispered in her ear. Astrid did not return his embrace and the absence of her arms caused him to step back. Watching her looking around the room at the mess he'd made, he felt a little embarrassed. "I'm glad you're alright. Who found you," he asked looking behind her to see if she was with someone.

"No one found me," she said as he placed the piano back in its place. "I came here on my own. Max, I…I never had any intention of hurting myself. I just wanted…to hurt you."

Max took one step closer to her, "You succeeded," he said quietly. He noticed her rigid posture and cool tone. She was obviously still upset with him, but at least she was safe. "There was blood in the car. Are you injured? Maybe we should have you checked out at the hospital." He noticed the bruise and cut on her forehead and there was something wrong with her hand. He tried to reach for it, but she backed away. He backed off, not wanting her to feel the need to leave again.

"I don't need a hospital." She looked up into his eyes and the expression on her face puzzled him. "I cut my hand myself."

"What? Why?"

"After the crash I sat in the car a moment thinking or maybe brooding is a better word. I cut my hand and spread the blood around the inside of the car, grabbed some cash from my wallet and left." She glanced down at the carpet then back into his face. "I wanted to stay away and make you suffer," she said as a tear made its way down her cheek.

"I understand, Astrid," he said wanting to wipe the tear from her face, but unsure if she'd welcome the contact.

"I wanted you to see how it felt to have no control, no power, and no ability to change the situation you were in. I wanted you to be worried and frustrated." Tears continued down her cheeks as she gazed into his crystal blue eyes. "I wanted you to wonder if I was hurt or dead. I wanted you to feel all alone and lost." Max nodded his head understanding her need to punish him. Wanting desperately to comfort her, he moved toward her, but she put a hand up to stop him. "I wanted to stay away, but I couldn't. It was a horrible thing to do and I'm sorry. Regardless of how much you've hurt me, it was a horrible thing to put you through." She was taking deep breaths trying to get herself under control. "Could you ever forgive me?"

His hand reached up and gently stroked her cheek as he smiled tenderly at her. "Of course I can. I don't blame you for wanting to punish me. I wanted to punish myself. Astrid, I do love you. I think a part of you knows that. You knew how much it would hurt me to not know where you were; to wonder if you were alright." He gave her a little grin. "It damned near destroyed me."

"I'm sorry," she whispered. "I'm a terrible, cold, heartless person. I don't blame you if you never…"

"Shhh," he said and unable to restrain himself any longer, took her in his arms and gently kissed her quivering lips.

"I'm everything my family always said, horrible, evil and treacherous."

"No," he said holding her face in his hands, "no, you're not."

"Yes, I am. You should hate me," she said sadly as the tears coursed down her face.

"Enough of that. Hate you? Not on your worst day," he said smiling softly. "You are none of those things you said. That's why you came back. Arranging the kidnapping was wrong, keeping it from you was wrong." He took her injured hand and examined the cuts. "Everything I told you about myself, the feelings I told you I felt for you, all of that was real. It was all real. I never lied to you. I kept things from you, but I never lied to you." He waited for her to respond, but she didn't. Taking a steadying breath he said quietly, "I have the eyes of a monster," he looked down at her hand resting in his, "but I wish you could believe that I am not one. I know I hurt you, but I didn't mean to. I never want anyone to hurt you ever again…especially someone you trust or that…," his eyes met hers, "that you should be able to trust." Precious, sea-goddess eyes searched his, but still she didn't give him any indication of how she felt. "Let me clean this up for you." He guided her to the sink and cleaned her wound. Examining the bruise on her head, he said, "Are you sure you're alright? This bruise looks pretty bad, did you black out at all?"

She slowly pulled away from him. "I'm just tired. I can't think about anymore of this right now." She put a hand up to her head and her words came out slowly. "I don't know what I feel or what I think you feel. I don't really know if you were truly upset I was gone or if you were just disappointed I'd left without telling you everything you wanted to know about the book."

"Cashmere, no," he touched a hand to her cheek, "I was worried about you…the woman I love. The damn book never even came into my head."

"I'm just tired. I'm going to go upstairs and lie down. Could we just talk about this tomorrow?"

Although hesitant to let her go before they finished working things out, he had to admit she looked exhausted and nodded his head saying, "Of course." She slowly started up the stairs as he turned his back to call the others and let them know she was alright. "Hey Tom, let everyone know it's alright she's…*helvete!*" he heard a crash and rushed into the foyer to see Astrid lying at the bottom of the stairs.

CHAPTER 22

Tom heard the phone fall and although he didn't speak Swedish, he'd heard Max use that particular expletive enough to know it was *hell* and something wasn't good. Stopping his car, he shouted into the phone, "Max! Max!"

Max rushed back to grab his phone he'd thrown and went back to Astrid. Breathing heavily he yelled into the phone, "Tom! *Hon föll ner för trapporna! Hon föll ner för trapporna! Få här snabbt!*"

"Max?" Tom said, shaking his head. He's never heard Max explode into Swedish before, clearly not a good sign. "Slow down! Tell me in English."

"*Få här snabbt!*"

"Max! Say it in English."

Max took a shaky breath, "She's...she's fallen down the stairs...get here quick."

"Max, don't move her!" Tom said. "Max!"

"What?" Max answered, distracted as he gently wiped the hair out of her face.

"Don't pick her up. I know you want to, but don't pick her up. She may have hurt her back in the fall. Max?"

"Okay, okay...," Max growled something incoherent trying not to panic, but lost the battle and yelled, "*skynda på...skynda på. För fan!*"

"Max...English," Tom shouted back, "English!"

Max took a deep breath trying to regain some control of his temper. "Some of it was hurry up...the rest...isn't worth translating." He shook his head and whispered, "Tom, just please...please hurry."

"Take a breath. I'm minutes from you," Tom kept his voice calm trying to reassure his friend who is usually so cool and in control. "Is she awake? Is she responding to you?" he could hear Max softly calling her name.

Max was gently rubbing her cheek noticing how cold it was. "No." he said worriedly. "She's not responding." He bent his head down to lay his cheek against hers, "*Inget ljud alls*," he whispered to himself. *No sound at all.*

"How'd she get there?"

"I don't know. She just came in a few minutes ago. We talked and then she said she was tired and was going upstairs to lie down. She was acting a little dazed, I just figured she was tired." He rubbed a hand through his hair frustrated with himself all over again for this whole ordeal. "*Det finns en knöd på huvudet alla lila och blåmärken.*"

"Say it again," Tom said patiently, hearing the sad tone to Max's voice.

Max closed his eyes a moment and swallowed hard, "There…there is a lump on her head," he paused to steady his breathing, "it's…bruised and purple. It happened in the accident."

"I'm almost to your place now, Max. I'm hanging up to call the paramedics," Tom said and hung up not waiting for Max to respond.

Max hung up his phone and leaned down to place a soft kiss on Astrid's cheek. "*Jag älskar dig,*" he said brokenly, "*Jag älskar dig.*" His words of love all he could think to say, he called Sara to let her know what was happening and see if she'd meet him at the hospital.

♣

As Max watched Astrid's monitors in the hospital room he felt his sister's eyes upon him, "It's alright, Sara. I know what you're thinking," he said letting out a long breath. "I deserve this. All of this."

"Max," Sara said softly, frowning at him, "You don't really believe that?"

Running a hand through his hair, he sat down hard in the chair next to the bed. "I know you think I'm just a mindless, heartless thug that doesn't deserve her and I won't argue with you. Just another bully like our father. A monster."

Quickly coming to his side, Sara reached out and grabbed his hands. "Max, I have never, ever thought that of you. I know I've…I've said some hurtful things lately," she said on a sniffle.

Max looked up at her and wiped the tears from her cheek. "Don't worry about it. We are siblings. No one is more effective for getting under your skin than a sibling," he said dismissively.

"Max," she said, not letting him excuse her behavior or to avoid the subject. "I'm sorry. Truly I am. I didn't want to hurt you. I've just…been so worried about you. You've tried so hard to protect yourself that sometimes…I just think maybe you've over protected your heart a bit. I think Astrid is very good for you and I want you to be happy." As she stroked his cheek, his eyes closed briefly to that tender caress and he took a deep cleansing breath.

"I appreciate what you're saying, but I see the censure on your face."

"It's just that," she stepped back to sit in the chair opposite of him, "I'm worried for Tom. He cares about her, too and…he was afraid something like this would happen because of…of all the secrets and…"

Max nodded his head, "I know," his heavy sigh hung on the air as they sat together listening to Astrid's monitors.

An hour later Jackson came in with coffee for Sara and Max. "Any change?"

"Not yet," Max said taking the coffee. "Sara went out to the courtyard to make a few calls." Jackson nodded and set her coffee on the table beside Astrid's bed. "Did you talk to Ivan?"

"I told him you were out of commission for a bit, but…you know him."

The two men fell silent for a few minutes, Max drinking the terrible coffee and Jackson going over to the window to stare out. As he walked back to sit next to his brother, Max said, "You know…you were right about telling her. It would have made all the difference if she'd heard it from me the right way." He smiled at his tall little brother, "I guess we all know you're the brains of the outfit."

Jackson looked at him and snorted, "Right. That's why Ivan has never given me a case of my own."

"Is that what's been bugging you?" Max had noticed that the last several weeks his brother hadn't quite been himself. "Jackson, I'm sure that he's only…"

"Max," he said waving a hand, "Don't. I don't need the music box."

"You never did," he said quietly, "I played it for Sara. I was trying to…take care of you two and protect you."

"Maybe you've been trying to protect too much."

"I know you're still upset about my not telling you before about the rack and…and all that business."

"Jeez, Max! Stop trying to clean up his mess. Stop trying so hard to make up for our parents short-comings."

"I wanted you to have a better relationship."

Jackson looked at Max as if his head had just spun around on its axis. "A relationship? With a monster?"

"He wasn't the same with you as he was with me. I thought…"

"No, he wasn't. He was completely indifferent to Sara and I. We only mattered to him as pawns against you, but you…you weren't indifferent, you cared and we knew it. We deserved to know what he was doing to you instead of constantly being told everything was fine. We weren't stupid or blind or as indifferent as he was. We gave a damn what was happening to you." Jackson ran his hand through his hair and sighed heavily. "That day I came to your room and your eye was swollen shut and your nose was broken…Father did that, didn't he?" Max nodded, but didn't look up. "You told me that you'd had an altercation with Manette's boyfriend. When we all came to America I asked her about it, but she wouldn't tell me anything. I think she considered it your job…so do I."

"It's in the past, Jackson."

Jackson walked over to Astrid's bed and gently touched her hand before turning back to his brother. "I hope you've told her more than you've told us. Or should I say me? Sara certainly seems to know more than I do."

"Jackson,"

"I guess she's able to handle the truth better than I am."

"She has gotten most of her information from the damn servants! They told her things she never needed to know. The day I left I gave her the music box and told her to play it for herself whenever she was sad. She was always so…fragile. I couldn't have left at all if you hadn't been there to watch over her. You were always stronger than the rest of us."

"Please don't try to blow smoke up my ass, Max. We all know, beat all odds, Max; stronger, tougher, never say die…Super Max!"

"My strength comes from the love our mother gave me; keeping myself going for her sake and to do what I could for you and Sara. Your strength is stronger because you forged your own heart and soul yourself with no mother and no father. You raised yourself to be the man that you are."

Jackson went to the door, "Don't you see? Watching you…trying to be you…trying to prove that I'm not just a screw up…that is what made me and so far…I haven't proven a damn thing to anyone. Not even myself." He left Max sitting alone, shaking his head in bewilderment.

♣

Astrid woke up and looked around trying to figure out her surroundings. The last thing she remembered she'd gone back to Max's house, but this was not a place she recognized. This was some kind of medical facility. She slowly turned her head and saw Max sitting, rather uncomfortably, in a chair beside her bed. He hadn't shaved, his hair looked as though he'd been rubbing his hand through it. She remembered seeing him doing that often when he was angry or stressed. There was a tube in her nose and an i.v. in her arm. What happened to her? Just then Tom came quietly into the room. He looked down at her and smiled.

227

"You're awake." Max was startled awake and immediately grabbed Astrid's hand.

"Why am I here?" she asked in a raspy whisper.

"What do you remember, honey?"

Astrid blinked a few times and glanced at Max, but his face held so much worry she turned away to look at Tom. Remembering what she'd done, she cast her eyes down and said softly, "I remember going back to Max's house. I…" Tears formed in her eyes and one spilled over causing Max's heart to quiver. "…I…I was angry and I…" she looked back at Max, "I'm sorry."

"Don't upset yourself. It doesn't matter."

She turned back to Tom, "I wanted to punish him. I…put the blood in the car and ran off. I'm sorry, Tom. I know he's your friend and I intentionally hurt him. It was…cruel and…"

"Shhh, Astrid," Max whispered.

Tom smiled gently at her, "Well, a little wake-up call might be just what he needed." Max looked up at him and frowned, but said nothing, not wanting to give Tom the opportunity to elaborate. "When you crashed the car, do you remember blacking out?"

"No, I…I don't remember."

"Well, you had a concussion and passed out after you got to Max's house," he said checking something on her chart. "You scared him so badly his Swedish came out like gunfire."

"Well, he was angry with me for…"

"No, Astrid," Tom said interrupting her and laying a gentle hand on her arm, "It wasn't anger," he smiled turning from her to Max and back again, "Face it honey, you're Superman's kryptonite."

She looked into Max's eyes, "I'm sorry," she said softly. He smiled at her and squeezed her hand. Turning back to Tom she said, "I remember being there, seeing the mess all over the floor, and seeing Max's head bent down as he stood at the fireplace and wondering…wondering if he could ever forgive me. I'm not sure about anything else."

"That's alright. It may come later. We've got another test to run this afternoon and then if all goes well, tomorrow you can go home." Tom closed his pen watching the couple staring into each other's eyes saying so much with no words and walked out the door unnoticed.

Max's phone vibrated and he looked down at it. "If you need to be somewhere…," Astrid started to say, but he shook his head.

"Only place I need to be is right here. I'm just…," he took a deep breath and sighed, "I'm just a little worried about Jackson."

"Has something happened?" He just shook his head, "Maxim, please share with me what's on your mind."

Max looked down at his feet frowning, but knowing if he'd just shared before things wouldn't be in such a mess, "It just feels lately like we're a little disconnected. Astrid, when the two of you talked…hell, I'm not sure what I'm asking," he said frustrated with himself and running a hand through his hair.

"Are you asking if he divulged any of your deep dark secrets?"

He looked at her smiling face and took her hand to place a kiss on it. "No," he said with a sad smile, "Cashmere," he frowned as is unsure of what he wanted to say, "Part of your being a witch is your ability to empathize with others. I remember when you first met him and you said to him that it must be difficult to be my brother. I'd like to know what you meant. I want to understand him, but lately…I know I'm a perfectionist, obsessive, maybe overbearing at times. I tend to be a hothead and I…"

"Max," she said with a patient smile and shaking her head. "The difficulty he has in being your younger brother isn't about you. It's about him. He gets a little lost in the shadow. No matter how hard he tries…his body doesn't fit it." Astrid reached out and stroked Max's cheek. "He's taller, thinner and an entirely different man. He's just having a little trouble understanding that and accepting that it's okay. He's standing behind a really large shadow."

"I don't want him behind me. I want him beside me."

"He has to figure that out for himself, but you are a good brother, Max. Just let him find his way." Max nodded and again breathed a heavy sigh looking at his phone. "You look tired," Astrid said softly, "You stayed all night, didn't you?"

"I'm fine. I dozed off in the chair a while."

"You don't need to stay. I'll be fine."

"I have nowhere else I need to be."

"I doubt that's true."

"Besides, I want to be with you," he said smiling and leaning in to give her a kiss. She didn't push him away, but he felt something was definitely still wrong between them. "I know you're still unsure about…"

"I'm sure Ivan has been trying to call you and really, Max, I'll rest better knowing you're getting some rest as well." Max stepped back uncertainly. "I just want to nap a little before the test later."

"Alright, I'll…uh…go home and clean up and see you this evening." The little smile she gave him as he walked out did nothing to change the feeling in his gut that there were still barriers between them.

♣

When he returned to the hospital, rested and cleaned up, Astrid was already asleep. Apparently after her test she'd complained of a headache. They'd given her a sedative to help her relax and she was resting peacefully. Max stayed a few hours watching over her, until he got a text from Ivan. Since he said it was related to Astrid and he was really doing no one any good just watching her sleep, he left to go see his boss and take his mind off of the thought that maybe she hadn't wanted to see him. As soon as he got to Ivan's office he recognized full pandemonium had descended. The secretary's desk had been taken over by two of their best I.T. guys and they were so intent on what they were doing they didn't even bother to look up at him. Inside the heavy oak door were two other agents of the alliance as well as Heiss and Tom. "What's going on?" he asked the first person that noticed him standing there, but they continued their walk over to Ivan's desk. Looking that direction he was surprised to see Ivan's brother, Erik standing next to the desk. Whatever was happening must be big as the illusive brother had not been active in

230

the alliance for some time. After he'd been severely injured he'd endured extensive surgeries to his right hand to try to regain the use of it. The fact that he wore a glove on it and was holding it behind his back, Max had the impression that the procedures had not been successful. He sometimes wondered if Ivan kept Erik hidden to hide his own failure to keep his brother safe or to keep other agents from contemplating the occasional danger they were all in. Seeing another agent whose face he recognized, Max asked again, "What's going on?"

"She's been spotted," the petit brunette told him. "Agent Griffith saw her in the hospital parking lot just a few hours ago."

"Who?" As the little brunette had moved off to show some paper to Ivan, he made a bee line for Tom. "Who did you spot, Agent Griffith?"

"Astrid's supposed twin," he said grinning. "There can be no doubt now about Astrid's story. She was having an MRI at the time that I saw this woman in the parking lot. Her story about the venal witch is true."

Max looked over at Ivan, "Well I never doubted her."

Ivan gave him a slight bow, "Are you going to stand there reveling in your being right or are you going to help catch her?"

Only now seeming to realize what they'd been saying, Max grabbed Tom's arm, "Wait, if you saw her at the hospital why did you leave Astrid unprotected?"

He turned and started out of the room, but Tom grabbed him. "She's been under surveillance since you brought her in. We know everyone that's been anywhere near her. She's perfectly safe, Max. I would not leave her in danger."

Max patted Tom's arm and took a deep breath. "I'm sorry. I know you wouldn't."

"It's alright, but you should know, her mother came to see her this afternoon."

"What? Why? How did she even know where she was?"

"Apparently one of the nurses asked if she had contacted her family and offered to do it for her. I think that's why that venal witch," he paused to look over at another agent, "What's her name?"

"Brenda," Max said.

Tom turned back to Max, "Like I was saying, I think that's why Brenda was at the hospital, she came with Astrid's mom. She didn't actually come into the hospital probably because she knows we're looking for her. In fact, Astrid's mom was trying to hide her own identity with sunglasses and a scarf and such."

The agent Max had spoken with earlier came back and Max looked down at her, noticing how she wrapped her arms around herself, much like he'd seen Astrid do when she was worried or upset. "Are we any closer to knowing why in the hell this woman is doing this to her own kind; putting all witches in danger, framing Astrid, and getting this family mixed up in all her mess?"

The little brunette's question hung in the air and she tried to hide her tears with her hand until Agent Heiss walked up. "Angelika," his Latvian accent for the first time to Max's ears sounded less robotic and almost tender, "Some people have no honor, no regard for life, and...to do this to this innocent young woman, no soul." He put his arm around the five foot woman and Max stood open mouthed and motionless a moment as she took the comfort offered by the enormous man next to her.

"There is a reason he is a guardian, Gunther. Try cutting him some slack," Ivan said reading Max's thoughts. "You are both difficult to understand and to deal with, but both of you are worth it."

Max looked at Ivan the Terrible and simply had no words for him. As Agent Heiss walked up to him he said, "Thank you for helping with clearing Astrid's name."

The tall Latvian looked down at Max. The kind expression he'd had on his face for the little brunette was gone and he'd replaced it with a sneer and his robot tone was firmly in place when he said, "The guilty should be punished not the innocent, but...I still do not like you."

"I don't like you either," Max said knowing they both sounded like school boys. When he heard Tom's chuckle he knew others were thinking the same thing and turned away to focus on the business at hand.

He spent the rest of the night with the other agents trying to hack into CCTV and contacting all the other agents in the North and South Dakota, Iowa and Wisconsin areas. Jackson showed up and helped out where he could. Ivan and his brother were dealing with Canada and the possibility that it was where she's been spending the bulk of her time.

CHAPTER 23

The next morning at the hospital Max was greeted with an even greater surprise than the one he'd found at Ivan's office. Astrid was up, dressed, and packed ready to leave, but she had a visitor. Entering the room, he slowly turned toward a woman in the room who had a definite look of Astrid about her. "Max, this is my sister, Kim."

"It's nice to meet you," he said cordially, but didn't smile. She didn't offer a smile either, but inclined her head slightly acknowledging the greeting.

He turned back to Astrid masterfully hiding his slight confusion to ask, "Ready to head home?"

"Yes, I...," she glanced at her sister waiting by the door, "Kim, could I have a few moments with Max alone, please?"

The sister dutifully walked out of the room and Astrid turned back to him. Before she could speak however, Max took several steps toward her asking, "Why is she here?"

"She's agreed to let me stay with her for a little while until I get things sorted out for myself," she said.

Max's mouth fell open for a moment before he blurted out, "Why in the hell would you do that?"

"I have the right to go where I choose."

"I know that," he said quickly, then took a deep breath to calm himself down, "Of course you do, but this isn't about rights. This is about safety! Astrid," he looked down at the floor briefly then took another step toward her looking deeply into her eyes, "If this is about the kidnapping…or the men I killed…I swear to you that you have no reason to fear me."

"I would love to use the excuse that my actions were driven by fear, but that's simply not true. I'm not afraid of you, Max," she said setting a hand gently on his left arm. "This isn't about you; it's about me."

"Yes, you. A grown woman who doesn't need a family that… locks her in closets, or steals her identity or makes her feel less than what she is."

"A grown woman," she said softly. The cashmere voice getting his attention more than a shout would have. "A grown woman who wound up in the hospital because her life was getting out of control and she didn't know what to do. I made a stupid choice and crashed my car to punish someone that…,"

"That deserved it."

"No. It was wrong and…," she took a deep breath and took his hands in hers, "Max, it's not who I am. You taught me that. I'm not a spiteful person, but I intentionally hurt you and that makes me believe that I need to step back from things and look at them more clearly. I was angry with you…not afraid and that's just not a good enough reason to do what I did."

"Astrid," he said softly, squeezing her hands gently, "these people have hurt you in the past. Do you really believe they're not going to hurt you now?"

"I'm not going to let anyone hurt me," she said firmly and he couldn't help but flinch thinking he was one of the *anyones*. "Thanks to you I am strong enough to face my situation. This is my life and I have to get figured out what I want out of it. That includes dealing with my family and deciding what part I'm willing to give them in my life." He shook his head, but didn't speak. "I know you don't like my choices, but they are mine to make. Manette brought me my things from your house. Thank you for everything you've done for me. I will never forget your patience and kindness."

"Where," he swallowed the lump in his throat, "where will you be?"

"I think right now, it's better if you don't know. Let me get things figured out and then…maybe I'll give you a ring and…we'll see. I still have the phone you got for me," she said softly.

His arms flexed with the effort to remain at his sides. Desperately trying to keep his emotions in check so that she understood his next comment was out of concern rather than desperation, he said calmly, "Please, Astrid," he blinked rapidly and briefly looked at the floor then back into her beautiful blue-green eyes, "If you need someone…if something should happen, please call me or…or Sara or Tom or Jackson, please just…call someone. Don't hesitate to call one of them because of your feelings toward me. I know you're upset with them for not telling you the truth about the kidnapping, but…,"

"Max, I know their loyalty lies with you just as it should. They've known you a lot longer and they trust your judgement."

He shook his head, "They all argued with me. They do care about you. Please call them if you need someone."

Astrid smiled and said softly, "Don't worry. I know I have friends I can call." He took a deep breath and she said, "Goodbye, Max. Take care of yourself." She turned to grab her bag and walked out of the room leaving Max standing alone.

Sara came to the hospital to see Astrid off, but the room was empty. She asked a nurse if she knew the whereabouts of Dr. Tom Griffith. The buxom blonde nurse smiled brightly, "Oh, yes. I know Tasty Tom! I'll see who's got him cornered!"

"What do you mean, cornered?"

The nurse laughed, "Well, we're all in a bit of a competition around here to snag him. Do you know him well?"

"Actually I…"

The nurse paused what she was doing and looked directly at Sara. Watery eyes, red nose, and sniffling, it was obvious she'd been crying. "Oh, you're one of his girls aren't you?"

"I beg your pardon?"

"They always come in crying, but don't worry, honey. He'll set you to rights, lucky girl."

"What? Uh…no. I'm not…What do you mean one of his girls?" Her earlier tears for Max and Astrid were quickly turning into tears of hurt for herself.

"Well, he does get a lot of friendly female visitors. They definitely keep him busy. A bit young some of them, but some guys go for that."

"What do some guys go for?" A short nurse with her black hair tied back in a ponytail asked as she approached.

"Girls rather than women," she answered.

They both laughed and the short nurse said, "Oh, Tom," in a way that made Sara want to scratch her eyes out.

Another nurse came up to them and they tried to hide their giggling. She was a beautiful brunette with a lovely smile that she directed first at Sara and then the other nurses. "Alright girls that's enough gossiping for this shift," she said with a laugh. "What's it about anyway?"

"The elusive Dr. Tom."

"I'm afraid with Tasty Tom we're all out of the running, we're too close to his age," she said giving Sara a wink.

"Maybe so," the blonde said, "but that doesn't stop me from trying, Evelyn. That sweet, shy way of his is too alluring to ignore. Eventually he'll want a real woman," she took a chart off the counter next to them.

"Sorry, Carrie," Evelyn told her as she walked away, "but you'll have to get in the back of a very long line."

"Hey, Sara," Tom said walking up to the two ladies. He gave Evelyn a little nod before turning back to Sara. "Everything alright?"

"No," Sara said turning and spotting Max down the hall, run straight into his arms. "Get me out of here, please."

"Sara, what's…?"

"Ask me all the brotherly questions you want to later. For now, just get me out of here."

Tom came rushing up to them. "Sara, what is it?"

Sara looked up at her brother and he got the message. "It's alright, Tom. I'll look after her." It was normally enough, but this time Max was stunned to see Tom stand his ground.

"No, it's not alright. Sara," he looked into her tear streaked face, "What is it? Is there something I can do to help?"

"I don't need *your* kind of help! Just leave me the hell alone, Dr. Griffith. I'm not one of your *girls*," she said angrily. Seeing her tremble in her brother's arms and looking at him with such pain in her eyes was too much for Tom. He ducked his head down and walked away. "Oh, Max," she whispered before turning her face into his chest and breaking down with heavy sobs.

Max walked her to her car and calmed her down. She didn't want to talk about whatever was going on and quite honestly he didn't feel like pressing the issue at the moment. Clearly he was no authority on women and little sisters fell into that category so he gave her a hug and watched her drive away. Shaking his head, he got in his own car and sat wondering where he was going to go to stop thinking.

♣

Max prowled around the empty house looking for something to occupy his mind. He'd spent so much time at the gym the last few weeks that Pete had practically banned him saying he was intimidating the other customers. With winter set in there was no gardening to be done out at the gazebo and the peace and solitude he used to feel...now just felt alone. As he prowled the house he noticed that although all the furnishings were the same, there was something decidedly different about the place now that Astrid had moved out. It wasn't anything he could explain or define, just a feeling of something lost. An energy that was no longer there. Even the comfort he used to get from the flowers seemed changed. As he walked past the mantel he couldn't stop himself from looking for the little glass piano that he knew wouldn't be there. There was a space where it was supposed to be and although it was a small space, it felt like a huge hole.

Going up the stairs he glanced into the room she'd occupied and immediately noticed the lack of spiral notebooks and pencils from the bedside tables. Manette had continued to provide the room with fresh flowers, but they almost seemed to droop a little knowing there was no one in the room to appreciate them. The little doily Astrid had kept on top of the dresser to place her jewelry on was gone. Walking toward the bed he noticed something on the floor and bent to pick it up. Smiling at the little blue manual pencil sharpener, Max shook his head. He given her an electric one, but she'd insisted on using the manual one at night, worried that she would disturb Max's sleep even though his room was two doors down the hall. The pillow he picked up and brought to his nose no longer held her smell. The sheets had been washed and every trace of Astrid seemed to have been cleaned away. He squeezed the pencil sharpener he'd placed in his pocket as he left the room and headed to the kitchen.

When he opened his coffee cabinet he noticed the special coffee Astrid had brought him from the American Swedish Institute was nearly empty.

"I've never seen you smile at an empty bag of coffee before," Manette said walking into the normally bright and sunny kitchen that today felt dark and gloomy.

Max looked up at her. "Well, I don't quite feel like me right now," he said quietly giving her a little smile.

"Is there something I can get you? Something you need?"

He smiled and shook his head, "What I need...you cannot give. For a small portion of my life I knew what if felt like to be loved. With all my oddities, moodiness, and many, many faults, she loved me," he said with another shake of his head, "Someone so wonderful loved me. I can't imagine going through the rest of my life without that."

"She still loves you, Max. Not the you she's seeing through her anger right now, but the real you that she fell in love with in the first place. She'll see that again...eventually."

"The problem is...she wasn't angry at the hospital. If anything she was very polite and," he looked out of the kitchen window a moment and

239

then back to his friend, "it was as if she was just saying good-bye to an acquaintance she'd seen on the street. Manette," he paused and looked into her eyes, "may I ask you a question?"

"Since you sign my paychecks I would have to say yes," she said smiling, but the smile soon faded looking into his pain filled eyes.

"Not as my employee," he said softly, "but as my oldest and dearest friend."

Manette reached out and took his hands, "Of course."

"Am I a good man?"

His voice was so calm and quiet and the way his eyes looked into hers she knew that although it seemed to her as a silly question, to him it was very serious and she asked him, "What does your heart tell you?"

"I...," he turned away from her to look out of the window again, "I honestly feel that I...I am trying to be, but...," he let out a heavy sigh looking to the floor, "when I look in the mirror and see my father's eyes looking back at me...I seem to see every mistake I've ever made right in front of me."

Manette wrapped her arms around him and said sincerely, "Even good men make mistakes, Max. Lily would be proud of the man you've become."

"I'm not so sure about that, but thank you," he said. The melancholy tone to his voice was not lost on her, but sensing there was really no more she could say she gave him another hug and handed him a small slice of pastry as if he were a child and a treat would make everything better.

Deciding it probably would, he ate it with a small grin and walked away just as his phone rang. "Yeah?" he said breathing a heavy sigh.

"We're having a crisis and I've got agents all over the place telling me they need personal time! Are you available now or not?"

Max almost smiled at Ivan's exasperated tone knowing it wasn't quite as much an epidemic as he was letting on. "Being that my personal life has imploded...I'm available."

"We got a report of a witch down at Minnehaha Creek. You're the closest not on assignment. She's apparently new to the area and heard about the spiritual energies over there. Just make sure she's safe and all. We've been trying to reach Agent Griffith, but he's not been returning calls or texts."

Max walked to his desk and sat down behind it, "Tom's got some personal things going on right now. I've got lots of time on my hands. I'll try to fill in for him."

"Well, you're not really a good replacement for his specialty, but I'm desperate." Max couldn't resist a little chuckle knowing the man was right, he wasn't a good replacement. "She's a hereditary witch named," he heard Ivan fumbling through his papers, "Name is…that can't be right…the report says her name is, Patty Ann. Isn't that the name of the character in Astrid's book?"

"Yes," Max said, "I'm on my way," and he hung up his phone.

"Max," Sara said from the doorway, "Is something wrong with Tom?"

Max stood up and grabbed his keys off his desk. "You know it is, Sara." He let out a deep breath at the confused expression on her face. "Honey, what is it you think Tom does in this alliance?"

Sara shuffled her feet looking down at the carpet as Max came around his desk. A finger under her chin had her looking up at him. "Same thing you do. Protect the witches from people who don't understand them."

"Aggressively, forcefully, beating the living daylight out of those that threaten them, and kill when necessary?"

She walked toward the window and pulled a tissue out of the box on Max's desk. "I don't know."

"Don't you?"

"Sometimes I think in all these years I've never truly known him and then at other times I would swear I knew him better than anyone. I can't imagine him doing the work you do. He's simply too sweet, too kind, I…Oh Max! I didn't mean…"

"It's alright, Sara. I know who and what I am. You know who and what Tom is."

"But I don't, Max! I...I apparently don't know at all! The way the nurses at the hospital describe him...," tears filled her eyes and she covered her mouth with the tissue unable to finish her sentence.

"I don't know how they described him, but I can describe him to you if you want." Sara turned to look at him and nodded her head. "Tom doesn't do my job in the alliance. We're not all a bunch of soldiers out to destroy the witch haters." He was rewarded with Sara's smile at his jest. "We all have our specialties. Mine just happens to be intimidation. I'm not really, as my nickname suggests, Hired Gun Gunther, any more than Tom is strictly what his nickname suggests."

"Which is?"

"Teddy Bear Tom," he said.

"You're kidding?" Max shook his head at her laughter. "What about One-Night?" Her brief smile coaxed out one of his own.

"That one doesn't fit me anymore," he said trying to glare at her, but not quite accomplishing it.

"Why is he called Teddy Bear?" she asked.

Max took her hand in his and looked into her eyes. "When we find witches who are children that have been...shall we say, unappreciated by their parents, or women who have been beaten and mistreated, Tom is the one who is called first. His compassion, kindness and ever abundant hope is what is needed first and foremost. The alliance is made up of many men with different specialties and his...is comfort."

"I...I can see that," she said giving him a weak smile.

"All those things you were telling him about meeting up with different men. I know you expected him to get angry, protective, or maybe express himself the way I do, but that's not his way."

"I just wanted him to care. I...wanted him to...," tears again filled her eyes.

"He does care. He has always cared, but he's not a Neanderthal like me that's going to tell you who you can go out with or forbid you to go somewhere. It would never occur to him that you were playing some kind of game; lying to him, trying to trick him. His compassion extends to your feelings and your right to choose for yourself. It was his understanding you wanted someone more…aggressive…that's just not his way. He can't be something he isn't so he's tried to let you find someone. It's been killing him, but he's done it."

"I don't want to *find* someone. I don't want him to be anything other than what he is, but…at the hospital they said…if he cares for me then why…why does he go out with young girls?"

Her attempt at anger made Max even more aware of her sadness. Max was truly bewildered and shook his head, "What?"

"They said he has girls, young ones that keep him busy."

"Honey, the only girls he has are the ones he helps through the alliance. Sometimes they've resorted to drugs or alcohol and he gets them into the hospital programs for that. Of course right now…he isn't helping anyone."

"Why," she asked, delicately blowing her nose.

"Because the thing he gives most to others is hope and he's lost his."

"I don't understand."

Max took her chin in his hand again and said firmly, "Are you really that blind?" The innocent, sad expression on her face answered his question and he shook his head wondering how it was possible that amidst all the darkness in his world she was able to stay so bright. "At the hospital you called him *Dr. Griffith*," tears once again rolled down her cheeks. "You cussed and got angry with him and you never do that. You don't even do that with me and we all know you want to. You told him to stay away from you as you cried in my arms. You told him you didn't need his kind of help." She reached for another tissue and he wrapped his arms around her. "Maybe…you were a little too caught up in your own feelings to notice, but…the pain was all over his face. Pain not just because you didn't want him, but he also felt the pain that you were in and knew that he couldn't help. It makes a man feel a bit…well, inadequate when the only help they can offer is not what's wanted or needed." Max stepped back and lifted her chin to look into her eyes. "On many occasions when I have been…let's just say a little angry at the world, he has said to me, *As long as there are angels like Sara in the world, darkness with never overshadow the light.* You are his hope and as far as he can tell…he's lost you." He reached around grabbed another tissue and handed it to her. "I have to go, honey. Will you please give some thought to what I've said? He's a good man…," he said, then giving his chest a rub, added, "Broken hearts are painful," as he walked out the door. Sara walked over to the fire and sat down on the sofa lost in thought.

CHAPTER 24

It was silly to think this new witch had anything to do with Astrid. It was an unusual name certainly, but that didn't necessarily mean anything, but *Astrid loved going down to the river,* he couldn't help thinking. As he raced out of the house he remembered the last time he'd raced there. He sat in his car, took a deep breath and reminded himself that it was all possible this had nothing to do with her.

Max smiled at the new little witch in the area. Patty Ann, named after her two grandmothers, was performing a seasonal ritual unaware she'd been spotted by anyone. In rural Georgia, where she was from, she'd often done her spells out in the open and no one had ever noticed her. Max explained to her about the alliance and that she'd be watched over, but she still had to exercise caution in public. Not everyone was tolerant to other's beliefs. As she drove away, Max couldn't help his disappointment that this little witch truly had nothing to do with Astrid. As he was driving he noticed the American Swedish Institute and laughed. Yet another reminder of Astrid. Using the excuse that he needed another bag of the coffee she'd gotten him hooked on from the institute, he turned his car into the parking lot.

It was as impressive as Astrid had described and the small courtyard had a peaceful and relaxing air about it. Deciding to indulge in the tour of the mansion, Max turned a corner and suddenly couldn't breathe. There she was, standing in front of him in a soft cashmere sweater the color of the Caribbean Sea. *Cashmere,* he thought to himself, *just like that first day I saw her; soft and delicate.* As the guests admired the architecture, Max admired the exquisite woman standing before him.

With a soft smile on her face as she asked him, "Guarding the witch?"

Max swallowed the lump in his throat. "No, I...," he grinned suddenly remembering why he was there, "I ran out of the coffee you bought me. Besides, I did promise you I'd visit one day. You were right it's...breathtaking," he said so warmly Astrid wasn't sure if he was talking about the mansion or her, his eyes said it was her. "May I ask...why you're here?" He'd missed her every day, but now that he saw her...and she was standing close enough to touch, he missed her more. *How is that possible,* he silently asked himself as he rubbed absently at his chest.

Looking shyly at the ground, Astrid said, "I've spent the last couple of weeks visiting the places I was the happiest. This is one of those places."

"I'm glad," he said sincerely. "Will you take fika with me? Talk with me a bit?" Feeling suddenly as nervous and inadequate as Tom usually was around Sara, he added quickly, "Have you had a chance yet to experience the café?" He grasped at every straw he could, "I have news about your book. I..."

"Max," her cashmere voice floated to him, "you don't have to use the book or anything else. I would like to take fika with you."

They sat sipping coffee in the little café overlooking Turnblad Mansion and reminiscing over the past few days as if they were talking with an old friend. The way they leaned toward each other and the way they gazed into each other's eyes, anyone passing by knew there was a lot more than friendship between them. Unable to put it off any longer, Max leaned forward and kissed her gently. A warm chill spread throughout his body. A strange sensation of comfort from the warmth that was Astrid and chill from the excitement of being able to touch her again. Raw emotion played over his face as he gazed into her eyes and said, "You are so beautiful."

Astrid leaned forward and returned his chaste kiss wrapping her arms around his neck and pulling him closer. "I've missed you, but I had…," she took a breath, gaining courage to tell him what she so desperately needed him to understand. "I had to show my family that I'm strong now. They can't bully me or control me anymore. I let them know I wasn't going to put up with anymore of their harassment." She smiled brightly, "It felt really good."

Max gazed into the blue-green eyes that slanted even more with her confidence radiating out of her. "I'm glad you showed them the Astrid I know; intelligent, compassionate, and brave."

"I had to leave them…disassociate myself from them…on my terms. Not yours and not theirs. Please…," she begged, holding his hand, "please, try to understand."

"I do and I think you should feel very proud of yourself."

"Max, I've…I've felt my Granna with me again." She smiled brightly, "I did what you said and put aside the hurt and just talked to her and…she's with me."

"I'm glad you've reconnected." She tipped her head down shyly and he noticed a bag in her lap. "You've made a purchase," he said, clearing his throat.

Astrid smiled brightly, "Yes, it's an ornament…you know, for the Christmas tree? I've never put up a tree or decorated before…it just seemed like a lot of trouble just for me, but this year…I've decided I'm worth it."

Max watched her face practically glowing and said, "Indeed you are. What is the ornament?"

"It's homemade from a little workshop in Sweden," she said taking it out of the bag, "They called it, 'a Butticki Tomte boy with book'," she chuckled softly, "but…I call him…Maxim." She held the little wooden doll in the palm of her hand as gently as if it was a real child. It had blonde hair and a red knitted hat and scarf and carefully in his hand he held a book that Astrid knew must surely be his favorite story.

For a moment, Max didn't know what to say, then with his throat tight and gently stroking her cheek, he said the only words that came to him, "I love you, Astrid. That hasn't changed."

She stared into his crystal blue eyes a moment then sat back in her chair blinking a few times and placing the ornament back in the bag. "The gift shop was just brimming with beautiful things. Christmas in Sweden must be truly enchanting."

"There is nothing like a Swedish Christmas. I'd love...," he swallowed and inched his chair closer to hers, "I'd love to take you there for *Jul*."

The eyes that gazed into hers were so warm she couldn't bear to turn away as she said softly, "I thought you said you were too much of a coward to go back and risk facing memories."

"With you there...I'd have my hero with me," he said with a grin.

His joke sent Astrid's mind back to the second day they'd known each other and he'd been attacked in the parking garage. It all seemed like such a long time ago. So much had happened since then. Leaning closer to smell his wonderful aftershave she said, "Maxim," then let herself give in and kissed him with all the passion she felt for him right in the middle of the cafe. With no further words spoken they left together hand in hand to spend the evening in each other's arms; at Max's house and in Max's bed making love as if the world were coming to an end and in each other's arms was exactly where they wanted to be when it did.

In the early hours of the morning, before the sun rose, Max received a call from Ivan demanding his presence. Smiling and giving a sleeping Astrid a kiss on her cheek, Max hurried out the door hoping to be back before she woke up.

♣

Jackson paced the study waiting for Max to get back from his talks with Ivan. He'd been gone all day and Jackson had spent all that time trying to figure out how to word what he had to tell his brother. It wasn't a good time to have to give him bad news. He was never in a good mood after speaking with his boss. He really hoped the old line of not shooting the messenger popped into Max's head. The front door slammed indicating Max was home. As Max entered the room Jackson looked like a deer caught in the headlights of an oncoming vehicle. "Jackson," Max said curiously. Jackson swallowed hard and tried to figure out how he was going to start the conversation he now had to have with his big brother. He rubbed his head back and forth a few times. "If you're doing that expecting a genie to pop out," Max said with a smirk, "I've got news for you." Jackson frowned and wiped his sweaty palms on his jeans as Max sat down at his desk looking at him. "I got everything sorted out with that damn Swedish warrior today. Everything is working out fine. To what do I owe the pleasure of your company?" He tried a little smile, but when Jackson just stared at him he tried another tactic. "Spit it out Jackson, what's your trouble? You know I'll fix it, just spit it out."

"I uh…I need to talk to you."

"Why do you look as though I'm going to devour you? Sit down, relax. By the way, I thought I'd take everyone out to dinner tonight. Where are Astrid and Sara? I imagine Sara will want to take Tom." He smiled at Jackson knowing the little romance kindling between Sara and Tom was driving Jackson nuts for some reason.

"That's what I needed to talk to you about."

"Tom and Sara? It doesn't bother me. I haven't been able to figure out why it bothers you." Max said turning on his computer.

"No. Not Sara. I wanted to talk to you about Astrid."

Max looked at him. "Okay, what about her?"

"She's gone." There he said it, how come he didn't feel relieved yet?

He stated it so plainly Max wasn't sure what he meant. "What do you mean, gone?" he asked curiously.

Jackson fidgeted with the keys in his pocket and looked briefly up at Max. "She's…she's gone. A cab came to take her back to the museum where she'd left her car yesterday and…she left."

"When?"

"This morning, shortly after you left."

Slowly Max stood up from his chair looking at his watch, "That was hours ago." After looking at his watch again, he ran a hand through his hair. "Why didn't you take her to get her car?"

"She asked me to wait here for you."

"Was she planning on going anywhere else? Did she say when…if she'd be back?" Max looked at his watch again then at his phone to make sure he hadn't missed any messages or calls. "Where else was she going," he nearly shouted.

Jackson wiped his sweating palms on his pants. "Please sit down. Sit down and I'll tell you what she asked me to tell you." Max sat down in the nearest chair and glared at his little brother. "She sent this notarized form to Ivan." He handed a copy to Max. "It gives all the rights to her first novel to you. She also left all the finished chapters of the second novel along with three spiral notebooks of notes in that box right there." He waved his hand towards a white file folder box with Astrid's doodles of flowers all over it. "She said it has everything she'd ever considered putting into the story. She wants no part of any of it." Max braced his elbows on his knees and put his head in his hands. "She's requested that any and all money that is generated from it be used to help anyone whose life had been damaged because of the things she'd written." Seeing his brother's distress Jackson spoke a little softer. "She also asked me to give you this when you got back." Jackson held out an envelope to Max.

Max looked up wearily. He had thought they were going to be okay. She hadn't told him she loved him since the crash, but he had hoped he had convinced her their love was real. Last night when they'd held each other it all seemed like it was finally working out. Maybe all it had really been was a final good-bye. Tired beyond his years he reached out and took the envelope from Jackson.

As he pulled the letter out, Jackson watched him; the big brother who had always looked after him and Sara was now crushed and defeated. He wished he knew something he could do to help. He hoped Astrid's letter would somehow soothe him, but within moments he realized that wasn't going to happen. Max jumped out of his seat knocking the chair over. He grabbed his keys off of his desk and ran out the door without a word. Jackson watched out the window as Max got in his car and sped off down the driveway. Taking a deep breath, Jackson slowly moved away from the window. It was all over; Max's real chance for happiness. He'd finally found someone he loved. Gently and quietly she'd melted the icy fortress down around his soul and he'd handed his heart to her, but it wasn't enough. He turned around and picked the letter up off the floor where Max had sent it flying. He crushed it in his fist feeling the need for the first time in his life to hit something, but being that it was an unnatural urge, the sensation went as quickly as it came. He didn't want to hit so much as he wanted to hold. He wanted to hold on to something; something to make him believe love could happen and could last. First his parent's terminal unhappiness and now Max's was stripped right out of his hands. Subconsciously he began to smooth out the letter in his hand. As he sat down he could hear his mother's music box playing in his head. The one Max always turned on when she was crying and he didn't want him and Sara to hear it. As if it mattered somehow, he laid the letter on the coffee table and continued smoothing out each and every crease he'd made in the paper until suddenly he frowned looking closer at what was in his hand. As he began reading a smile slowly spread across his face.

Max,

I know I shouldn't listen to anything my family says to me, but I couldn't help worrying when they said you only loved me because I had you under a spell. I had already worried about the same thing ever since you made me aware of powers. The day we spent at the gazebo you even told me that I'd put a spell on you. I know you were just kidding, but I couldn't get the thought out of my mind. I wanted you to have free choice to love…or not to. I hoped that if I left you alone for a while that any spell I may have done would be broken. At the institute when you said you still loved me I started to let myself believe it was real…until this morning. When I woke up alone and Jackson told me you were going to be meeting Ivan…all the doubts came back.

251

While I stayed with my family I got all the information I could about the woman my mother called Brenda. Yesterday before I saw you, I met with Ivan and told him everything I knew about her and my family's association with her. I also told him of a new book I want to write of children's fairy tales...all with happy endings! He really liked my ideas and we're looking forward to working on them.

So if it's not the book, and it's not information on my family, and it's not a spell...do you love me for just me? As for how I feel...I love you, Maxim. You've everything I ever wanted, but thought I'd never have. If you want me...if you love me, meet me at the gazebo at sunset. If you're not there I'll understand and move on. Even if you don't come I wish you well. You're a good man and deserve to be happy. I hope you find someone someday that you feel you can love enough to commit to.

Hoping to see you,

Astrid

Jackson's smile faded as he noticed the sun setting outside the window. What would she do if Max didn't get there in time?

♣

Max was wondering the same thing himself as he raced down the road. Would she leave? Where would she go if she did? Would he be able to find her? What was worse was that she would be thinking he didn't love her. She'd think her love for him meant nothing. He almost laughed at that; it was everything. Doing eighty miles an hour in a midnight blue Jaguar had already garnered him some attention from one cop and now he was being chased by two, but he wasn't stopping. The sun was almost set.

♣

Astrid sat at the gazebo watching the sun go down. She had let herself really believe Max would be there. As she sat in the dark a moment trying to pretend she was just deciding where to go, it was impossible to ignore the fact that she really didn't want to leave. Walking over to where he'd carved their initials into the pillar, she wanted to think maybe, just maybe he was simply late. If traffic was bad or...she shook her head. Tracing the M.G. plus A.M. in the wood, she wondered, *was it really just pretend? Was he just...playing a part?* Her finger traced the heart surrounding their initials three times before she realized she was stalling again and walked back into the gazebo to grab her handbag. There would be no tears this time she'd promised herself. Don't bet if you can't afford to lose. *It's for the best, right,* she asked herself, *you don't want him if it's not real.* She looked at her watch. The sun had set seven minutes ago. He wasn't coming, it was time to move on. It was time to make a new life without him. The trouble was she wasn't sure where she was going or what she was going to do. She walked down the gazebo steps and across the short walk to her car. *You're still stalling,* she fussed at herself as she sat in the car. Finally starting the engine, she pulled onto the road. She could hear sirens approaching and looked up to see a car speeding right towards her with three police cars in hot pursuit. It turned sideways in front of her blocking her exit and she recognized the car. "Max," she whispered, her hand going to her throat, almost afraid to believe it was really him. He jumped out and ran to her car. She sat stunned a moment as he tried to open her locked door.

Max shouted, "I know I'm late, but I'm here!" Two officers jumped from their vehicles and grabbed Max pulling his hands behind his back. Astrid opened her door as he begged, "Please, honey. Don't leave." They tried pulling him away, but he was fighting them. "I'm sorry I'm late. I was in a meeting all afternoon!" The officers pulled him back away from the woman who held his heart in the palm of her hand. "I don't care about the book. I don't care about the information on your family. I just love you." Sweat beaded across his forehead and dripped down his back and he didn't know what was worse the struggle with the officers or the struggle to find the right words to convince her how desperately he needed her. She stood shell-shocked as the blue lights flashed in the dark and dirt was kicked up in the scuffle. "I love you, Cashmere," he said softly. The officers forced him onto the ground putting a knee in his back to keep him still to handcuff him. His heart was hammering in his chest, but he didn't resist anymore. Looking up he searched her face. She hadn't responded and he didn't know if she believed him or not. They hauled him toward the police car and he felt a desperation he'd never felt before. "Please, Astrid. Please believe me. Don't...don't leave," he pleaded. "I won't...," he couldn't seem to catch his breath, "I won't be able to find you...I..."

Astrid hurried towards him nearly laughing at the absurdity of it all. "I do believe you," she said though happy tears. Her hand reached out to caress his face, "I love you," she said as the cops put him in the back of the car.

Finally able to take a deep cleansing breath he gave her a tremulous smile. "Call Tom," he told her through the window. "I'll be alright, now. Don't worry, just...be home waiting for me?" He asked.

"I'll be there," she promised.

♣

Max came in the front door quietly noticing all the lights were off in the house. Tom had managed to get him bailed out in record time and he was anxious to see Astrid. He hurried up the stairs to her room and crept in only to find an empty bed. Looking around he noticed her spiral notebook and pencils weren't in their usual place. The top of the vanity held no brush, comb or anything else of Astrid's, the drawers in the chest were empty. He frowned beginning to get worried all over again. She'd said she believed he loved her. She'd said she loved him, so why weren't her things back where they belonged? He sat on the foot of the bed and then it hit him. Laughing at himself, he marched out of her room and into his own. *Of course,* he thought, *she'd be in...* His thought stopped as he opened the door to his bedroom to find it dark and empty just like he was beginning to feel. *Where is she*, his tired mind asked. He didn't bother to take his clothes off or do any of the other readying for bed routines. He was tired, frustrated and he just didn't know what to do next. Spending most of the day dealing with Ivan, then racing to catch Astrid in time at the gazebo, then hanging out in a jail cell with a bunch of drunks, only to come home to an empty house. It seemed every time he thought things would be okay, life laughed in his face. Stretching out on the bed exhaustion took over and he let it, not sure if he wanted to eventually wake up or not.

CHAPTER 25

Astrid woke up and tried to straighten her legs. She'd fallen asleep in Max's chair with her legs underneath her. She didn't know how long she'd slept, but it was long enough to have cut off the circulation. As she slowly crawled out of the chair and stood, she glanced at the mantel clock. It was four o'clock in the morning. She had hoped Tom would be able to get Max out of jail quickly, but obviously things weren't going to be so simple. Walking to the foyer, she considered the staircase. She really should go up and get some sleep in a bed, but she wanted to be right at the door when Max came home. Besides, the thought of being in a bed without him wasn't appealing. Now that she knew he loved her, she didn't want to spend another night alone. She passed the stairs and went into the kitchen to fix a cup of coffee. She'd use Max's favorite blend, just in case he came home soon. She could never smell that delicious scent without thinking of him. Hoping Max would at least be home by breakfast, she spent the next few hours thinking up a breakfast menu and checking to see if she had the ingredients.

At eight o'clock the door finally opened and Astrid ran to it from the sitting room where she'd once again fallen asleep. "Hi!" Sara said coming in the door. "I hope you being here means everything is alright with you and Max? Jackson told me about the note you left, about him meeting you at the gazebo." Sara's smile was big enough to light up the whole room. "How romantic!"

Astrid tried to hide her disappointment that it wasn't Max at the door and smiled. "It was, very. He was late and just when I thought it was over, there he was."

"I noticed his car isn't out front, so where is my lovesick older brother anyway? I have to tease him, it's a sister's duty."

"He's not here. He got arrested."

Sara turned around from hanging up her handbag. "What? What for?"

Astrid gave her a sheepish grin. "Well, since he was running late to meet me, he was speeding. He was really, really speeding to the point that he had three cop cars coming in behind him as he drove up to the gazebo!" Both girls enjoyed a laugh picturing the scene. "I called Tom to bail him out, but apparently it's taking a while."

"What gazebo?"

"Oh, just uh…one we found one day," she said remembering Max's need to keep a few things, what he considered his weaknesses, private.

The ladies started for the kitchen when the door opened again. Sara noted the way Astrid spun around quickly, it was obvious she was hoping to see Max step through the door, but it was Tom. "Finally!" she said peering around him anxiously, "Where is he? Where's Max?"

"Isn't he here?"

Sara put her hands in her hips, "If he was here would she be asking 'where is he?'" Although she smiled, Tom turned away from her.

Looking at Astrid he said quietly, "I bailed him out just a couple hours after you called me. I even gave him a ride to his car they'd left on that piece of property out there in the middle of nowhere." He saw the worry etched on Astrid's face. "I'm sure everything is fine. Let me just try calling him." Astrid clasped her hands together to keep them from shaking as he dialed Max.

"Hello?" came a gruff voice at the other end.

Tom put a reassuring hand on Astrid's shoulder. "Where are you?"

"Leave me alone." Max grumbled and hung up the phone.

Astrid and Sara looked at Tom waiting for information. "Well?" Sara said.

"He hung up. He told me to leave him alone and he…he hung up."

Tom and Sara looked at Astrid as if she had some insight, but clearly by the expression on her face, she didn't.

Tom started dialing again. "Don't hang up again!" He practically yelled into the phone just as Jackson came in the front door. "You've got people here concerned about you. Where the hell are you?"

"Look, I'm fine. I just want to be left alone to think things out."

Jackson turned to Sara, "Who is he talking to?"

"Max." she said motioning with a finger for him to be quiet.

"Max, what happened? Is it something to do with Ivan? Is it another case?" Tom glanced at Sara and softened his tone. "You may not like it, you may consider it baggage, but the people in your life care about you." Turning his back to the others and staring at the carpet he added solemnly, "Not everyone does...don't abuse it Max." Sara heard his words and the realization of how she'd made him feel made her chest ache. "They need to know what's going on."

The minutes seemed to tick by as Tom held the phone waiting for some kind of response from Max. When he finally spoke his words seemed slurred as if he was drunk or half asleep. "I hear you, Tom. I'm okay just...give me a little bit to get my thoughts together and I'll call you back."

"Well," Astrid asked when Tom put down his phone.

"He says he'll call us back when he gets his thoughts together. I don't know, he sounds odd like he's worn out or has been drinking or..."

"Or what? Injured?"

"Astrid, he said he was okay. He just seemed a little...lost."

Sara put her arm around Astrid. "It'll be okay," she said trying to calm her own fears. "Have you spoken to Ivan recently," she asked Tom, "Could he have given Max another assignment?"

Tom shook his head, "I am not made aware of assignments he gives other agents," he answered without looking at Sara, "It is possible, but normally Max would simply say he was on assignment unless...,"

"Unless?"

"There are times when situations can't be divulged," he answered cryptically.

"Tom," Jackson said trying to get his attention.

"You mean dangerous times," Astrid said quietly, "If he's hurt or there is any type of danger...," she turned toward the window lost in thought.

"Astrid." Jackson said.

"How did he seem last night when you bailed him out," Astrid asked.

Tom smiled remembering the oddity of the situation. "He seemed happy. For somebody who'd just been arrested and thrown in a cell, he seemed happy."

"Astrid." Jackson said again. Receiving no answer he said, "Sara."

She ignored him and asked Astrid, "You said everything worked out last night though, right? Everything between the two of you was worked out."

"Yeah." Astrid said shaking her head in confusion. "It doesn't make sense."

"Sara." Jackson said a little louder.

Finally hearing her twin's call Sara answered him, "For heaven's sake Jackson what is it? If its breakfast you want it's already on the table, go eat!" She turned away from him and put her arms around Astrid to walk her to the sitting room.

"Damn it! All I wanted to ask was if Max is missing how come his car is behind the garage!" He stomped toward the sitting room to slump in a chair.

The three others quickly followed. "What?" Tom said. "Why is his car parked behind the garage?"

Jackson ignored them as he had felt ignored moments earlier. "Jackson!" Sara yelled at him, used to his pouts, "Why is his car behind the garage?"

"How the hell should I know?" He frowned at his sister, "I don't only think of eating, you know!"

Sara reached down and took his hand. They may be twins, but sometimes she felt like the older sister. "I'm sorry, Jackson. We are worried about Max."

Tom had already started dialing Max again, "Why is your car behind the garage?"

"Because I don't trust automatic car washes and that's where the hose is. I thought I said leave me alone and I'd call you." Max grumbled.

"Max, wait…"

Astrid took the phone from Tom and pleaded softly, "Maxim, please." She tried to hold back her tears, but she was so frightened for him she couldn't. "I just need to know that you're okay."

"Astrid?" he whispered into the phone. He closed his eyes savoring the sound of her voice saying his name in the way he thought he'd never hear again.

"Yes. Please don't hang up. Where are you? Max, why is your car here and you not?"

Max scrambled to get untangled from the bed sheets. He could hear the tears in her voice, "Cashmere," he said in a stronger voice. "Where are you? Where…wait…," he ran a hand through his hair trying to get his brain to activate. "What do you mean my car is here and I'm not? Where are you?"

"I'm at your house."

"What?" he shouted.

"I'm at your house, we all are. I waited all night for Tom to bail you out, but you never came home and…where are you?" Astrid waited for a reply and instead heard footsteps running down the staircase. "Max," she whispered as he came into view. She pushed the phone into Tom's hand and rushed to him.

Max grabbed her and crushed her against him. With his voice full of emotion he said into her ear, "I came home and…I couldn't find you. You said you'd be here…but you weren't." His breathing was ragged and he knew he was holding her too tightly, but he couldn't bring himself to loosen his hold. "I thought I'd lost you again," he whispered.

"I was here," she said through her tears, "I was waiting for you and fell asleep in your chair."

It dawned on Max what she was saying and he closed his eyes nuzzling her hair. They'd simply missed each other.

Sara walked over to them. "So, you fell asleep downstairs and this idiot fell asleep upstairs and you've both been wondering where the other one was?"

Astrid didn't care if they found it funny. All she cared about was that he was finally in her arms, "Just hold me," she whispered, "Just hold me."

Max did as he was asked and Sara laughed turning to smile at Jackson and Tom. Jackson smiled back and shook his head, but Tom looked sadly down at the floor and started to walk to the front door. Stopping him with a hand on his arm she asked, "Where are you going?"

"Well, now that everything is alright I...I don't want to be in the way."

The sad look in his eyes was all the more painful to see knowing she was responsible for it being there. "Tom, don't go. Remember what Max said you're...you're part of our family."

"No, I uh...I have some things to do."

"Like getting away from me?"

Tom swallowed and stared at the back of the door. "Sara," he said softly, "you don't want me here...the way I want to be...I..." When she took his hand gently into hers he couldn't finish his thought.

"I do want you here," she said so softly it made the back of his neck tingle.

"But not the way I...," he tried pulling his hand from hers, but she held on.

"Tom," she said softly looking up at him. Looking into her eyes he was unable to refrain from reaching his hand out to her cheek, but just as it got there he pulled it away. Sara reached up and placed his hand against her cheek. Slowly he started to bend down to offer her waiting lips a kiss, but Jackson came up behind him loudly clearing his throat. Tom straightened back up and blinked a few times without looking at her. "Go away, Jackson," Sara said in frustration and put her hands around Tom's neck to pull him back to where he'd been. Waiting, hoping he understood that she was making her choice and it was him. Slowly he resumed his descent and tenderly kissed her eager lips. They were soft and warm and welcoming and he'd waited so long that he couldn't hold back a small tremble. She held him tighter and he deepened the kiss.

He pulled away from her inviting lips. Still holding her warm, soft cheek in his palm he said, "Sara," he looked down shyly, "You know, I'm hopelessly in love with you."

Trying desperately to catch her breath as she looked into his beautiful smoky green eyes she thought she might just burst with happiness. "Well, that's alright," she said with tears welling in her eyes, "I'm hopelessly in love with you, too." He rested his forehead on hers a moment and then kissed her again this time wrapping both arms around her to hold her against his heart. Quietly she said, "I'm hoping that…since you love me, you'll forgive me."

"Yes, I forgive you," he said, keeping his cheek against hers.

Sara giggled, "You haven't heard what I want forgiveness for."

"I don't care," he said, "You're forgiven."

Sara took his hands into hers and said seriously, "I appreciate the get-out-of-jail-free card, but I really have to tell you." Understanding her need for seriousness he nodded and listened as she unburdened her heart. "I never went out with any of the people I claimed I was going out with. I never went out with a married man. Never met him at Running Aces. The guy who came with me to the hospital that day…I paid to come."

Tom frowned and shook his head, "Why?"

"I was trying to find out if you cared. I honestly," she pressed his hand to her heart, "honestly, didn't know I was hurting you. I was used to Max and Jackson's explosions and…you never explode."

"Sara," he stepped back bowing his head, "I'm…I'm not like them and I can't be something I'm not. If you need someone more…I guess…forceful…"

"No," she said quickly. "I know you're a gentle man and I should have known to look for some other signs that you cared. I was just…in love…and I didn't know what to do about it." She stopped as a tear slid down her cheek, "Mostly I was afraid…afraid you only saw me as a little sister."

Tom wiped the tear from her face and the look he gave her was most definitely not brotherly, "I have ached for you all these years," he whispered, "if you ever doubt…if I seem oblivious to your worries, please just…"

"I don't doubt anymore," her hand reached up to wrap around his neck and slide her fingers into his hair, "the way your eyes are looking into mine tells me everything I need to know." Bending down he kissed her again choosing to forget there were three other people in the room with them.

Jackson stomped over to stare out of the window as Max watched him. Tom and Sara had been a long time coming, but inevitable. Sara had boyfriends before. She wasn't a child. The fact that it still bothered Jackson was a mystery to Max. "Jackson," Max said walking up to him.

Jackson turned around and, ignoring Max, headed for the dining room for breakfast when something caught his eye. "Hey, I've looked everywhere for this," he said as he picked the Pancake Pie book off the shelf of Swedish books.

Jackson sat a moment to look through its pages and Astrid turned to Max. Not waiting to be asked, he answered the question on her face, "It was time to stop hiding it," he said looking into her eyes.

Sara and Tom stood together in the foyer and seeing the looks Max and Astrid were exchanging, Jackson set down the book and stormed into the dining room. "Well, breakfast is ready, let's eat," he said and took his seat at the table to eat without waiting for the rest of them.

Giving up on his brother, for the moment, Max wrapped his arms around Astrid, "Looks like our family is expanding. Knowing Tom the way I do, I'm sure he'll be wanting a wedding!"

"Wedding?"

He shrugged his shoulders, "Seems like the natural way of things. That's how he'll see it anyway. Marriage…isn't the worst idea I've ever heard." He looked at her and grinned, but the grin died off noticing her frown just before she turned to move away from him. "I don't necessarily mean right now," he said suddenly realizing he tipped his hand too soon, "I mean…once you're sure I'm not going to screw up again or…Astrid," he swallowed and said lightly, "if you don't want marriage…"

"No, it's just…well, marriage and what sometimes follows."

"You mean children," he said finishing her thought.

"Do you want children, Maxim?"

The softness in her tone indicated to him the importance of the question and he took a few moments gathering his thoughts before answering. "I have to admit that I hadn't given much thought to marriage and children…until recently. Now, the idea of marriage sounds rather nice, but…as for children…well, my father…"

"You are not your father," Astrid said as he let go of her to get the remote for the fireplace.

"No, I know that, but…," he came back to her and gently took her face in his hands. "It doesn't seem to stop me from behaving like him. Astrid, I need to know you can forgive me for…for having you kidnapped and tied to a chair…I…," he swallowed the lump in his throat, "I would never do anything like that again. Not to anyone. Not ever again. It was cruel and barbaric and I never want you to think of me as a monster. Your opinion of me matters more than I can tell you and…," his eyes held tears and his brow furrowed. "I guess I just need to hear it that…that you forgive me."

Astrid understood just how much her opinion of him mattered and smiled tenderly at the man she loved. "I forgave you for that some time ago. Maxim, you are no monster. It was a mistake…if anyone can understand making mistakes it's me," he shook his head, but she continued, "I know you needed the information for Ivan. It was wrong, but I understand. I guess I put you between a rock and a hard place for a little while," she said with a smile. "Now, back to this about marriages and families."

Max stepped back and shook his head, "Why does everything seem to always circle back around to that bastard."

"It doesn't," she said stepping back. "This has to do with, Sara, Jackson, Tom, and...," her voice softened making his neck tingle as she said, "and maybe...us."

She reached out and took his arm trying to get him to look at her, but he turned toward the window. "It still comes back to him." He glanced back at Astrid, but she shook her head and frowned   . "Before I was born my father was just a normal, doting husband. Mother had no idea how jealous he would become." Max stepped over to his desk looking down at the lily in the vase as he heard the others sitting down and enjoying their breakfast. Long ago his mother had tried explaining his father to him, but try as he might, it still baffled him. "The night she gave birth he had an important meeting and didn't get there until late. She was just putting me to her breast for my first feed when he entered the room. She looked up at him smiling; so happy I'd been a boy she could present to him. Instead of seeing a happy and proud father standing there, she saw him scowling at her precious bundle. Thinking he'd just been worried over how ill she'd been, she ignored it. Time would work it all out, she thought. When it went on and three days passed and he still hadn't held me she knew something between them had changed." Astrid was looking down at the carpet, her hands resting against her abdomen as he approached her. "I don't want things to change that way between us. I don't want to think I could become him, but there is a part of me that...worries and another part of me that..."

He didn't finish and Astrid sensed such sadness from him that she dreaded what he'd say next, but she had to know. "A part of you, what?"

"A part of me...would like to be a father." Astrid let out the breath she'd held as tears welled in her eyes. Misinterpreting their origin, Max continued, "I know what you're thinking and I understand. You're afraid I'd scorn my own child like he did." She shook her head, but he went on, "I have searched my soul, Cashmere and I just," he came to her and took her hand in his, "If it were to come to that...I could not live with myself if I ever hurt a child, any child much less my own."

"Don't you see?" she said though her tears, "That's why you couldn't be like your father."

"There was something in him that turned him into the monster he became and," he tucked his head down, "obviously whatever it is I'm not immune. Only a monster would let strangers kidnap a woman, tie her to a chair, and try to force her to give him information."

Astrid laid a hand over his lips, "We're past that. You're not a monster. You made a mistake."

He wiped a tear from her cheek, "Let's not worry about it now. I don't want you to be upset."

"I'm not upset."

"Astrid, you're crying," he said with a chuckle.

"Because you said...," she wiped at her tears, "you said that you wanted to be a father."

Closing his eyes briefly, thinking he finally understood. "Astrid, I'm sorry. I should have thought...," he shook his head aggravated with himself, "if you can't have children it doesn't matter. We could always..."

"No," she shouted shaking her head unable to find the words she was looking for. Turning away in frustration with herself, she spotted Max's book lying on the sofa and suddenly knew exactly what to say. Picking it up she turned to him and said, "In five months...," she took a deep breath, "Will you read this to our child...your child?"

"In five...?" Max didn't move, didn't blink, and didn't breathe. *A child? In five months? Is that what she said? Your...my...child?* Looking at Astrid's left hand guarding her tummy and the radiant smile on her face it was clear to his mind what she was saying, but his heart was taking a little longer to catch up. Max slowly sat down on the clock coffee table and held his head in his hands.

CHAPTER 26

"The doctor confirmed it last week," she said with a nervous giggle, "It must have happened the first time we…" Astrid's happy tears stopped and she knelt down in front of him. When his head came up, she was surprised by the tears in his eyes. "Maxim?"

His brow furrowed slightly as he inquired softly, "You would," he stopped to take a breath, "You would entrust me with a child?"

"Of course I would," she said with a smile, "Even if you hadn't met me at the gazebo I was going to tell you about the baby. Whether you loved me or not I knew you'd love this child." One tear escaped down his cheek and she caught it with her thumb as she caressed his face. "You mentioned once that your eyes were just like your father's, but you're wrong."

"I'm afraid I'm not. I look in the mirror every day and see that monster looking back at me. The same eyes that would look down at…at this child. My child," he whispered. Sitting up straighter, Max swallowed and cleared his throat, "Sara and Jackson have mother's eyes. I got the icy, cold eyes of that worthless bastard I call Father."

He tucked his head down and she gently took his face in her hands lifting it for him to look at her. "No, these eyes aren't like ice. They're like warm and comforting crystals. Since we met I've been drawn to them and every time I've been frightened or worried and looked into them I have felt a warmth and a solace that I've never felt before. These eyes," she stroked his cheek, "these eyes will look down at our child with so much love it will no doubt be the most spoiled rotten child in the world. You will spoil it with love and affection, time and attention, and it will never doubt how much it is wanted." Max didn't respond and concerned for the direction his mind might be going, Astrid said, "You know, my mother tried to make me believe that you started that fire in my apartment."

Max looked at her with his mouth hanging open, "What?"

Astrid nodded and smiled, "That was when I knew that she would never have a part in my life again. That's when I knew...my brothers burned my apartment," she gently lifted Max's face to look at her, "didn't they?" He nodded and looked back down at the floor. "You didn't want me to know my own family had done such a horrible thing to me."

"My father is the one that burned my books that day. I didn't want you to have to feel the pain of knowing that people who were supposed to love you; family that was supposed to be your support, would try to take away the things that mean so much to you. I didn't...I didn't want you to know that pain."

"I know, Maxim. That's why I want you to raise this child with me; you are so incredibly compassionate. I truly believe you will make a wonderful father." Unable to find the words to say, Max simply rested his forehead against hers savoring the sweetest moment of his life. "But...there is one thing, Maxim. One thing that I admit I...I do have doubts about."

Pulling himself together, he gazed into her eyes, "Yes?"

"You told me the first day we met that...," she took a nervous breath and stood up to walk away, but he took her hand and stood next to her, "You said you weren't married because you hadn't found a woman you could promise to be faithful to...and...and what is a marriage without...that commitment and...," unable to look into his eyes another moment, she turned her head, "I would want marriage, but...am I enough for you to...to feel you could...," Astrid stopped and looked into his eyes, "I would want you all to myself."

Max smiled, looking deeply into the eyes he knew so well, "My darling girl, I have waited my whole life for someone to love me so that I could prove I could be the husband my father was not and here you are. I have waited my whole life for the opportunity to prove I could be the father my father was not and here the two of you are," he said placing a gentle hand on her tummy. "I can without hesitation promise you my love, my protection, and most assuredly my fidelity." Taking both of her hands in his, he said with a smile, "If you don't mind a quick wedding, we could spend *Jul* in Sweden for our honeymoon."

Astrid smiled and rested her forehead on his saying softly, "*Jag älskar dig,* Maxim Gunther."

"I love you, too," he said sealing his declaration with a kiss then with a twinkle in his eye he added, "By the way…you are aware we have twins in the family." She giggled as he wiggled his eyebrows and went to tell his siblings his news.

I hope you enjoyed The Book That Must Not Be Named.

The next in the Witches Guardians Series is

The Heart in His Art

Other books by Pepper Phoenix include

The Voice of Annwyn

And

The Visions of Annwyn

All available on Amazon.com